HEARTWARMING

Her Veterinarian Hero

——

Elizabeth Mowers

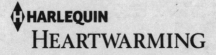

♦H HARLEQUIN
HEARTWARMING

HARLEQUIN®
HEARTWARMING™

Recycling programs
for this product may
not exist in your area.

ISBN-13: 978-1-335-42673-4

Her Veterinarian Hero

Copyright © 2022 by Elizabeth Mowers

For questions and comments about the quality of this book,
please contact us at CustomerService@Harlequin.com.

Harlequin Enterprises ULC
22 Adelaide St. West, 41st Floor
Toronto, Ontario M5H 4E3, Canada
www.Harlequin.com

Printed in U.S.A.

Elizabeth Mowers wrote her first romance novel on her cell phone when her first child wouldn't nap without being held. After three years, she had a happy preschooler and a hot mess of a book that will never be read by another person. The experience started her down the wonderful path of writing romances, and now that she can use her computer, she's having fun cooking up new stories. She's drawn to romances with strong family connections and plots where the hero and heroine help save each other. Elizabeth lives in the country with her husband and two children.

Books by Elizabeth Mowers

Harlequin Heartwarming

A Promise Remembered
Where the Heart May Lead
Her Hometown Detective

Visit the Author Profile page
at Harlequin.com for more titles.

To Michaela.

You are the sunshine of my life.

CHAPTER ONE

"Is this really where we're going to *live*?"

Olivia turned the car onto a long, narrow driveway through a dense wood, as her fourteen-year-old son, Micah, knitted his eyebrows in a discerning scowl. The long, three-day drive from California had tested her patience with her son so much, she could have swallowed her tongue after biting it so many times.

Olivia gripped the wheel tighter, praying her decision to pull Micah out of school for an extended fall holiday had not been another terrible mistake. As Micah told it, she had been making plenty of those over the last two years.

"Mom," he said, his face pressed to the passenger window. "Is this it? Seriously?"

The heavy bed of gravel shifted beneath her tires. Stones flew up under the body of the car with a series of clinks and pings to announce that, yes, their long journey to Roseley, Michigan, was finally at an end. This was home—for now.

It was one of Olivia's favorite times of year—that window when the last few warm days of summer still lingered but the cool nights had cued autumn's entrance. She supposed she could be satisfied that she had made it to Roseley in time for that. Trees still swayed with green leaves but also flecks of goldenrod, burnt orange and cranberry. After a quarter mile or so, she and Micah made the bend and the trees cleared to reveal a tiny Victorian cottage. Its north-facing side was blanketed with a light bed of moss, while the hillside behind the south corner of the house was covered with thousands of wildflowers still holding on to the last breaths of summer. The yellows and whites and violets cascaded down the sprawling hill and around the cottage. They seamlessly spilled into the garden beds tucked around every inch of the cottage perimeter just as the first yellow maple leaves of the season floated to rest on top of them. It was a sight that would only last another day or two, so Olivia drew a breath of gratitude and buried her frustration with her son somewhere down deep where her other frustrations lay.

"Yes, Micah, until you hear otherwise, this is it."

"You said it was on a lake."

"It's near the lake."

Micah sighed loudly, shoving his fists into the front pocket of his sweatshirt. "I'd better get a cool room."

Olivia managed a meek smile. She had no memory of her aunt's cottage being any larger than a two-bedroom, but she had decided to break that to him after they arrived. They had not needed any more contention on their road trip.

Olivia eased the car to a stop as her aunt Hattie, covered head to toe in loosely draped clothing, effortlessly glided out the front door. Whipping a wide-brimmed straw hat from her head, she tousled her cropped auburn hair, which carried a heavy white streak above her left temple. Her smile spread wider than her outstretched arms, which were punctuated with flailing fingers.

"There she is!" Hattie cried. Olivia had barely managed two steps in Hattie's direction when she was encompassed in a fierce, full-body hug. It was two years since Olivia had seen her aunt, but instead of waning over time, Hattie's enthusiasm only seemed to have strengthened. "My darling girl," Hattie said, wrapping a tender palm behind the back of Olivia's head and pulling her snugly to her shoulder. "My blood."

Hattie smelled of earth. Of sunshine and morning breezes and black dirt crumbling like chocolate cake between your fingers. Her unbridled energy for life infused Olivia with the memory of a childhood lost and yearned for. Two peas in a pod, her mother had often said of her sisterhood with Hattie. As Olivia melted into the nape of Hattie's neck, she sighed. Her aunt's scent carried memories of the mother she had lost several years ago. Bittersweet.

"I missed you, too," she said when Hattie finally released her. Her aunt's brilliant smile softened as she studied her niece. Her eyes crinkled with the weight of her sixty years. The sun had worshipped her as much as she had it. Darkened spots peppered her cheeks and nose and forehead in an array as dense as the Milky Way.

"You're the vision of your mother," Hattie said, cupping Olivia's cheeks between her hands. "Perfection." She pecked a kiss on Olivia's nose before wrapping an arm around her waist. "How'd he do?" she whispered as Micah slumped from the car. Olivia barely spared a look before Aunt Hattie was closing the gap with Micah at twice his speed. "And this cannot be Micah. Have you been eating growing pills? The last time I saw you, you were no taller than my bosom."

Micah's face twisted as Hattie enveloped him into an unreciprocated hug.

"Hi, Aunt Hattie," he said quietly.

"So, what are you into these days?" she said, carefully eyeing him and stroking the hair off his brow. "I know I sent you comic books for your last birthday, but I have a sneaking suspicion you've moved on. Yes?"

Micah made a noncommittal shrug as Olivia piped up.

"He plays a video game called *Doom*."

"Video games?" Hattie cried. "No one who moves up here wants to spend time playing video games. Nature's playground awaits you, kiddo. Do you like fishing?"

Micah shrugged.

"You like fishing," Olivia prompted.

"Hmm, I see." Hattie ran a hand through her messy locks. "What about rock climbing? Dirt biking? *Cliff jumping?*"

Micah's lips spread into a thin smirk. "I've never done any of those."

"Aha!" Hattie said, leading him toward Olivia. "Then you are in for a treat. We will keep you busy up here. You'll be saying *Doom*

Shmoom by the end of the week." She turned them both to face her cottage. Releasing a sigh that could only be pride, she asked Olivia, "Do you like it?"

"It's charming."

"Isn't it, though? I only spend every waking minute on the upkeep."

Olivia admired the place they would call home for at least the month. It was a giant downgrade from their four-bedroom McMansion in the suburbs, and it looked like heaven.

A familiar friend shuffled down a low-grade metal ramp off the porch steps. Olivia chuckled at the sight of him.

"Hello there, Boomer."

Micah knelt to pet the eight-year-old English bulldog. With a tan, stout body and white markings on his face and underbelly, he wagged his bubblegum tongue to and fro as he looked up at Micah.

"His hip dysplasia is getting pretty bad." Aunt Hattie sighed. "He still had to come out and welcome you."

"It's been a long time, Boomer," Micah said, nuzzling his round mug. "I haven't seen you since you were a puppy."

"Pretty close," Hattie said. "Friends watched him the last time I visited you. That would have been a long flight for him, and I didn't want to be distracted at the—" Hattie stopped short and shook her head in apology.

"We're doing okay," Olivia said. "A change of scenery is just what we need."

"*Boomer* is just what you need. He's a good listener, Micah."

"Can he sleep in my room?"

Olivia cleared her throat and looked at her aunt. "I haven't discussed sleeping arrangements."

"Good," Hattie said. "We can tackle that together. First, let's get your car unloaded. After a nap we can have dinner in town. Yes?"

Without waiting for a reply, Hattie opened the trunk and hoisted one of only a few suitcases out of it. "Whoa. Liv, dear, you travel light."

"I'm trying to simplify my life."

"I like it. Good for the soul." With Micah and Olivia carrying bags behind her, Hattie dragged a suitcase into the cottage and up a narrow wooden staircase. When she reached the top, she called, "Well, my loves, this is it."

Olivia cleared the low overhang at the entrance to the only room at the top of the stairs. It was a small space that smelled of cedar chips, but it had a beautiful view of dense woods. She moved across the aged hardwood floors, aware that every step was reciprocated with a delicate creak beneath her feet. There were two twin-size beds with matching white bedspreads, a desk, a shared nightstand and a closet. Hattie tied back the sheer, snow-white curtains and leaned back to face her niece.

"It gets the morning sunshine, so drop the blinds before you go to bed."

Olivia eased her way across the room, taking in every nook and cranny. She strummed her fingers along the cherry nightstand and grazed them over a silver framed photograph of her, Micah and Jeb. Micah was only a toddler in the photo, and Jeb was...

"You thought of everything, Hattie."

Hattie lifted her shoulders. "I've had the three of you smiling at me in the living room for ages but thought it might best suit you in here."

Olivia's eyes moistened as she turned to Micah, but he had other things on his mind besides an old photograph of his father.

"We're sharing a room?" he mumbled.

"Ah, it won't even faze you after a few days," Hattie said. "Your grandmother and I shared a bedroom until she went off to college, and I was lonelier than an owl's hoot when she left."

"This is different," Micah insisted.

"Nonsense. Who knows you better than your mother?"

Micah shot Olivia a scowl before silently dropping his suitcase on the far bed.

"We'll make do," Olivia said. "Thank you for having us."

"Yeah, thanks," Micah said.

"You are most welcome," Hattie replied. "Once you get your suitcases unpacked, we can store them in the garage to get them out of your way."

Micah flopped on his bed and pulled out his Nintendo Switch.

"Why don't you get unpacked, Micah," Olivia said.

"I'll do it later."

"Come on, kiddo. We can unpack and then rest up before dinner—"

"I said *later*."

Olivia wanted to pull the "mom card" and just make him do it. However, she didn't want to start their new venture as roommates off on the wrong foot. Micah rolled toward the window away from her, his game console pressed inches from his nose. Hattie caught Olivia's eye before leading the way down the stairs. "Cup of tea, Liv?"

Olivia helped Hattie fix the tea and then

followed her to the back sunroom. "We're off to a great start," she mumbled.

"What happened on the drive?"

"A better question is, what's happened since Jeb died? Where do I begin?"

"It's been a hard two years for the both of you. You need to cut yourself some slack and remember that a lot of it is just his age."

"Is it?"

Hattie curled into an oversize chair and studied her niece with the unwavering focus of a guru. "Tell me about the camp."

Olivia sipped her tea, contemplating the last few months. "His teacher nominated him. He encouraged Micah to write an essay about what the outdoors means to him. Apparently, it was very good, not that he would let me read it. It won him a summer at the Nature's Heirs Camp."

"I've heard of that one. It's about as exclusive a camp as they come."

"Swimming, hiking, white water rafting, camping—"

"Baseball?"

Olivia sighed. "That was the best part, but Micah hasn't picked up his glove since Jeb died."

"I thought that kid slept with his glove."

"Jeb and I used to laugh about that, but now

he won't touch it. In fact, he won't do much of anything. He refused to attend camp."

Hattie sighed, her focus turning to a cardinal perched just outside the window. "He's just sad. I'm sure baseball is very painful if it brings up memories of his father. What does his counselor say?"

"Dr. Redwood has been great, but he just retired." That was why Olivia hoped it'd be okay to move up here before transitioning Micah to a new doctor at the same practice. "I know it's not the best time to take a holiday, what with the school year just starting, but I'm at my wits' end with him."

"It must be difficult for you, considering he's the kind of patient you would normally help."

Olivia rested her head back against her chair, recalling so many conversations she'd had with colleagues over the past two years. She knew all the stages of grief and all the ways to help a child process death, loss and trauma, but when it came down to helping her own son, why did she feel so inadequate? When she'd first learned what art therapists did, she had immediately known she wanted to dedicate her life to it. But recently, her failure to help her own son had made her question not only her vocation, but her ability to mother.

"I thought the camp would be a push in the right direction," Olivia said. "But the more I try to help, the higher he builds a wall between us. I've been wrong about a lot lately."

"Well," Hattie said. "I'm sorry he has to settle for visiting me instead."

"You don't play second fiddle to anyone, Hattie. I'm happy to be here, and I think, to some degree, Micah is, too."

"Hmm," Hattie said, taking a deep sip of tea. "It'll take a few days to get settled, but I'm only giving him until tomorrow before I hide that video game."

"Thanks, but he'll end up blaming me for it."

Hattie quirked a brow. "That's what a teenage boy does with his mother, because he knows she can handle it."

"Some days I'm not so sure."

"You're a fine mother, and you're doing your *best*. It's what the women in our family do—always."

"I have to get out for a little while," Olivia said, setting her teacup on the table. Suddenly the urge to escape smacked her like a northern wind.

"Of course," Hattie said. "There's a lot happening in town—"

"No," Olivia said, standing. "I need to jog."

"I never understood your runner's high."

Olivia didn't want to admit that her runner's high was less about getting something good and more about expelling something bad. She had three days of pent-up frustration with Micah just waiting to burn off.

"Take your time," Hattie continued. "The lake is beautiful this time of year."

Olivia hurried to change into running clothes, already remembering one of her favorite spots on Roseley Mountain. It was a secret place from childhood that she could feel calling to her. It beckoned her to come discover it again, and just like it was when she was a child, she was certain no one else would be there.

CHAPTER TWO

TYLER ELDERMAN HIKED the trail winding up Roseley Mountain as Ranger, his loyal German shepherd, trotted dutifully beside him. If there was any place in the world where he could realign his emotional barometer, hiking through these woods silently with Ranger would be it.

He stopped at a steep slope and glanced up ten yards to a heavy mound of dirt. In the spring he had moved so quietly he had walked up on two fox pups. On that day, the spring rains had made the ground covering so green and dense that Tyler would have sworn he could see it growing. He had watched, just to be sure, and that was when he'd spotted the pups rolling in the grass just in front of the dirt mound. They had been playing like puppies, without a care in the world. At first, he hadn't believed his eyes. It wasn't a common sight to see fox pups out and about during the day. He'd figured the mound was most likely their den, the opening hidden on the backside of the slope. Ever since that day, he'd carefully hiked this patch of path hoping to catch a glimpse of them, now grown adults, but every hike since then had been unfruitful.

Tyler turned and watched Ranger, who was hyper focused on sniffing a decaying tree stump on the edge of the path. The dog maneuvered his black-and-tan body around the stump, his jet-black nose most likely cataloging every scent he found there.

He recalled his summers at Uncle Gary's house, watching chickens roam free over several acres of property. He'd never seen a chicken so happy as when it was pecking at a bug and just being a chicken.

"Gotta let 'em be themselves," Gary had said, his large belly bouncing with laughter. Gary had taught him a lot of good lessons over the years—many within the walls of the veterinary practice that Gary and Tyler's dad had run, which Tyler now ran with his uncle. For some reason, the bit about the chickens had stayed with him whenever he worked with animals. Ranger seemed never so happy as when he was walking alongside Tyler, smelling every different calling card nature provided, and just being a dog.

Once the German shepherd appeared to glean everything he wanted to know about the stump, he looked up at Tyler as if to say, "Thanks for waiting. Where to now, boss?"

Tyler led the way farther up the mountain to one of his favorite points, Falcon's Peak. He loved walking Ranger off leash, especially when they reached the lookout point and could sit together and stare out over the woods, lake and the edge of town. It filled him with a deep pride that he could trust his dog to stay by his side, no matter what critter went scampering by. Still, some folks didn't like to come around the bend of the mountain and find a ninety-pound dog, all fur and muscle, staring at them.

After glancing around to be sure no one else was there, Tyler stopped and stretched, then signaled to Ranger that he could venture out on his own while Tyler rested his legs. Following where his nose led, the dog wound his way up and down the path like a trolley car on rails that no one could see but him.

Tyler wiped perspiration from his brow. It had been a long morning at the clinic, with several appointments that had kept him moving from sunup until…just now. He heaved a sigh of equal parts satisfaction and exhaustion as he watched the branches sway and listened to the birds call from above. It was a movement of branches he caught out of the corner of his eye that instinctually looked out of place. When he'd been a teenager, he'd walked up on deer more than once on this trail, and for a moment, when he'd noticed the branches move, that was exactly what he thought he had done.

But this, he quickly realized, was no deer. Deer didn't wander out on narrow ledges above a fifty-foot drop.

When Tyler jerked his head, giving full attention to the edge of rock slab jutting out at the top of Falcon's Peak, he spotted a ponytail. He had glimpsed it for only a moment. It had swung from behind a tree that had roots growing out from the steep drop at a forty-five-degree angle. The tree was the only thing keeping anyone or anything from falling off that ledge. If they did fall, they'd transform into a pancake on contact. Apparently, that risk hadn't stopped someone from skirting around the warning signs and climbing out to the place where the rock shards shifted under your feet faster than a sliding avalanche.

A knot tightened in Tyler's stomach. His feet moved fast as he sprinted to the tree. He skidded down the steep slope, his backside dragging over the dirt to keep himself from tumbling forward. He was at the edge of the rock slab in less than a few seconds. After securing a foothold at the roots of the protruding tree, he grabbed a deformed branch at the base of the trunk. Without a second thought, he thrust an open hand in the direction of that ponytail.

The thick, dark brown curls most likely belonged to some teenage girl, too ignorant for her own good. She couldn't possibly understand how dangerous a predicament she'd put herself in or she'd have kept a distance from the edge in the first place. Tyler had passed a few high schoolers on his ascent up the mountain, their laughter quickly fading once they'd spied him coming up the path. If this girl had left her peers and he managed to save her from doing a nosedive, he'd give her a verbal reprimand she might never forget.

The ponytail swung, and just as he caught sight of the rest of the person it belonged to, he wrapped a firm grip around the girl's bicep and squeezed. She wobbled on her feet and let out a yelp.

"Steady," Tyler said, his voice a controlled command. "You're right at the drop-off. If those rocks shift, you'll go over the edge, but I've got you."

The girl instinctively dropped to her bottom, forcing Tyler to lower himself to the ground with her. She tried to scoot up the

gnarled roots of the tree, but without anything solid to grab on to, she began to panic.
She kicked out her feet, flailing wildly as the
rock shards did begin to shift. They fell like
confetti to the ground far below. It was just
as Tyler had feared.

"I'm slipping!" she screamed. Tyler tightened his hand around the tree branch. His fingers burned as if boring holes into the bark.
As gravity pulled at her, and the full weight
of her body tugged at him, he squeezed her
bicep so hard he thought he might snap her
arm like one of the twigs scraping at his face.

"I've got you," he said, his voice husky.
"Stop moving. I'll pull you up."

He expected her to fight it, to flail for traction out of fear. As the adrenaline surging
through his veins had made his palms sweaty,
he knew that if she squirmed, she'd slip right
out of his hand.

Luckily, she didn't.

Tyler heaved his hardest, his muscles
straining so hard he thought they'd split his
shirt. If he'd rock climbed a thousand times
over the last twenty years only to have the
sheer strength to save this girl now, he'd say
a prayer of thanksgiving for having picked
up the hobby in the first place.

He hoisted her up and back toward him

until she could wedge the heel of her sneaker over a tree root. She managed to get some leverage. Once she wasn't dead weight anymore, Tyler repositioned his grip on her bicep. Carefully, he pulled her arm up and around his neck, then jerked to cinch her around the waist. The brim of her baseball cap scraped against his face as her body clung to his. He was never so relieved to hold a perfect stranger so tightly.

"Grab that tree branch," he said, jerking his head for clarification. Once she did, he helped her the rest of the way up the topside of the tree. He hoped the heavy summer rains hadn't compromised the tree roots' integrity, but once she was wrapped up in his arm and had found her own traction, instinct told him they could trust it. He eased them away from the drop-off until they could both get their footing and scramble up the slope, clawing at the earth as they went.

At the top, the girl broke from his arms and dropped to her hands and knees like a storm-tossed sailor who had miraculously made it ashore.

"Are you okay?" he asked as he caught his breath. His arms ached and his brow dripped with dense sweat. He sat back on his heels and wiped hands down the length of his face, grateful they were both on solid ground. Her back was to him, rising and falling hard as she caught her breath.

"You scared me," she breathed.

"I scared *you*?" he said, shaking out the cramps in his hands. He could almost laugh, almost find humor in her words, only because he felt so relieved to not watch her fall.

Ranger, most likely hearing them, came running from somewhere farther up the mountain. Tyler released a short whistle, reminding Ranger to ignore the girl and run straight to him. He wrapped his arms around Ranger's neck and kissed the top of his head. The girl cocked her head to glance back at him, though her face was shadowed under her sunglasses and baseball cap.

"You were like some ninja, scaring me half to death. I didn't hear you until you grabbed me."

Tyler made his way to his feet. "That was the point, miss. If I'd said anything, you might have fallen."

"I *did* fall," she said over her shoulder, her voice assertive. Now that she had caught her breath, she was putting it to good use to blame him for their little tango. "You grabbed my arm, and I nearly fell off the cliff."

She made her way to her feet as he huffed in response.

He tried to keep his voice level as he said, "It's a good thing I grabbed your arm. Heaven knows if I hadn't…" He stopped, considering her for a moment. Somehow, she hadn't seen the giant warning sign about the drop-off. It was cast in bronze and pretty difficult to miss. If she'd purposefully bypassed it… had she intended to fall all along?

His ego had been ready to rear its ugly head and set things straight about just what had happened not two minutes earlier. He was itching to confront her about taking such a dangerous risk. But now, instantly, none of that seemed important.

"Look," he said, grappling for the right words. "I've had my fair share of rough days over the years. Everyone does. If you're struggling right now or need someone to talk to, I can help you find—"

"Good heavens," she sputtered, turning and whipping off her sunglasses in a fury. "I wasn't trying to kill myself, if that's what you think." Her black eyelashes fluttered wildly; angry brown eyes narrowed, evidently eager to clear the record. He needed to swallow the shock that had come over him once he got a good look at her face.

The teenager he had been making assumptions about was no teenager at all.

It was a woman glaring at him: she looked like she had the same number of years on her face as he did. Hidden under a baseball cap, dirt smudged along her cheeks, she was not at all who he had been expecting. She was beautiful. Beautiful, fierce and unprepared for the full impact of Ranger's protective instinct.

Ranger lunged between the two of them, standing tall as the look on the woman's face shifted from angry to shocked.

"Easy, boy," Tyler said, taking a step forward to stand beside his loyal companion. "Let's not give this nice lady another reason to hate us today." At Tyler's words, Ranger's body relaxed, and he peered up at him waiting for a command. "Sit," Tyler said, gesturing with his hand. He always felt a sense of pride when Ranger complied, but never so much as in this moment. The woman was just an arm's length away and her eyes had grown to the size of saucers.

"He won't hurt you," Tyler said. "He's just protecting me."

"I can see that," she said. "I'm sure glad he listens to you."

"I hope you do, too."

"About what?"

Tyler shifted as he pieced together a response. What she'd done had been so irresponsible he didn't want to think about what might have just happened.

"What are you doing up here?" he finally said.

"Jogging."

"Over the side of the peak?"

She scowled. "I haven't been up here in a very long time. It *changed*."

"Which part exactly?"

She wiped her cheeks on her shoulders, her voice breaking as she pointed an accusatory finger at the tree that had helped save her life.

"I used to sit for hours under that tree."

"It must have been a long time ago."

"It was. Too long." She pinched the bridge of her nose and squeezed her eyes shut. "I just got into town, and I wanted to climb down and find my old spot... The bushes have grown over the edge. I couldn't see it dropped off there until I'd already made my way down and I didn't know... I just didn't see that it...it..."

He nodded, finally understanding. "A few years back a bad storm took a part of the cliff off. The town reinforced it as much as it could, but it's dangerous if you climb past the barriers."

"Yeah, I figured that out," she said. "But I'd hardly call a couple hip-high wooden posts *barriers*."

"And the giant bronze warning sign," he said, raising a brow.

She twisted her mouth in concession and knelt to offer Ranger her hand. After he had given it a polite lick, she ran her hands through his fur and scratched him behind the ears. Tyler knew the peaceful effect a dog could have on a person. He had seen Ranger work miracles with folks over the years, taking an anxious adult or an excited child and calming them down. Heck, if the woman felt anything like him, she would bury her nose in Ranger's fur and wrap her arms around his neck the way he wanted to right now.

As she moved, her slender hands shakily moving over Ranger's fur, he admired the pretty face under the baseball cap. Her profile was a study in feminine curves: full lips, round cheeks and a nose that looked like a perfect dollop of pudding. Wanting a closer look, he squatted to the ground to join her.

"What are you doing up here?" she asked.

"Hiking."

"Do you live nearby?"

"Yeah. I grew up here. I know this mountain like the back of my hand."

"Lucky for me, huh?" A slight smile almost breached her lips and when it did, Tyler caught his breath.

He could only assume that the near fall to his death had altered his senses, because suddenly, at her smile, everything around him was brought sharply into focus for the first time in a long time. The orange leaf tips waving in the breeze had never looked so bright. The songbirds' melodies had never sounded so spirited. Even the slight taste of blood on his tongue from accidentally biting his lip made him grateful that he was still alive and able to taste it. He knew it couldn't just be her that had jolted something inside him. It had to be everything else bombarding him, too. Didn't it?

He tried to tear his eyes away from her face, to will himself to look at Ranger or the trail. But he couldn't.

"I like your dog," she said. Ranger licked at her face as if returning the compliment. The woman didn't shy away from it. Instead, she offered him her other cheek to lick. "What's his name?"

"Ranger."

"You're a good friend, Ranger. I can tell." When she lifted her eyes to Tyler's again, he asked as gently as he could manage, "Are you really okay?"

She stared at him just a beat too long, perhaps gathering a reply that fell somewhere between honesty and self-preservation.

"Yes, I think so."

"I have to point out that you're shaking like a leaf."

"Am I?" She scrambled to her feet and hugged herself, rubbing her arms. She wasn't built like a delicate flower. She was athletic, strong, and he could tell she wasn't used to playing the damsel-in-distress. But as terrifying as the tumble on the ledge was for him, he could only imagine how scary it might have been for her. He might have had full confidence in his strength to pull her to safety, but she had had to trust a perfect stranger. As Tyler wasn't very good at trusting even the people he knew best, he wouldn't have traded places with her for anything.

She turned to face the ledge and then looked back at him. "What almost happened just now…it was…"

"Scary?"

Her face fell grave, and she blinked solemnly as if the realization of what had happened or, worse still, what *could* have happened, hit her.

"My life didn't exactly flash before my eyes," she said. "But my son's face sure did."

"I think that's normal. Good, actually."

"You do?"

He had said it because it was the truth, but when her eyes moistened, he knew he'd say just about anything to keep her from crying. "I think it means you have something to live for."

He recalled where his mind had gone for those brief moments when his life had also hung in the balance.

Nowhere.

No faces flashed before his eyes, as all of his life decisions up to that point had intentionally made it so.

"I shouldn't have yelled at you," she said, her shoulders softening for the first time.

He smiled. "That wasn't yelling. That was your fight to survive still surging."

She popped her fists to her hips. "I'm trying to apologize here, and you're letting me off the hook too easy."

"Miss, there's no need to apologize—"

"I haven't been called a 'Miss' in a long time."

A knowing smirk came over his face. "I didn't hurt your arm, did I?"

He knew he had nearly squeezed the life

out of it. He could almost see the bruises forming on her tawny brown skin.

She rubbed her bicep and shrugged. "It'll be sore tomorrow."

"Just as long as you live to see tomorrow."

She rolled her eyes in concession. "I guess I have you to thank for that."

"Was that an official thanks, then?"

Her face broke into a wide smile that made him want to stumble closer to its warmth. He could also tell by the way she tightened her ponytail and slipped her sunglasses back over her eyes that she wasn't sticking around.

"It certainly was," she said, slowly easing past him and Ranger one step at a time. "You're definitely my hero."

He lifted his brows. "Hero, huh?"

She hummed a note of amusement and took off jogging back down the mountain trail at a steady pace.

"Don't let it go to your head!" she called, but he knew it was too late for that. She'd gone to his head like a glass of champagne.

"You're welcome," he called, but her curly brown ponytail had disappeared around the bend, taking the rest of her along with it.

CHAPTER THREE

OLIVIA PACED HER jog faster and harder down the mountain trail. The adrenaline from almost getting killed had scared her from crown to sneakers. A stupid mistake on her part had nearly left Micah with another parent to bury and mourn when he'd already left his home and school to come with her to Roseley.

As her feet pounded the trail, she wondered just how long she would have had to be missing before Aunt Hattie called the authorities. How long would it have taken before a search crew had found her broken body at the bottom of the peak? She hadn't even told Aunt Hattie or Micah where she was going. From sheer desperation to get away and clear her head, she'd left Micah pouting on his bed and sprinted out the back door.

She shuddered at the thought of Micah learning the devastating news. Hattie would have been there to comfort him and care for him, but if he'd had to lose a second parent before making it to adulthood—

Olivia wiped her moistened eyes and let out an audible "No!"

The shout of her own voice often interrupted her negative, destructive thoughts, and since losing Jeb, there had been plenty of those. Heck, she'd done her fair share of ruminating before Jeb had died, too, and it had usually been about him.

Fortunately, she reminded herself, she was fine. Micah would have his mother for another day. He could continue to complain and roll his eyes at her as if she hadn't just been shocked out of her baseball cap on what was supposed to be a pleasant jog. Luckily a man had appeared out of thin air and saved her from an early grave, and if she'd had to choose a rescuer, she couldn't have picked a better one than the strong, handsome stranger.

Olivia slowed to a stop to catch her breath. She'd been so shocked at what had just happened on Falcon's Peak she hadn't even caught his name. She couldn't send him a thank-you note or a gourmet cookie basket or whatever else you were supposed to do when someone saved your life. *Hey, thank you, kind sir, for risking your life to save mine. I hope you like homemade mini muffins.*

Olivia hunched over, hands pressed to thighs, and released a hearty laugh at the thought. Her mother had always been one for good manners and had instilled in her the value of saying thank-you, but even she would laugh at Olivia's train of thought. It had been a very long day.

Once she made it back to her car and settled into the driver's seat, her thoughts shifted from gift baskets back to her rescuer. He had been staring at her so intently she was sure his hazel-green eyes would be seared into her memory forever. And when he'd asked her if she was okay, really okay, the genuineness in his voice made her question if he wasn't about to wrap her in his arms and hold her right there on the mountain until the adrenaline had passed and she'd stopped shaking. Would she have let him?

Between arriving in Roseley, managing Micah's adjustment to Hattie's cottage, and then nearly dying, the day had been challenging enough without piling on her attraction to a perfect stranger. She tried to shake away the flush that came over her at the memory of the man's voice, warm and steady like a crackling fire. The energy exuding off him reassured her that she was safe again, and to believe him so easily was a first for her. At least, it was the first time in a long time she'd believed in a man's words.

She was eager to get back to the cottage and hug Micah. Maybe she'd squeeze him tight enough to forget the fear that still seized her at the thought of falling. That feeling was understandable to her—probably was to anyone who'd gone through a near-death experience. But to also feel desire, a desire to see the stranger again, made her stomach flutter. Since Jeb had died—heck, even when he was still alive—she'd felt so detached from her desire and need to be loved and cared for—a direct result of years of neglect and a marriage that had turned loveless. Now, even entertaining the thought of having someone protect or care for her, the way the stranger had, felt a bit intoxicating. Maybe too intoxicating.

By the time she'd gotten back to the cottage, thrown herself into the shower and tugged on clean clothes, she was determined to wipe the entirety of the afternoon's events completely from her mind. If she ever bumped into her hero again, she'd smile and offer a sincere thank-you, but that would be it. A second encounter could never be as engaging as their first one, as both of their emotions and senses had been firing at max capacity on the peak.

Aunt Hattie honked the truck horn from

the driveway, sending Olivia to the bedroom window.

"Hattie?" she called down. Hattie slung an arm out the driver's-side window and craned her neck up at her.

"Shake a leg, honey! Bayshore happy hour already started!"

Olivia turned to find Micah napping. She sat on the side of his bed and swept a hand over his sweaty forehead. He was a hot sleeper and had been since he was a baby. So many summer nights she'd sat rocking him on the front porch, waiting for Jeb to call from whichever city he was in. So many nights she'd had only her own loneliness and Micah's perfect rounded forehead to keep her company.

Micah stirred and pulled a pillow over his head.

"Hey, kiddo," she said. "It's time for dinner. I have a crazy story to tell you."

"I told Aunt Hattie I don't feel like going. She said there's sandwich stuff in the fridge."

Olivia rubbed his shoulder gently.

"But it's our first night in Roseley." She wanted to fight against his protests and scoop him into her arms and smooch kisses all over his face. Instead, she tried jockeying for a quiet dinner together. "We don't have to eat at the restaurant. What if we pick up food and take a drive around town? I can show you where all my favorite—"

"I've been in the car for *three days*."

"Yeah, I know but…"

"We can take a drive tomorrow. Okay? I'm tired."

Olivia bit back a few tears, the stab of Micah's rejection twisting in her gut. She knew teenage boys could be temperamental with their mothers. Every experience like this one just reminded her that he was progressing through the next developmental stage of life. Still, it didn't make the shot of reality sting any less.

"I'll bring you back some dessert," she said, easing off the bed. She made her way to the truck and climbed in the passenger seat of Hattie's old rusted-out Chevy. "Micah's staying in tonight."

"Leave him be," Hattie said. "He probably needs to be alone." She shifted the truck into Drive and took off down the driveway. "Speaking of which, where did you go this afternoon?"

"Roseley Mountain."

"Beautiful day for it. See anything interesting?"

"Interesting?" Her jog had been nothing

but interesting, not that she was prepared to talk about it.

"Yeah," Hattie said. "I was up there last week and passed nearly a dozen other hikers. It's not the reclusive spot it once was. Was it crowded?"

"No, I wouldn't say so."

Olivia scrambled to think of something to change the subject, but the only thought pinging around in her head included a set of hazel-green eyes.

"Meet anyone new on the trail?"

"Meet?" The word popped out before she could help it. Hattie zeroed in on the higher pitch her voice made and raised a brow.

"Yeah, *meet*. This town is crawling with all sorts of interesting folks. Who'd you see?"

Olivia fiddled with the radio station, tuning for a song that would distract her from the memory of her stranger's strong arms. Technically, she hadn't *met* the guy. They hadn't exactly exchanged names. Sure, she'd been pressed against him and, sure, she'd pet his adorable German shepherd and, *sure*, they'd shared an experience that would forever tether him in her memory for as long as she lived. However, when it came to officially *meeting*…

"I bumped into a…" Olivia wasn't quite

sure how to explain what had happened unless she was prepared to explain all the details.

"Friend?"

Olivia shrugged. He certainly wasn't a foe. "Uh, no. A stranger. I took a little tumble when I was jogging, and a guy helped me out."

"Tumble? Did you trip?"

Olivia shrugged again. Did nearly falling off the side of a mountain constitute a little trip? "Sort of."

"On the trail?"

"Off the trail."

"In the woods?"

"Um… Falcon's Peak."

Aunt Hattie's head swiveled like a barn owl, her eyes just as curious. "Let me sum up so far," her aunt said. "You went jogging up Roseley Mountain and took a tumble near the peak when a stranger helped you."

"Right."

"Helped you how?"

"Helped me…" Olivia now felt grateful Micah was not riding in the back seat of the truck. "To my feet."

"Is that all?"

Olivia scoffed and began digging through her purse for her lip gloss. "What else would there be? Sometimes the story isn't a story at all." She peered at her reflection in the visor mirror, smeared gloss over her lips and slammed the visor up again. "Geesh."

"My auntie senses are tingling here, Liv. I can play a verbal cat and mouse game with you if you want, but wouldn't it be easier to just tell your dear, sweet aunt what really happened? Ooh, or are you waiting for cocktails?"

Olivia chuckled. The release of laughter felt good after such a long day. "Why do you always think there's more to the story?"

Hattie shimmied her shoulders. "Because there *is*."

"How do you know?"

"I know your tell, honey. You'd make an awful poker player."

"What tell? I don't have a—"

"You twist your mouth the same way your mother did when she shouldn't tell me something but hoped I'd drag it out of her. I was the first one to learn she was secretly dating your father and they were expecting you." Hattie poked a gentle finger to the dimple at the corner of Olivia's mouth. "Same twist… right there. Blood doesn't lie, love."

Olivia met Hattie's smile with one of her own and then heaved a breath. "Okay, okay. I nearly met my maker not an hour ago."

"Died?"

"Yep. I was too close to the ledge and this man came out of nowhere and saved me. Literally saved me, Hattie. Hero stuff."

Hattie was staring so intensely she tumbled onto the gravelly shoulder before swerving to right the truck.

"Hattie!" Olivia cried, gripping the center console. "The road! I tell you I almost died and you're about to kill us!"

Hattie's eyes darted excitedly between Olivia and the road. "You're fine, dear. I know what I'm doing. Now get back to the good stuff. The full-blown hero stuff. What did he look like? Good-lookin', did you say?"

"Aren't you concerned I almost *died*?"

"You look alive enough to me. Spill it and don't leave out any details, please."

"Liv, love, you almost died?" Olivia mocked. "I'd be devastated. I could cry right now just at the thought of it!"

"I'm glad you're okay," Hattie said, patting Olivia's hand affectionately. "*Are* you okay?"

"Yes. I think so."

"Good. I love you, honey."

"Thanks."

Hattie patted Olivia's hand again and turned her attention to the road. They drove in silence for a while, and Olivia was satisfied to see some concern registering on her aunt's face. She appreciated the kindness in Hattie's voice, too.

She watched out the window, letting the tall grass along the road blur for a couple miles before it transitioned into asphalt and brought them to The Bayshore Bar. The day had not been without its challenges or surprises, and when they finally pulled into the parking lot, seeing all the other cars and people gave Olivia hope that the evening would be one for celebrating. She'd had a very rocky beginning and middle to her day, but now she was about to enjoy her aunt's company. A beautiful evening looking out over the water was just what she needed. She'd just managed a smile when she spotted Hattie smirking.

"What?" Olivia said. The register of Hattie's voice dropped an octave as the words slid from her mouth, slow and pointed.

"Was he hot enough to melt your butter?"

"Hattie!"

"It's been a while since anyone around here has had a story worth listening to."

"Hattie."

"Oh, come on. Who can you trust more than me?"

Hattie crookedly swung her big truck into two parking spaces. Her mention of butter melting had made something inside Olivia cringe as if she was being disloyal to Jeb. Plus, it was weird having her aunt's face light up like they were thirteen-year-old girls hiding under a bedsheet with a flashlight and whispering about boys.

She thought back to the days when she did feel excitement. She'd been just out of her teens when Jeb had first started calling. He had been older and confident, so headstrong and ready to take on the world, that she'd felt honored to tag along with him—in the beginning.

"He doesn't melt my butter," Olivia said with a disgust she had not really meant. "Not that I'm in a position to notice stuff like that... notice men, I mean."

"I only wondered if he was good-looking. I didn't imply you had feelings for the guy."

"I'm very grateful he was there when I slipped off the ledge—"

"You slipped off?"

"It's fine. *I'm fine.*"

She recalled the moment when he had gotten her to sturdy ground. She could still feel his arms, as firm as tree trunks, holding her close.

All at once Olivia's cheeks felt hot.

"Look," she said. "He saved me, and I

thanked him. I doubt he'll even remember it in another day or two. I certainly won't. It was insignificant, hardly worth mentioning."

Hattie shut off the truck. The Bayshore Bar, a restaurant on Little Lake Roseley with a deck overlooking the water, was crowded for a weekday. That was most likely because it was still warm enough to sit out on the deck and catch the last few summer rays. That was all Olivia wanted to do now.

"I'm glad you told me, no matter how insignificant you say it was."

"Me, too," Olivia said. They made their way into the restaurant. "We don't need to talk about it again."

"If that's what you want."

"It is."

Olivia shivered away how emotionally exposed she felt from telling anyone else what had happened on Falcon's Peak. Almost dying was too terrifying to relive, and the jolt she'd gotten from talking to the stranger still felt confusing. Sure, as an art therapist she was good at guiding children to talk about their feelings, but for the moment, she was content to suppress her own.

Hattie slipped an arm around Olivia's waist and gave her a squeeze as they waited for the hostess.

"Now that I've got you in town for a while, I don't want you disappearing on me."

"Fat chance. I need someone to help me with Micah."

"Geesh, if you had died that would have really ticked him off."

Hattie howled at her own joke, and though it seemed too dark to dare laugh at, Olivia couldn't help joining her. If she didn't laugh away her frustration with Micah, she knew she'd probably cry—hard.

Hattie patted Olivia's cheek fondly. The handful of bangle bracelets around her wrist clinked to punctuate her words. "I'm glad to have you and Micah here."

"We won't overstay our welcome," Olivia said. "I'm not sure how long we'll stay, but I promise it won't be too long."

"Stay forever," Hattie said. "I'm tickled pink to have you both. And to toast your first night in Roseley we need some fun, fruity drinks. I'm going to hit the bar. I'll meet you at our table."

Hattie hurried off before Olivia could stop her. She appreciated Hattie's zest for life and she was happy to celebrate her first night in Roseley.

She had no sooner crossed the deck, fol-lowing the hostess to a table, when she spotted a familiar face. Standing at the railing, the setting sun highlighting those strong shoulders she couldn't get out of her head, was her rescuer, with his eyes locked on her.

CHAPTER FOUR

TYLER LEANED BACK and breathed in the fresh lake breeze. He liked when the waves were choppy enough to crash against the deck and spritz his face. After the afternoon he'd had, it felt like a christening.

He waited for his take-out order and watched people chat and mingle on the deck. His dad had always loved to come here, too. By the time Tyler had hit late grade school, they had made it a tradition to grab burgers and sodas here after a long day of fishing. But that was a long time ago, and the food had never tasted as good since Dad died.

As his gaze floated back toward the entrance, someone interesting caught his eye. He had to blink a double take.

Repositioning himself to fully face the door, he watched the woman from Falcon's Peak stride across the deck. He liked that she hadn't yet seen him. He could watch her as she was, how she must usually behave when a thousand ccs of adrenaline weren't coursing through her veins. She was graceful, easy on her feet, and noticeably surprised when she finally spotted him.

He made his way toward her, and they both stopped short at her table.

"How's the arm, slugger?" he said.

She rubbed her bicep instinctively. "Hi. Fine, I guess."

"Are you sure? I think I nearly ripped it off this afternoon."

"It's okay. I won't hold it against you if it bruises."

"It already is. I wanted to tell you to ice it, but you ran off on me so quickly—"

"I didn't run off." She straightened. Her eyes widened in protest and Tyler had to fight to suppress a grin.

"No, of course not," he said. "That was a bad choice of words on my part." She readjusted on her feet as he cleared his throat and started again. "What I meant was, make sure you ice it. I'd hate to see it hurting you later."

Since their last encounter, she had piled her hair on top of her head. The wisps framing her face were curling more by the minute from the evening humidity. Without the baseball cap he could get a better look at her. Her brown eyes had looked nearly black on the mountain, but now, facing the setting sun, they warmed to brown.

"Thanks. I'll do that."

"I didn't mean to keep you from—"

"Did you already eat?" she asked. He dipped his head closer, looking for clarification.

"Are you asking me to join you?"

"Oh, no. I don't want to be rude if you're eating all alone, so yes, of course, you can sit here. But honestly, I was just making conversation."

This time he winked. "I'm waiting for a take-out order but thank you. How about you?"

"Celebrating with my aunt."

"Do you have a new lease on life?"

"Something like that. Today is my first day in Roseley."

"You almost bit the dust on day one? And I don't even know your name."

She stuck out her hand and shook his firmly on contact. "Olivia Howard. Nice to officially meet you."

"Tyler Elderman. What brings you to Roseley?"

"Visiting for now. We don't have any plans to move here—yet."

"We?" The word felt covered in barbs as

he spoke it. Still, picturing Olivia with someone who qualified as the other half of a "we" made him curious.

"My son, Micah, is fourteen. Recently, life for us has been challenging." He remembered her mentioning her son earlier. Her eyes skimmed the water as she seemed to muster more of an explanation. "We came up here looking for a slower change of pace, I think."

"You'll find it. Roseley has a way of reconnecting people to what's important. It brings the good stuff into sharper focus."

"Yeah?" she said, brightening. "You have no idea how much I want that to be true."

"Is it just you and your son?"

She nodded. "We're staying with my aunt. I took a leave of absence from work and…"

He waited for her to finish, but as she seemed at a loss, he felt he should help her.

"Let me welcome you to Roseley. How long will you be around?"

"Hard to say. I don't have a plan."

"Sometimes the best things happen when you don't."

"Ha. I'm not so sure about that."

"It's true," he insisted. "I didn't have a plan for this afternoon but look who I met."

She cracked a smile. "You almost got yourself killed. Tomorrow you should at least write a to-do list."

He laughed as the waitress hurried over with his carryout order.

"*Your* to-do list," he said with a departing grin, "includes icing that arm. It was nice talking with you, Olivia Howard."

"You, too, Tyler."

He strode back across the deck as his cell phone vibrated on his hip. It was a text message from Gary, who he'd promised dinner.

What's taking so long?

"Hold your horses," Tyler muttered to himself on his way out of the restaurant. "I wish it had taken a little longer."

OLIVIA STEPPED INTO gardening boots and out into the backyard. Like every day that week, Hattie had already been up before the sunshine, picking up fallen sticks and clearing her garden beds. The threat of a night frost had been on locals' lips the day before. Sure enough, Olivia had woken to a cool, brisk morning. She had left Micah snoring in their room and had found Hattie outside, bidding goodbye to her summer flower beds.

"How long do you expect Micah to sleep

today?" Hattie asked, shielding her eyes from the morning sun and glancing up at the bedroom window. "I need to transplant my hostas and could use his strong back."

Olivia tucked her hair under a bandana.

"Ten. Eleven. Who knows?"

"Again?" Hattie said, shaking her head. "That will not do. The winter snow will be here before we know it, and he'll sleep away all the fun of autumn. Come on. Let's get that child of yours up and about. There's plenty to do today."

"It's not worth the aggravation," Olivia said. "He'll be grumpy for the rest of the day if I wake him now."

Hattie made for the back door.

"Since you arrived, he's been grumpy no matter what you do."

"Really, Hattie," she called. "Just let him sleep a little longer."

Her aunt stopped and turned to stare down at her, her normally pleasant face contorting.

"Liv, darling, are you scared of your son?"

Olivia let out a snort. "Excuse me?"

Hattie planted each of her garden-gloved fists on her hips. "You let him skip our celebratory dinner at The Bayshore Bar—"

"*You* did, remember?"

"You still haven't made him unpack his

suitcase. He kicked his stinky shoes onto my coffee table last night and left his dirty dishes in the sink. He was up wandering the house until two o'clock in the morning, while you and I were trying to get some beauty sleep."

"I didn't know he'd kept you awake." She felt a twinge of regret at that.

"I can't believe he didn't keep *you* awake. You sleep not three feet from him. La Casa de Hattie needs some new ground rules, and the management—that's you and me, love—need to lay them down."

Olivia's mouth fell ajar. After years of counseling and researching child development, her son sounded like a typical teenager to her.

Micah had always been a pleasant kid, despite Jeb's long absences on the road. He had certainly been a kid she'd loved to be around and for so many years the two of them had been buddies. Then Jeb had died, Micah had entered into his teens and overnight he'd started acting like he knew better than she did. The last two years had been so hard she already felt like she was pacing herself, rationing her energy stores just to get through his next several years of teenage angst. Jeb's death had felt like a bomb going off in her life, so she now chose her battles with Micah carefully, sometimes choosing to make peace and hunker down so she had the energy to face another day.

"Hattie," she said. "I think setting expectations is a great idea. However, it's more complicated than simply barging into his bedroom at this hour."

"Liv, dear. He needs discipline, hard work and clear expectations. Letting things go now will only make it harder later. He's going to be a man with a driver's license, pressuring you to fork over the car keys, before you can say *curfew*."

"I know that," Olivia said, her voice breaking. "Don't you think I already know that?" Her little boy was not so little anymore. When he had been a toddler, she'd helped him understand the passage of time by counting the number of sleeps between events. "Mama," he'd ask, pulling at the hem of her nightgown. "How many more sleeps until we visit Grandma?" Olivia would smile and hold up fingers for a visual cue. "Three more sleeps until we see her, Micah," she'd say, smiling. "Three more sleeps," he would repeat.

Now she could feel the number of sleeps before Micah entered adulthood dwindling as fast as sand through her fingers. "How many sleeps until my window of influence with you is over, Micah?" she'd sometimes whisper late at night from the doorway of his bedroom. "How many sleeps do I still have to turn this around?"

"Liv…" Hattie said, her tone challenging.

"He's adjusting," Olivia said, sputtering the words defensively. "I know he needs to get moving but—"

"March your mama legs up those stairs and get that boy up for the day. If you were back home and he was in school, he'd be in first period by now."

"He was up until two last night, and it's only seven o'clock in the morning."

"Then he'll be good and tired for bedtime tonight."

Olivia tried to scoff away Hattie's orders, but Hattie was having none of it.

"Either you're going to be the bad guy, or I am, kiddo. I'm fine accepting that role for a little while, though a part of me thinks I'd be enabling you."

Olivia's forced laugh dissipated quicker than morning dew under the hot sunshine. She moved toward her aunt. "Enabling me to do what, exactly? We've only been here a few days. He's getting adjusted, Hattie. The last time I checked, we weren't on an army base. You're acting like I'm the worst mother in the world for not putting my kid on a strict schedule."

Olivia matched Hattie's stare, as firm as an army colonel, but inside she could feel herself unraveling.

"You're a terrific mother," Hattie said.

"You don't seem to think so."

"I do."

"But?"

"You've lost your nerve where he's concerned. You used to have it. You still had it at Jeb's funeral when I last saw you, but somewhere in between then and now…" Hattie released fingertips from her lips like an Italian chef bidding goodbye. "Lost."

Olivia peered up at Micah's window. Was parenting *supposed* to be this hard? If there had been any profession in the world that should have prepared her for motherhood, shouldn't it have been psychology? Recently her vocation had seemed to prepare her for parenting as much as a ski instructor was prepared for welding steel.

"I will talk to him today," Olivia said. She could already feel her inner cheerleader rallying ideas for how to fix things. "I'll encourage him to go to bed earlier tonight. It might take a few days to get him on a schedule but—"

"Weak."

"Hattie—" Olivia began, but her aunt's face had slipped into determination. Spinning on her garden bootheels and marching into the house, she disappeared before Olivia could stop her. Within a minute, Hattie had drawn the shades and opened the window by Micah's bed. From the yard, Olivia could hear voices. Though she couldn't distinguish what they were saying, she could imagine the exchange, especially the protests spattering from Micah like grease in a hot cast-iron skillet.

Olivia turned her focus to Hattie's flower beds, wanting to avoid getting in the middle of her aunt's tour de force. She knelt at the edge of the garden and tugged at the last weeds of the season. When the stems ripped, leaving the tops of the gnarly root taunting her from the soil, it made her pull even more furiously. Even though it was Hattie forcing Micah out of bed, *she'd* be the one he blamed.

All she had wanted when arriving in Roseley was a little peace. She wanted to return to a time when the days were long and happy. Her memories of this place were deeply rooted in memories of her mother— that much she at least recognized. Sometimes a longing for Roseley had really just been a longing to be with her mom again, the two of them squeezing onto her grandparents' large wooden swing and talking the afternoon away. Her mother had always been good at taking a long, humid day and turning it into a memory.

When she'd been Micah's age, she'd craved her mother's company, but Micah certainly didn't crave her company now. And sadly, since Jeb's passing, he also didn't seem to crave anything else. That was what worried her most.

Her throat tightened and she promised herself she'd figure things out with Micah. She wasn't sure how to do that, but she loved Micah too much to quit.

The back screen door banged against the frame, shifting her attention. Micah stormed out into the yard, his clothes disheveled and his hair a mess. He had tugged on his sneakers without tying them and had grabbed a handful of granola bars from the kitchen as breakfast.

Olivia sat back on her heels and watched him. Despite his gawky limbs and soft cheeks, he had begun growing into a man. It wouldn't be long before he was a foot taller than her and nearly twice her width at the shoulders. He was the spitting image of Jeb at the same age, aside from the dark eyes and darker complexion he'd inherited from her.

"Mornin', honey," she called, trying to keep her voice as calm and pleasant as she could manage.

"Mornin'," Micah said. He trudged past her and disappeared into the woods behind Hattie's backyard. Hattie trailed behind and stopped when she reached the flower beds.

"Tomorrow will be easier," she said, patting Olivia on the shoulder. "He'll be grumpy the first few times we wake him, but eventually he'll even out his sleep schedule."

"Where do you think he's going?" Olivia said, still staring toward the woods.

"I hid some things out there for him to find. How do you feel about him using power tools?"

Olivia's head snapped up. *"Unsupervised?"*

Micah hadn't demonstrated that he could handle loading the dishwasher, and Hattie wanted to arm him with a table saw or drill?

"No, dear. My mistake. There's just a handsaw and a hammer and nails. There's no electricity in the woods."

Olivia let out a breath of relief. "I don't understand. What did you ask him to do out there?"

"I didn't ask him to do anything." Hattie

went back to work, pulling weeds as Olivia stared after her confused. "But I hauled a huge pile of scrap wood and tools out there before you two arrived."

"For what?"

"I'm not sure. We'll see what he makes of it once he finds it."

Olivia returned to pulling weeds, letting Hattie's words settle over her. Her aunt spoke in riddles much the same way her mother used to. She wondered what the pile of wood looked like. She wondered how on earth Micah would figure out that it had been placed in the woods for him, as some sort of gift. Finally, she sat back on her heels again.

"Hattie, how did you know Micah would even walk into the woods?"

Hattie raked her gloved fingers through the dirt. "When a man's soul is unsettled, he escapes into the wild."

"Do you consider your woods the wild?"

Hattie smiled. "They'll have to do."

CHAPTER FIVE

TYLER SHOOK OUT his hand and stared up at his favorite rock cliff. It was the one he preferred to climb on mornings like this, when the sky was clear and promised to brighten to the perfect shade of robin's-egg blue. He liked to get to the mountain to test his equipment while it was still dark, while the sun was still stirring. It was a short climb to the summit, something he could manage before he had to open the clinic for the day, so by the time he usually reached it, the sun had breached the horizon and all of Roseley was waking for the day.

Today, however, would not be one of those days. His hand still ached and shook when he tried to clamp it shut. It was normal, considering what he'd done earlier that week on Falcon's Peak, but it meant he wouldn't be grabbing any climbing holds anytime soon.

Tyler breathed in the fresh morning air and listened to his favorite friend, a male house finch, sing his arrival just like he did every morning. Tyler knew it had a nest in one of the conifers nearby, but he had yet to pinpoint it. Instead, he enjoyed listening to the warbled short notes the bird sang, ending in his usual upward slur. By the time Tyler made his way back to his truck, he had a feeling it was going to be a good day.

Back in town, Tyler unlocked the front door of his veterinary practice as the ladies of Roseley's walking club hustled up the block. One of them shot a waving hand into the air and hollered, "Yoo-hoo! Dr. Elderman!"

Tyler offered a quick wave as CeCe Makes, a stout woman who commanded any room she entered, reached him and handed over an index card. She and the other ladies marched in place as CeCe explained it.

"Gary's booth reservation for the Fall Festival is lot 34. He can start setting up the day before, beginning at eight a.m."

Tyler tucked the card in his pocket before turning his attention to Mallory Robinson. She ran The Lollipop and, though her culinary sweets were for humans, she occasionally made an order of pet-friendly treats for him to pass out at the clinic.

"I think we'll be ready for another order of cookies, Mal," he said.

Mallory flashed a thumbs-up. "I'll whip up a batch later today."

Joan Baskins, a newer arrival to Roseley, leaned ever so slightly to glance past Tyler into the clinic.

"How's your uncle these days?" she asked. The other women tilted their heads closer, tuned for his answer.

"Busy. We have more business than we know what to do with."

"That's a good problem to have," Joan said. "You can always hire more help, but you can't always scrounge up more business."

"Good point." He and Gary ran the veterinary side of things and they had employees to run the front desk, billing and scheduling. They didn't need another full-time or even part-time employee. What they could really use was another pair of hands from time to time.

"Come on, ladies! We have to keep our heart rates up!" CeCe Makes shouted, twinkling her fingers goodbye. "Forward march!"

The walking group hustled down the sidewalk like a roving gang. Tyler entered the clinic and switched on the overhead lights as Gary wandered out from the back room.

"What are you doing back here?" Tyler said. "You missed the walking group."

Gary's face dropped in disappointment. "They're early. They must have changed their route."

"Only you would memorize their route."

"Being in the right place at the right time is less about luck and more about careful observation, nephew. I'll recalculate for tomorrow."

Tyler considered this. Being on Falcon's Peak when Olivia had needed him had felt like all luck at first, but he supposed his careful observation, where swinging ponytails were concerned, hadn't hurt, either. He wondered how Olivia was faring and if she would make a return visit to the mountain.

"Ty?"

"Hmm?" Tyler jerked his attention to his uncle, unaware he'd zoned out for a moment.

"The walking group? Did they say anything?"

Tyler ran a hand down his face, scrambling to shift his train of thought from Olivia and her hiking routine. He surveyed the clinic like the Cliffs Notes to an exam question were written on the walls.

"What do you think of bringing a volunteer on board?" he said.

"A volunteer? To do what?"

"Help set up before surgeries. Sit with animals before we put them under anesthetic.

Sit with them as they wake up. I could come up with any number of things if you give me a minute."

"That's usually a paid position and one we can't really afford right now."

"Hence it being a volunteer. Maybe we can find a retiree who's looking to—"

"Retiree? Why do I feel like you already have a person or *persons* in mind?"

Tyler offered Gary the registration card. "The walking group is already used to getting up early and we could use an early bird. That's a fact."

Gary studied the card. "I'm not opposed to bringing someone on as long as he or she is doing it for the right reasons."

"Love of animals?"

Gary winked and tapped the side of his nose as he continued.

"Make up a sign and put it in the window. In the meantime, I had to schedule a last-minute appointment for you this afternoon. Hattie Pike called about Boomer."

Tyler frowned. "What's wrong with him?"

"She wasn't sure. He might just need a checkup."

"This afternoon, huh." Tyler pulled out his phone, checking his schedule. How likely was it that Olivia would go jogging on Roseley

Mountain at the same time again today? He hadn't seen her for the last several days, not that he had gone hiking to look for her. With a sore hand he couldn't rock-climb, so hiking was his next favorite choice. Plus, if he did happen to see her again, he wouldn't mind. It would be a natural meeting, passing on the trail and, as Gary told it, being in the right place at the right time—

"There you go again," Gary said. "Earth to Dr. Elderman."

"What?"

"The other night you handed me my food and then stared at your sandwich for nearly five minutes. What's up with you?"

"Nothing."

"Something. You've been acting weird all week."

Tyler shoved his cell phone in his pocket. "My week didn't go entirely how I planned."

Gary leaned closer, now interested. "A lady?"

"What?" Tyler scoffed. "No. Why do you always assume it's a lady?"

Gary patted Tyler on the shoulder before returning to the back room. "Chalk it up to wishful thinking."

"What time did you schedule Boomer again?"

"I told her to drop in after four."

That ruled out a hike on Roseley Mountain at the same time he'd seen Olivia. But it was probably for the best. The chances of bumping into her three times in less than a week were slim to nil.

AFTER A COUPLE hours of working in the garden, Olivia had found Hattie standing in the kitchen with a contemplative look on her face.

"Is everything okay?" Olivia asked.

"Micah asked about my old photo albums. I know I have a big box of them somewhere, but I can't seem to put my hands on them." She sighed.

"What about in the shed?"

"May lightning strike me silly if I stored them out there. They would be warped in a month in this Michigan weather. I'm sure they'll turn up eventually." Hattie fluffed her hair and turned her attention fully to Olivia. "What are you up to this afternoon?"

Olivia didn't want to admit that she'd planned on going for another hike. Without a job to fill her days, she had mentally been gearing up to tutor Micah, in the hopes that she could keep him academically on track while she figured out their next moves. However, she hadn't yet broken that news to him. After Hattie had practically pulled him out of bed by his sideburns, she preferred to table the conversation about tutoring until tomorrow.

"My day is open. Do you need help with something?"

"I'd appreciate some, yes. I accidentally double-booked myself."

"You? Double-booked?" Olivia grabbed an iced tea out of the refrigerator. "Things certainly have changed around here."

"Don't I know it. I will rest for a month once this Fall Festival is over. Boomer got sick a few times last night, and I wouldn't mind having the vet check him out."

"Oh no. A virus?"

Hattie lowered her voice. "He has a sensitive stomach. I suspect someone has been feeding him human food."

"Micah?"

"Yes, unless you've been the one slipping him treats."

Olivia made her way to the living room and found Micah crashed on the sofa with Boomer. She knelt beside them and examined the dog.

"Not feeling very well, huh, buddy?"

Micah winced. "I think I'm the reason. When Dodger was alive, he could eat out of the trash all day without it affecting him."

"Dodger was a different breed. Boomer has to stick to his dog food." Olivia studied the pup for a moment before glancing up at Micah. "I'm taking him to the vet later. Would you like to come with me?"

Micah shrugged. "I can, if you want."

Olivia nodded, trying her best not to appear overly enthusiastic. *I want*, she thought.

That afternoon, Olivia had no sooner pulled onto Main Street, a couple of blocks from the Roseley Veterinarian Clinic, when Micah motioned for her to pull over.

"Do you mind if I run into a shop and then meet you down at the clinic?"

Olivia pulled to the curb and squinted out Micah's passenger window to the shop he was referring to. She wondered what he needed in an office supply store.

He hadn't waited for her reply before barreling out of the truck and slamming the door shut. When he turned and found Olivia still watching him, he frowned and waved her off, his typical response when he felt she was smothering him.

"Well, I guess that's that," she muttered as she pulled back onto the road. Olivia looked down at Boomer, who was blinking up at her. She scratched the lovable bulldog under the chin.

"Boomer, *you* like spending time with me, don't you?" Boomer affectionately licked her hand. "Yeah, that's what I thought."

Olivia crept the truck up the street, taking her time to note each store on either side. She and her mother had always loved making a day of walking the streets. Even if they didn't end up buying much, Olivia could always count on visits to The Lollipop to select penny candy, Pleats and Patches to sort through the table of discounted fabric swatches, or Grandma's Basement to admire the antique treasures.

The wave of nostalgia that washed over her when she spotted the familiar store signs and painted window displays caught her momentarily off guard.

"You don't suppose Micah would want to go shopping with me, do you, Boomer?" She had no sooner uttered the words than she rolled her eyes at herself. It felt like wishful thinking just then.

She pulled into an angled parking spot in front of the clinic and lifted Boomer out of the truck when a familiar voice called her name.

"Oh my goodness! Liv! Hey, Livvie!"

Olivia turned to spot a beautiful redhead dashing toward her from across the street.

Olivia squealed when she recognized the bright smile. "Caroline!" she cried, embracing her friend.

"I thought that was you!"

"It's me!"

The two women laughed, holding each other as if the other might try to escape.

"Hattie told me to keep my eye out for you, but I didn't believe you were moving back until now." Caroline beamed.

"Not moving back, but I'm definitely here for a while."

"And the baby?"

Olivia laughed. "He's fourteen."

"A teenager! Gosh, does time fly. I'm sure he's sprouted half a foot since the funeral. I'd love to see him. And you." Caroline checked her cell phone. "And if I wasn't so darn late for an appointment, I'd take you out for coffee and chat your ear off all afternoon."

"I have to get Boomer to the vet anyway."

"Now that you're back, we can't waste any time, Liv. Can you meet Friday afternoon at The Lollipop? My treat?"

Olivia pretended to consider her schedule even though it was wide open. For the first time in her life, she had more time on her hands than she knew what to do with. It was a little unnerving. "I would love that."

Caroline squeezed Olivia's hands before hurrying back across the street. "I'm *so* late. I'm sorry, but we'll catch up Friday. I'll text you later about the time. And bring Micah!"

Caroline dashed down the sidewalk, turning to wave one last time before disappearing around the corner. Olivia sighed happily and looked down at Boomer, who had plunked himself to sit sidesaddle on the pavement at her feet.

"Boomer, Caroline has no idea how much I needed that."

CHAPTER SIX

TYLER ADMINISTERED A vaccine shot for a sweet, four-month-old kitten named Marble as it finished licking a smear of food off the exam table.

"A little tuna fish and Cool Whip go a long way, huh?" he said. Mrs. Hanford nodded as her daughter, Beatrix, smiled and showed off a mouthful of braces decorated with red and black bands for Falcon school spirit.

Tyler continued, "The next time you need to get a shot, Beatrix, tell your mom you will require a tub of Cool Whip…or ice cream… or something delicious and distracting."

He led them out of the exam room and to the front desk.

"Marble," he said, handing the kitten's chart to Julia, his receptionist. "You were a pro. Julia has some treats for you, on account of your excellent behavior."

Julia offered Marble a little gift bag. "Fresh from The Lollipop."

"Thank you, Dr. Elderman," Mrs. Hanford

said. "It's nice seeing you back at the clinic. You know, I remember you hanging around here when you were a little boy. That was two cats ago for me."

"After working at several other clinics over the years, I realized there's no place like home, Mrs. Hanford."

"Your dad would be proud."

Tyler swallowed a lump. All he'd ever wanted as a kid was to become a veterinarian and work alongside his father. "Have you seen my apprentice?" his father would say to patrons. "The second generation is already logging his clinic hours." His dad had always been proud to see him working in the clinic as a kid, so he would most certainly be proud now. If only he was still around.

"Thanks, Mrs. Hanford. And I still remember your first cat. It was scared of its own shadow."

"Wallflower. That's right."

"It took Dad and me a long time to win her over."

"You were just as patient with her as your dad was." She smiled, leaning closer. "I almost forgot to ask. How's your mother?"

Tyler's stomach clenched at the mention of Sandy. She was an exercise in practicing more patience than he usually had in reserve. He had received a text from her earlier that week and had felt grateful that his quick reply had appeased her. He could visit only so often without it taking a toll.

"Sandy is fine, thanks for asking."

Fine. It was a strange word to describe a woman who never came close to seeming it.

"Dr. Elderman?" Julia said, leaning forward and dropping her voice to a whisper. "Eh-*em.*"

Tyler waved goodbye to Mrs. Hanford and Beatrix before leaning over the reception desk. "Yes?"

Julia's dark brown eyebrows waggled up at him as she emphatically whispered each pointed word of her next sentence. "Your next appointment is here."

"And?"

"Well," Julia said, leaning closer. "As soon as you walked in, her jaw hit the floor. Old high school flame, I'm guessing?"

Tyler turned. Olivia Howard stood at the far side of the waiting room with Boomer. True to description, she seemed to be picking up her jaw.

"Not quite," he said, as he made his way to her. "Olivia?"

"Hi," she said. Like waves crashing against the sand, her face broke into a wide smile as she hurriedly explained. "I had no idea you worked here."

By the look of her face, he believed her.

"Let me guess," he said. "You're Hattie's…"

"Niece."

"Aha. The aunt you're staying with."

"Yes. My son, Micah, is running an errand but he'll be by in a little bit. You can meet him, too."

Tyler led Olivia to an exam room, avoiding any eye contact with Julia or Gary, who had made his way to reception as if sensing "a lady" was in the vicinity. When they'd reached the room, Tyler gently scooped up Boomer and placed him on the exam table.

"Does anyone in the household have a peanut allergy?" he asked. "I want to give him a little peanut butter."

"I think that's fine. Hattie does that when she needs to feed him medicine. He's gotten sick a few times over the last day."

Tyler unwrapped his stethoscope from around his neck. "Why don't you stand on the other side of the table and give him some love while I examine him."

"Sure thing." Olivia calmly stroked Boomer the same way she had petted Ranger on Falcon's Peak. The gesture was just enough to trigger that memory regardless of how hard he'd tried to ignore it. "I didn't realize this was your practice."

"Partly mine. My dad passed away years ago, so I came back to town recently to help run the place with my uncle. It's a family business again."

"That must be nice, but I'm sorry to hear about your dad."

"It was a long time ago," Tyler said quickly, keeping his focus on Boomer. He had gotten good at accepting condolences about his father, both before he'd passed away and then after. "I was in high school."

Olivia shook her head sadly. "When you lose a parent, no amount of time feels long enough ago."

Tyler caught her line of sight, noticing that her eyes had turned misty. "Very true."

"I'll bet your uncle is happy to have you here."

"He's happy about almost everything."

She smiled. "One of those personalities, huh? When I was expecting my son, one of the baby books described infant temperaments as different types of flowers. He sounds like he was a sunflower or daisy."

"That's pretty accurate. He always looks on the bright side. I'm sure you'll meet him when we're done. Gary never lets a new face slip by him."

"That's fine, just, uh…" Her lips tried for words she couldn't seem to form. Tyler eased back on his feet and waited. He appreciated having an excuse to watch her. She was calm, gentle, though assertive in how she walked and stood. He could tell he made her a little nervous, but he found her unease charming.

"Olivia," he said. "I didn't tell him about what happened on the peak, if that's what you're wondering. I didn't tell anyone."

"No?"

"No."

She breathed a sigh of relief. "It's not a big deal if you did," she said. "Still… I'm glad you didn't. Thanks."

"You're welcome."

Tyler checked Boomer's eyes and ears, taking his time to give the dog a thorough examination.

"Has he been eating?" he asked.

"Happily. My son was feeding him human food. Hattie suspects that's the problem with his tummy, but she still wanted to get him checked out."

Tyler could feel Olivia's eyes on him as he checked Boomer's teeth and gums. When he glanced up and found her staring intently, he suppressed a smile. He quickly reminded himself that he shouldn't care about the beautiful brunette standing opposite him, aside from caring that he could help her aunt's dog feel better. He'd had countless pet owners standing in the exact same spot over the last couple of years and none of them had knocked him off his life course before. This appointment was the same as any other, or at least that was what he continued to remind himself.

No matter how sweet she seemed, getting involved with her, at least in anything more than following up in a few days to see how Boomer was doing, was a recipe for trouble. In his experience, relationships could turn sour as quickly as a carton of expired milk. He'd tasted his fair share of sourness in the past to know he never wanted to try it again, no matter how sweet a person standing opposite him seemed.

"You mentioned that your son will be joining us," Tyler said. "You said he's fourteen?"

"Good memory."

"And you're both staying in Roseley for the fall. Slower change of pace, wasn't it?"

"You're wondering why I pulled him out of school, aren't you?"

Tyler shrugged as he checked Boomer's lymph nodes. "The thought crossed my mind."

"My husband passed away two years ago. Car accident."

Tyler stopped short. The words may have tumbled out of Olivia's mouth in a hurry, like a rehearsed line she'd practiced and delivered many times, but he knew better. He'd approached grief that same way, sometimes falling back on a handful of standard things to say when he didn't want anyone to see how tightly the grief gripped him. By the way Olivia petted Boomer, her face looking completely unfazed by what she'd just told him, he knew her insides were probably a squall of emotion. At least, that was how he had felt for so many years after losing his dad.

He lowered his hands from the dog and gathered his next words as carefully as he might collect snowflakes.

"I'm so sorry," he said. "When you talked about losing a parent before, I thought you were referring to your own."

"I was," she said, matter-of-factly. She clenched her jaw as if steeling herself from revealing much more. Tyler nodded, sensing she had more to say. Finally, she continued. "And I wasn't. Micah and I were close before the accident, but the past two years have put a strain on us. When Hattie offered me her help, I couldn't pass up the opportunity."

"I'm glad you have her."

"Me, too," she said, still stroking Boomer. "Especially when I start homeschooling Micah. Part of me thinks that's a terrible idea and will add even more strain between us, but I don't want him to fall behind."

Tyler did his best to maintain a pleasant, nonjudgmental face. When he was Micah's age, homeschooling with his mother would have been torturous, but for more complicated reasons than what Micah probably faced. Olivia seemed sweet, like she was genuinely trying to do the best for her son. It was refreshing to watch.

"You know," he said. "If things are already strained between the two of you, I have the name of a good tutor."

"Really?"

"It's worth considering. You might know her family, too. Did you say you grew up here?"

"No," Olivia said. "Just summers here with my mother."

"The Collymores run the The Hardware Shop. Their daughter, Maggie Joyce, just graduated from college in May and, as far as I know, she hasn't found a teaching position for the fall yet. She might be a good fit. I can get you her cell phone number."

"Huh," Olivia said. "Thanks. That might be a good idea."

By the time they had returned to the reception desk, Olivia's son had arrived.

"How's Boomer?" the teen said, squatting to tussle on the floor with the dog.

Tyler dipped his hands in his trouser pockets. "I think he's doing great. You must be Micah."

Micah stood and offered his hand with the confidence of a CEO. Micah also looked him right in the eye, something Tyler both noticed and appreciated. "Micah Howard. Pleased to meet you."

"Dr. Elderman."

Olivia quickly segued as Tyler shook the teen's hand. "Micah, Dr. Elderman and I were just talking about what you're going to do in Roseley this semester. He had a fantastic idea for you to—"

"Help in the clinic." The words were out of Micah's mouth so quickly and assertively that Tyler almost believed it had been rehearsed.

Olivia fumbled to correct him. "No, hon. Meet with a school tutor."

Micah went to the window and pulled Tyler's Help Wanted sign off the glass. He held it out to Tyler and beamed. "I'd be a perfect addition to your team, Doctor. I love animals, *all* animals, and I'm very responsible."

Tyler suppressed a smile, both impressed with Micah's enthusiasm and amused at how flabbergasted Olivia looked by it.

"Uh, Micah," she began. "You have schoolwork—"

"With a tutor? That won't take the entire day, will it? I should be able to knock my schoolwork out every day in just a few hours. That leaves me plenty of time to work here."

"It's a volunteer position," Tyler said. "We're looking for someone to come in early in the mornings before the first patients arrive. There would be a lot of mess and dirty work. We're sometimes handling animals who aren't always at their best—"

"Sounds great," Micah said, brightening.

This time Tyler had to smile. "Does it?"

"You like it, don't you?" Micah turned to his mother. "Mom, you don't mind if I work here, right? I overheard you and Hattie talking about giving me more structure. What better way than for me to volunteer?"

"Honey," Olivia began, carefully. "I don't think Dr. Elderman was looking for a…a… student. Right, Dr. Elderman? Don't you need a *seasoned* volunteer?"

Tyler rasped the stubble on his chin. When he had first pitched the idea to Gary about bringing on a volunteer, he'd pictured one of the ladies from the walking club. But now Mrs. Hanford's words were ringing in his ears. He'd been far younger than Micah when he'd started helping his dad and uncle in the clinic, and it had been the best thing for him. He'd learned discipline and responsibility. He'd learned how to care for things that were vulnerable and needed him to be at his best. Most importantly, he'd learned to love what would become his vocation, and he'd done it while working alongside two men who he respected above all others. If Micah yearned for the same thing, who was he to tell him he wasn't old enough to do it?

"Well," Tyler began slowly. "I need someone responsible *and* consistent. If we need you here at six thirty in the morning you can't be late. You can't call off at the last minute. And I need someone with a calm demeanor. You would help me prepare the animals for their surgeries. You'd have to sit with them when they are coming out of the anesthesia. All of those things take a firm yet kind disposition."

"Micah," Olivia cut in. "Maybe we should talk about this first."

"But someone else might get the job in the meantime." Micah turned to face Tyler. "Dr. Elderman," he said, his brow pinched in seriousness. "Would you consider hiring me on a probationary period? Take me on for a couple weeks and see how I do. After that we could discuss a permanent placement."

Tyler had never heard a teenager pitch an idea with such conviction. He glanced at Olivia.

"It's up to you, Olivia," Tyler said. "I'm happy to give it a try if you are."

Olivia warily eyed her son. "If you stay on top of your studies *and* you pitch in with chores around the house—"

"Done." Micah beamed.

"And," Olivia said. "You make time for us. You and me, kiddo."

Micah rolled his eyes, either at the demand to spend quality time with his mother or because she'd called him kiddo in front of other people. "Fine. Can I do it then?"

Tyler could feel Olivia's hesitation, but the more he studied the teenager, the more his own history at the clinic came flooding back to him. This place had been the source of so many happy and fulfilling memories for him, especially when life had turned on a dime and he'd struggled to find even a glimmer of hope from day to day. Maybe, just maybe, the clinic could help Micah, too. When Olivia looked at Tyler, he softened his expression to imply she should say yes.

She released a sigh that sounded like an agreement, and something inside him leaped before skidding to a halt. He was helping her again. Sure, he wasn't risking his life this time, but hiring Micah still felt like he was risking something for her sake. It was as if he was putting something on the line, giving up something he'd had not two minutes ago. Maybe he knew deep down that saying yes to Micah meant he would get to know Olivia. She'd be more than just some woman he had saved once. He'd be invested in her, in her son, in her story, at least to some degree.

That kind of risk, putting himself on the line for another person, even if it was something small, was the kind of thing he'd sworn off ever doing. He knew putting himself out there, investing some part of his time and energy in other people, was the best way to get hurt. It was the hole in the dam that weakened the entire infrastructure he'd spent years building up. He'd had the flood waters break through once before when he was not much older than Micah, and he'd vowed he would never let it happen again.

However, as he watched Olivia's face glow with maternal pride, he realized that his small concession, his agreement to hire Micah temporarily, also felt important somehow.

"Yes, Micah," Olivia said. "You can work here."

Micah stuck out his hand, eager to seal the deal. As Tyler grasped it and found Olivia's stare, he knew that to some degree, he'd sealed a deal with his own fate, too.

CHAPTER SEVEN

HATTIE SLAMMED THE hood of her Chevy truck and wiped her grease-smeared hands on an old bar towel.

"Did he do okay?" she asked, eyeing Olivia.

"It seems that way." Micah had met with his new school tutor and started a new job all in one day.

They both turned at Micah calling to Boomer from the backyard.

"I had no idea before that he wanted to work with animals," Hattie said. "He could have knocked me over with a feather at dinner the other night. Gosh, the way he was rattling on and on about it…"

"I know." Olivia leaned a hip against the truck. After she and Micah had returned home from the clinic, he hadn't stopped talking about how great he thought the job would be. He'd talked of little else leading up to his first day. "For so many years it was all baseball. Come to think of it, that was usually the only thing he and Jeb ever talked about."

"Did you and Jeb ever have pets?"

"No, but Micah loved playing with our neighbor's dog, Dodger. It died a few years back. We were always so busy with baseball, I think Micah knew better than to ask for a pet." Olivia let her words hang for a beat. Micah had never asked for anything else. Sure, Jeb had pushed so hard to get him started, throwing a ball when he'd barely been able to grasp one in his little hand. But she'd played a part in it, too. She'd helped build their home and their life around baseball, whether it was Jeb's games or Micah's. For her son to not want to play anymore, not even talk about the sport anymore, made her question if it had been his heart in the game the entire time…or just Jeb's.

"Hattie, you should have seen him coming out of work today," Olivia said, wondering if she was seeing her son's heart for the very first time. "You would have thought working at the clinic was the equivalent to scoring free passes to the World Series. I could have gotten him to promise me the moon just for letting him volunteer there."

"Good for him," Hattie said. "I wish him a

lot of success. If you don't mind me asking, what did you make him promise you?"

"That's right." Olivia strummed her fingertips along the top of the Chevy hood and contemplated how to put Micah's promise into action. "It's time to cash in."

A HALF HOUR LATER, Olivia proudly admired a makeshift art studio she'd set up in Hattie's garden shed, complete with paints, canvases and sodas. She knew setting the mood was an important element for what she wanted to do next.

"Hey, kiddo," she said, strolling across the backyard to where Micah and Boomer were lounging. "I ordered a pizza. I thought you and I could eat and work on something for Aunt Hattie."

"Like what?"

"Signs for the Fall Festival. I volunteered our creative services. Would you mind helping me?"

Micah picked up a stick and lured Boomer along as he followed Olivia to the shed. He stopped short at the doorway.

"Whoa, Mom. Where did you get all this art stuff?"

"I shipped it ahead and just unpacked it.

You know I can't go very long without my art supplies."

"True," Micah said, straddling an old stool. "When you said you were taking a sabbatical from work, I had a hard time picturing you completely art-free."

"Seven days. I think that's a record for me."

Micah raised a brow. They both knew that wasn't true. After Jeb had died, she'd gone thirteen days, and once she'd found her way behind an easel again, the process of creating had been a catharsis. It had not just been because her husband had died, but because she'd felt like she'd lost him a long time before. It had been difficult accepting condolences when she'd been unhappily married to begin with, but art had helped get her through.

Olivia had assembled a table out of a large piece of strand board and two wooden horses. With a plastic tablecloth smoothed over it, it was good enough for a casual dinner and painting project.

"What kind of signs does Hattie need?" Micah asked.

"Decorations for the main entrance. You can paint whatever you want. The theme this year is…wait for it…autumn."

Micah let out a harrumph. "Boring enough but I think I can handle it." He picked up a paintbrush and carefully compared the variety of acrylics Olivia had set out. Her son had never taken to art the way she had, but she felt proud that he never hesitated when it came to trying it. He was bold, confident that he'd create something good, something unique, something he could be proud of. It made her think that sharing her vocation with him over the years, using art to help express himself, had paid some dividends, even if she couldn't always see them.

"Maggie Joyce seems nice," Olivia said, mixing cadmium red and lemon yellow for the perfect shade of orange. Truth be told, Maggie Joyce seemed like a godsend. She was eager to work with Micah and as a new college graduate, she'd had lots of ideas about how to expand on the homeschooling curriculum that Olivia had bought.

"Yeah, she's pretty cool."

"Do you have any homework yet?"

"Nah. I can get everything done during the day."

Olivia rinsed her paintbrush. "The clinic job should be interesting. What did Dr. Elderman have you do for your first day?"

"They had two spays and one neuter this morning. Tyler let me—"

"You mean Dr. Elderman?"

Micah rolled his eyes. "Yeah, well, he let me join him while he did checkups and sick visits. Cats, dogs, snakes—"

"Snakes?"

Micah snickered, most likely pleased to hear a thin thread of discomfort in his mother's voice. Olivia let the lull in conversation expand between them. Experience had taught her that children needed the downtime between topics to process their thoughts and feelings. They needed to gauge if it was safe to share, safe to say what was on their minds. The silence was almost more important than the talking.

After a few minutes, she could feel Micah stealing glances at her. Finally, he readjusted in his chair.

"You know," he said. "I've been thinking about becoming a veterinarian."

Since Jeb had died, Micah hadn't offered a hint at what he wanted to do as an adult. If someone had asked her to guess, she would have assumed it hadn't changed from two years ago when he still dreamed of becoming a professional baseball player. "Oh? What made you consider that?"

"Well," he said, swirling viridian green over his canvas. "Animals make me happy."

"Yeah?"

"Mmm-hmm. I think so. I used to be so happy playing baseball, especially when Dad came to my games, but I don't want to do that when I grow up. I'd rather work with animals, maybe even work on farms. There are livestock veterinarians, you know."

"Oh. I didn't."

"Yeah. Gary was telling me—"

"You mean Dr. Elderman?"

Micah rolled his eyes more dramatically this time. "*Dr. Elderman Sr.* told me there are veterinarians who work with large animals."

Olivia dabbed her brush into a squirt of white as she tried to picture Micah on a farm. Visiting a Michigan cider mill when Micah had been five was about as close to farm life as he'd ever been. Still, he was too young to limit his options. Just because he'd never been to a farm didn't mean he wouldn't love working with farm animals. "It sounds wonderfully messy, Micah. I'm sure you'd love it."

Micah focused on his canvas.

"But I like pets, too," he continued. "Amphibians, dogs, cats…any of those are interesting. What would I have to study to get into veterinary school?"

"You know, I'm not sure but Dr. Elderman could probably tell you that."

"Yeah," he said, satisfied with that answer.

"I think that's great, Micah."

"You do?" He hadn't looked up from his canvas, but his paint strokes had stalled out as if waiting for Olivia to now say more.

"I really do. I think Dad would love it, too."

Micah shrugged his shoulders, unconvinced.

"He would," Olivia insisted. "He'd be proud of you."

Micah worked his jaw. It was the same reaction Olivia usually got whenever she mentioned Jeb. That was why talking to Micah about the car accident had never gotten easier over the last two years. Even Dr. Redwood, his counselor, hadn't made much progress. As soon as Olivia or anyone mentioned Jeb, Micah began raising an emotional drawbridge. But Olivia knew she couldn't give up. She had to talk to Micah about the big things, too.

"Pass the neon green," he muttered, rinsing his brush. Once he had a hold of it, he squirted a large blob onto his paint palette. The paint oozed over the sides of the well into the other paints.

"You know," Olivia said, pretending she hadn't noticed. "Dr. Redwood suggested we find a new counselor in Roseley. We're on such a roll, getting your job at the clinic and finding Maggie Joyce—"

"You mean M.J.," Micah said, his delivery mirroring hers from earlier.

Olivia managed a patient smile. "Right. We might as well go for the hat trick and meet with a new counselor. There's no reason we can't get lucky again."

"What do I need a new counselor for?" He raised his eyes, challenging. "Isn't two years of counseling enough?"

Don't shut down on me, kiddo. We have to get through this together.

"I don't think it's about being enough. I know I'm still processing things about the accident and losing your dad."

"Then why aren't you meeting with a new counselor?"

Olivia tensed. She meant to find a new one in Roseley, she really did. She just wanted to get things right for Micah first. He was the most important priority in her life, though he might not ever understand that until he had his own children.

"I'm going to," she said. "In fact, the counselor I found might be a good fit for me, too."

"Have you already scheduled me an appointment?"

"I'm getting ready to. While we're sorting

out our new…" Olivia bit the inside of her cheek. Her mind raced to come up with a word other than *normal* because there was nothing normal about any of this. There was nothing normal about losing a spouse and helping your child grieve.

"Routine?" Micah offered. She met his eyes, hoping to see a sign that they were still in this thing together. They might not have the same closeness they'd shared before Jeb's death, despite how hard she tried, but they could get back on track. Couldn't they?

"Routine," Olivia repeated. She reached across the table to touch Micah's hand, but he pulled away before she could make contact.

"I know what you're doing," he mumbled. He pushed the canvas away from him. "You know I'm not one of your clients, right, Mom?"

"Right. You're the most important person in my life."

He'd cooled to her so suddenly, just as it always went. His face darkened, the light behind his eyes slowly shutting off like someone closing a restaurant for the night.

"You can't do art therapy with me on the sly. I know what you're up to."

"I'm not up to anything. I love spending time with you." She wanted to explain that she also wanted what was best for him and she believed that included a new counselor. "Hattie asked for our help—"

"I don't feel like helping anymore. I'd rather hang out in the woods before bed."

"But I ordered pizza. It'll be here any minute."

Micah slid off his stool. "Just leave me a plate in the microwave. I'll get it when I come in." And just like that, he disappeared out the shed door and into the woods like an apparition fading into the night.

TYLER AND GARY lingered at the reception desk.

"The kid did pretty well for his first day, don't you think?" Tyler asked.

Julia grabbed her purse and locked the front doors. "I thought so," she said.

"He laughed at my jokes," Gary said with a chuckle. "We know he's smart."

"A bunch of us are grabbing drinks tonight at The Bayshore Bar," Julia said. "Would either of you like to come?"

Gary shook his head. "I have practice in an hour, but thanks, honey."

"Ty?" Julia said. "What about you? You should join us for once."

"Nah," Tyler said. "Not tonight."

"Not tonight. You sound like a broken record." She looked to Gary to help her. "Your
uncle and I are worried about you."

"Oh, is that right?" Tyler said, lifting a
brow.

Gary hooted with laughter. "Yeah, Julia.
Is that right?"

Julia squared her shoulders in defense.
"Gary," she said, narrowing her eyes. "I told
you today that we need to get Tyler out and
about and you agreed with me."

Gary laughed harder now. "Define 'agree.'"

"Well," Julia said, defensively. "You didn't
disagree."

"I would never disagree with you, sweet
Julia." Gary strolled toward the front window,
thumbs stuck in his belt loop. "Although,
Tyler, you might want to get out of here while
you have the chance."

Julia joined Gary at the window. After a
quick glance, she cinched her purse and broke
for the door.

"This is what you get for not coming out
with us, Ty. See you tomorrow and *good
luck*." Julia pushed through the front door
and held it open for someone farther down
the sidewalk, still out of view. "Hello, Robin!
Nice to see you again!"

Tyler groaned. Having drinks with a

bunch of twentysomethings never sounded appealing unless it was the alternative to what now awaited him with Robin. She was an unpleasant blast from his past.

"No appointment," he muttered. "How unusual."

"Do you want me to take her?" Gary said. "I think it's my turn."

"I doubt she'll let you."

The words were no sooner out of his mouth than Robin Elderman strode into the clinic. In a denim skirt and a tight black tank top that depicted dancing chili peppers and the words Too Hot To Handle, she looked like she was ready for a day of summer fun, not a visit to the vet. Her little dog, Fidget, poked out of the large leopard print handbag slung over her shoulder.

"Hi, Robin," Gary said sweetly. "Nice to see you." Tyler had to hand it to his uncle. He could speak with kindness to almost anyone. Robin flashed a toothy grin, her natural charm and magnetism pulling all focus to her in an instant. If the room had been packed with twenty talking people, she would command it just as easily. It was a trait he had admired when they'd first met.

"Gary," she said, beelining to him and grabbing him around the forearm. She gave him a little shake like she hadn't seen him in ages. "How've ya been?"

"Well."

"Good, good. And, Tyler," she said, turning briskly to bolt in his direction. "I just had to get over here and see you right away. Fidget hurt his paw, poor thing. You have to look at it. You just have to."

Tyler suppressed the first response that came to mind. He didn't *have* to do anything. Robin certainly never felt convicted to do what anyone else needed.

"What's wrong with it?" he managed, motioning for her to follow him to the reception desk. He gave the desk a little pat. Robin fluffed her hair and popped a hip.

"Shouldn't we go to a proper exam room?" she said, the irritation on her face only matched by that in her voice.

"This isn't an appointment, Robin," Tyler said. "We closed twenty minutes ago."

"I'm family."

"Family?"

"Technically, yes, you and I are still bound. You can't help family?"

"Your idea of helping and my idea of helping are two very different things, Robin. So are our ideas of what it means to still be… bound."

Gary hurried over, easing the handbag off Robin's shoulder as she leered at Tyler. Gary scooped up Fidget as Tyler took a controlled breath.

"If you won't help Fidget, I guess I can surmise just what kind of doctor you really   ," she snapped.

"Robin…" Tyler said in a warning.

She could shift from magnetic to magma in the blink of an eye, though he knew his disposition brought it out of her. The truth was, they brought it out in each other. Try as he might, he still couldn't let the past live in the past. The hurt was still there. It might be covered and patted down to help him get on with his life, but when tidal-wave-Robin swept back in without warning, she exposed the bits still festering. Those bits wriggled and writhed like parasites hiding in the sand.

"Hi, sweetheart," Gary said, placing Fidget in the crook of his arm. "Let's focus on you for a second, shall we? What's troubling you?"

Robin powered on, taking Fidget's paw into her manicured fingers. "It's his paw. See?"

Gary examined the dog as Tyler snatched his car keys and made for the door.

"Take it easy, Gary," he called, pushing out into the early evening sunshine, eager to escape the same old verbal sparring that brought out the ugliness in him. "I'm calling it a night."

He felt like a completely different person when he was around Robin, and it wasn't just because she was a person he couldn't stand. *He* felt like a person he couldn't stand when he was with her, and no matter how he tried, he couldn't change that.

Tyler slipped his sunglasses over his eyes just as a familiar face came into view.

"Well, hey there, stranger," he called, feeling his familiar self bubbling back up to the surface again.

Olivia dashed across the street. In denim shorts, her long brown legs looked like they crossed the street a full second before the rest of her.

"Hey," she said. "I hoped I might catch you."

"I'm just heading out." Poor Gary might be stuck at work for another half hour, but he seemed to have a better temperament to manage Robin in a way he couldn't anymore.

"Good. I wanted to talk to you about Micah."

"Okay."

"Um…how'd he do today?"

Tyler shrugged. "Great."

"Yeah?"

"Why wouldn't he? Is there something I need to know?"

"Oh, no," Olivia quickly supplied. "Of course not. He's a hard worker. I didn't have any concerns about him doing the job."

"No?" Tyler dipped his hands into his front pockets.

"Nuh-uh. All good on that front."

"But, still, you drove here to ask me about his first day?"

"Yeah," she said, quietly. "I did."

Tyler's eyebrow hitched. "What's on your mind?"

She looked as if she was gathering up her words. "Did Micah talk about anything today?"

"Anything…" Tyler said. "That sounds like a very loaded question."

"Did he open up about his life? The past?"

Tyler had to think. It had been as lovely and uneventful a day as he could have hoped for. The appointments had been fairly routine, and Micah had done a good job of helping and not getting underfoot. "It's surprising he never had any pets because he's pretty natural around animals."

"Natural?" Olivia said. "Really?"

Tyler shrugged. "I'd say so. I'm glad to have him on board."

Olivia's face burst into a bright smile. "Oh, that's great. I'm glad to hear that."

"You seem like you're worried."

"No, of course not. Not worried at all."

The door behind them swung open and Robin exited the clinic like she was walking off a yacht. Little Fidget blinked up at them.

"He's fine, Tyler, in case you're wondering," Robin said. "Gary said his paw looks a little irritated, probably from a new kitchen floor cleaner I bought."

"Glad to hear it," Tyler said calmly.

"Oh, are you?" she said with snark. Tyler let her words dangle uncomfortably like low-hanging fruit, but he refrained from answering. One lesson his father had taught him about being married was that if he didn't have anything nice to say, he should pinch his mouth shut as tightly as he could, for as long as he could.

Robin drew her pink-stained lips into a proud pout and turned to Olivia.

"He's a Pomeranian, in case you're wondering."

"He's adorable." Olivia grinned at the dog.

"Thank you. Three years old and spoiled rotten."

"His collar matches the rhinestones on your shirt."

It was true. Fidget's collar looked like it had been bejeweled at the same place Robin shopped for clothing.

Robin gave her shoulders a little shimmy. "That's because we're both a lot of fun!" She released a hearty cackle as Olivia ran a hand over Fidget's tan fur. "Are you a friend of Tyler's?" Robin asked, tipping her nose in the air.

"My son is volunteering here," Olivia said.

"Volunteering? Can't you afford to pay him, Ty?" Robin teased, but Tyler's eyes narrowed, unamused. "I just had to pop in for a minute," she continued. "I had to get Fidget checked out before we leave this weekend. I'm meeting my girlfriends in Florida for a few weeks. I can't have Fidget getting sick when we're traveling."

Tyler said with a strained smile, "You wouldn't want his illness raining on your parade, huh? The more things change, the more they stay the same."

Robin ignored his comment as she tended to ignore much about the past or his accurate recalling of it.

"Nice to meet you," she said to Olivia before strutting up the sidewalk.

"Technically," Olivia whispered to Tyler. "We never officially met. Does she come in here a lot?"

"When it suits her." Tyler watched Robin get into her car and fuss over Fidget, the type of fawning adoration she had always seemed to reserve strictly for her pets. "Her name is Robin Elderman, and she's my stepmother."

CHAPTER EIGHT

OLIVIA'S WEEK HAD been a series of emotional ups and downs, but when she opened her eyes Friday morning and remembered that she had plans to meet Caroline for a late afternoon dessert, she beamed. She hoped the easy rapport she had once shared with her friend would resurface quickly.

Luckily, it did.

They had no sooner gotten their desserts at the counter of The Lollipop and slid behind a high-top table in the front window than Caroline launched into a conversation about her job and planning her cousin Faith's outdoor wedding. Caroline's joy for life felt contagious and reminded Olivia of summer playdates they'd had together as children when Olivia and her mother had been in Roseley visiting Hattie.

"And now *you're* back," Caroline said, squeezing Olivia's arm. "Can life get any better?"

Olivia smiled as widely as she could manage, thinking of a few things she might improve, given the chance. "This place has changed, huh?" she said, glancing around the shop. "Mom wouldn't recognize it now."

The bright lights inside The Lollipop were a noticeable upgrade from the vintage look Olivia remembered. They also brought out every color of the rainbow, which adorned the walls and furniture and confectionary treats. The booth seats were pink vinyl with sparkly flecks and silver banding. Tall glass canisters filled with bubblegum, jawbreakers and hard candies lined the back wall. A three-foot-tall carousel with miniature white ponies and a red-and-white tent top spun in the center of the store. The ponies methodically rose and fell as faint music played from an antique player piano. The melody's tink-tink-tink signaled a happier, romanticized time.

"Mallory remodeled a few years ago," Caroline said. "She now rarely plays the piano."

"It's now just for show, huh?"

Caroline was quick to correct her. "Just for special occasions."

"At least the desserts haven't changed."

"You've got that right." Caroline dug a fork into her chocolate eclair. "So, what's your plan?"

"In Roseley?"

"You must have one."

"I had planned to homeschool Micah, but Tyler found us a great tutor."

"Tyler?"

"Elderman. He runs the vet clinic."

"Ah, of course," Caroline said. "I know Tyler. We went to school together."

"He's nice. I mean, helpful and such."

Caroline's face flickered to imply that Tyler was more than just helpful. Olivia was relieved when Caroline didn't press her. She knew Caroline would love the story about how she'd met Tyler on Falcon's Peak, but there was something about that encounter that made her want to protect it. Sharing it with Hattie had left her with the feeling that she'd given some of it away.

"If homeschooling is off your plate, you should help Hattie and me with the Fall Festival."

"Are you working on it, too?"

"Of course. My boss loves to promote herself and—" Caroline wafted her hand in a grandiose gesture "—find me more work to do."

"The way you were talking about Sheila before, it sounds like she sometimes…"

"Takes advantage of me?" Caroline asked.

"That's because she does. I love what I do, Liv. I just don't like working for her."

"Strike out on your own."

"In this small town?" Caroline said with a sigh. "Maybe I should. How hard can it be, right?"

Olivia broke her cookie into pieces but couldn't bring herself to eat it. Wasn't she essentially striking out on her own? Since Jeb had died, she'd thought about what kind of life she now wanted for her and Micah. Jeb had liked to work hard and play hard, and fighting against that rhythm had never felt worth it.

But now that he was gone, she felt drawn back to her roots and a life of simplicity, like the one she'd had growing up. She wanted that kind of life for Micah. So, she decided, she wasn't a woman striking out on her own. She was a mother trying to carve out the best life for her and her son. It still felt just as difficult.

"Is Micah joining a baseball team around here?" Caroline asked. "It's the end of the season, but maybe he can find some boys to play pickup games with."

"He hasn't been interested in baseball since Jeb died."

"Whoa. That's a big shift." Caroline eyed

her carefully. "Every email you ever sent me was always filled with stories about his games. Baseball seemed like a big reason why you couldn't visit often."

It was true. As much as she liked flying to Michigan for a week in the summer, those visits had gotten more sparse, especially after her mom died. It had been years since she'd been back.

"It was hard to find time to get away, yes."

"Are you worried about him?"

"Immensely. But not because of the baseball. He's not the same kid, Caroline."

"You're not the same woman. How could you be?"

Olivia finally nibbled on her cookie. When she'd been in art school, she'd been fascinated with a final project a classmate had completed. He'd drawn a simple sketch of his face. Then he'd laid a transparent piece of vellum on top and traced the sketch. Then he'd laid a piece of vellum over the copy and traced again. He'd done this hundreds of times, making a copy of a copy of his face. When he'd finished, he'd made a stop art animation of the drawings. The changes to his face looked subtle over the length of the movie, but at the end, when he'd shown the class the first drawing of his face and the last one side by side, they had looked like two different people. Sure, they had shared a resemblance, but they were not the same person anymore.

Olivia had thought of her classmate's project frequently over the past two years. She felt changed at a molecular level since Jeb's death, but it took a friend like Caroline saying it out loud to confirm the changes were visible to everyone else, too.

"What would Jeb say about that?" Caroline asked. "The baseball, I mean."

"He'd insist Micah get back out there and play play *play*." Olivia deepened her voice to mimic Jeb. *"Winners always hustle."*

"He sure was driven."

"He was hardworking, yes." Olivia had always admired that about Jeb.

"Does Micah like working at the clinic?"

"Loves it. Speaking of which, I have to pick him up in an hour." She'd agreed to let him go back for a shift this afternoon—it was Friday after all, and the school week was over.

Caroline's face contorted. "That doesn't give us much more time to unpack all your issues, Liv."

"What issues?"

"Jeb Howard's widow escapes the big city on a whim for a quiet life on Little Lake Roseley? The headline practically writes itself."

"It wasn't on a whim," Olivia said in protest. Since her husband's death, her phone calls to Hattie had become more frequent. Her aunt's support had gotten her through those first days and months, and by the time Hattie had offered for her and Micah to move to Roseley for a little breather, she'd been more than ready to accept the invitation. "I had to do something drastic. Micah won't talk to me anymore."

Her friend's gaze softened. "You're a good mother, Liv. Even if he's not talking, I'm sure he's listening. Is there anything I can do to help?"

Olivia patted her friend's hand. "This," she said. "Just being here with me means the world."

OLIVIA AND CAROLINE meandered down the sidewalk together, admiring the storefront windows. When they entered the clinic, Micah was waiting for them.

"Aunt Caroline!" he said, his face breaking into a smile. He hadn't seen Caroline since Jeb's funeral, but Caroline had always had a way of connecting with people.

Caroline wrapped her arms around Micah and gave him a squeeze. "Hi, sweetheart. I hear you're Roseley's next up-and-coming veterinarian."

"Hear that, Dr. Elderman?" Micah said to man standing at the reception desk. "The word is out."

"You must be Tyler's uncle," Olivia said.

"Guilty," he said. "You can call me Gary."

He patted Micah on the back. "Micah did fine work today. There was a pit bull giving him a little trouble—"

"Pit bull?" Olivia said. "Are you okay?"

"Don't worry, Mom," Micah said. "Pit bulls get a bad reputation, but they're not all prone to aggression. This one, Tumbler, had a sunburn."

"Really?" Olivia said. "I didn't know dogs could get sunburns."

"It's true," Micah said, leaning against the reception desk like he'd been studying ailments in dogs his entire life. "Pit bulls are prone to them on account of their short hair. Poor little guy."

"He wasn't so little," Tyler said, emerging from the back. His eyes darted to smile hello to Caroline before settling on Olivia and offering a gaze so warm she could feel it resonating all the way down to her toes. He then turned to Micah. "Are you taking off?"

"I can stick around longer if you need me."

"Nah," Tyler said. "I appreciate you coming back in this afternoon. Everyone wants Friday appointments. I'm gonna close up and cut Gary loose. He needs to get warmed up before his game."

"Game?" Caroline said.

Gary puffed his chest. "I play catcher for the Roseley Baseball Dream Team."

"Baseball?" Micah said. "You?"

"Don't look so surprised," Gary said, patting his belly. "I can still move."

"It's also not what you think," Tyler said. He and Gary exchanged a look. "But you should check it out tonight, if you're free."

"Yeah, we can go," Micah said. "Right, Mom?"

"To a baseball game? Tonight?" Olivia said. Tyler watched her with a passive face. Micah actually seemed interested in baseball again for the first time since losing Jeb, and it was all she could do to suppress the complete surprise on her face. "Micah," Olivia said. "Do you really want to?"

Micah nodded. "It sounds like fun."

"We'd love to go," Caroline said. "I don't have plans. What time is it?"

"Seven o'clock," Gary said, quickly making for the door. "I always play better when people I know are in the crowd. Tyler, are you finally coming tonight?"

Tyler balked slightly. "I didn't say *I* was coming."

"Yes, you did," Micah said. "You implied it."

"I take that as a yes!" Gary called on his way out the door. "Don't stand me up again, nephew!"

Tyler exhaled and said, "I guess my evening plans are made."

"Ours, too," Caroline said, hip-checking Olivia.

"Do you stand up your uncle a lot?" Olivia asked.

Tyler shrugged. "Let's just say I don't go out much. I think if I don't show up tonight Gary will make this family business a solo enterprise. He'll change the locks on me."

"Then we won't let you fall into old habits," Caroline said with a grin. "Shall we all grab dinner beforehand?"

Micah led them to the door. "The Sandwich Board. CeCe dropped off free mini subs the other day and they were amazing."

Amazing? Olivia thought. Was this her Micah speaking? He wanted to go to a baseball game and go out to dinner and he was using words like *amazing*? Something inside her leaped at the prospect of seeing the old Micah come alive again.

"I have to shower and change," Tyler said, motioning to his medical scrubs. "But I can do that in the back."

Caroline hip-checked Olivia a second time. "We don't mind waiting, do we, Liv?"

"Of course not," she said. "Take your time."

Tyler nodded appreciatively before disappearing into the back room. "I won't be long. I'll meet you at The Sandwich Board."

Olivia followed Caroline and Micah out onto the sidewalk.

"I'm going to run an errand first," Micah said. "I'll catch up."

Before Olivia could clarify, Micah darted down the street, disappearing around the corner. She decided to take advantage of the few moments alone with Caroline.

"Did you see Micah when Tyler suggested we go to the baseball game?" Olivia said. "His face actually lit up."

"That's the Micah I remember."

"It's great, isn't it?"

"So great. You just spent the last two hours talking about how you wanted to support Micah and now the perfect opportunity has landed in your lap."

They walked for a few moments in silence,

Olivia anticipating the evening with Micah watching a baseball game, when another thought hit her.

Spending time with Tyler.

By the way Micah jumped at the chance to attend the game, it was noticeable how much he enjoyed spending time with Tyler. The handsome veterinarian was probably becoming something of a mentor to her son, helping him discover interests he had probably always had but had never gotten the opportunity to explore. Tyler was certainly calm, encouraging and supportive, so she could understand why her son would enjoy spending time with him.

What had her so confused was why *she* was looking forward to spending time with him. When he had glanced back at her before disappearing into the back room, it had made her stomach flip-flop so hard, she'd thought everyone else could hear it. It had been a very long time since she'd been excited to spend time with Jeb and even longer still since she'd cared to spend time with any man other than him. So, to find her nerves skittering now, at the thought of an evening with Tyler close by, had her feeling very confused.

"Liv," Caroline said, looping an arm

through hers. "I've seen this expression on you before."

"What expression?"

"The 'I'm worried other people will know what I'm feeling before I completely know' expression."

"I don't do that," she said, remembering Hattie's words earlier about her mouth twist. She was really going to have to pay attention to that.

"I'm just excited to spend the evening with Micah," she said. "He hasn't been interested in much lately, aside from working at the clinic. I'm sure some of that has to do with working with Tyler. Do you know him well?"

"I've known him for years. Like I said, we went to school together."

"Were you two…friends?" The thought occurred to her that Caroline might have dated Tyler. Caroline was a wonderful person who would be a great match with the guy, at least based on what she knew of him so far. It made sense that the two of them might have wanted to spend time together if they had run in the same circle in high school.

"In Roseley, it's easy to go way back with most everyone in town. I had a lot of classes with Tyler and grew up knowing his dad, who was the nicest guy around, if you ask me."

That made a lot of sense to Olivia. For Tyler to be so kind, it figured that he'd had a great dad.

"And his mom?"

"Uh, I see Sandy around town from time to time."

"Is she nice, too?"

"Hard to say. She keeps to herself mostly."

"Any siblings?"

"Nope. He's an only child."

That much he had in common with Micah. Perhaps Tyler and her son connected on more levels than she realized, for Micah to love working at the clinic so much.

"Did he always want to be a vet?"

Caroline giggled. "You know, I'd have to check my notes to get more of his backstory."

Olivia rolled her eyes at herself. "I guess I'm getting ahead of myself. I was just curious about who my son is spending so much time with these days."

"You know, Liv. Tyler is probably a great influence on Micah…"

"Yes, I hope so."

"Any chance you're interested in him?"

"Goodness, no," Olivia said, the embarrassment of even being asked such a question making her cheeks go hot.

"No?"

"Why would you think… No."

"Oh," Caroline said. "It's okay if you are."

"I'm not. I couldn't be. It's too…soon."

Caroline slowed to a stop and faced her friend. "It's okay to like someone again, you know."

"I know." She knew it was okay to eventually move on from Jeb, but convincing her nervous system to not go into overdrive at the thought of doing just that was another story. Her plan for the evening was to completely focus on bonding with Micah. She would compartmentalize her growing fascination for Tyler's green eyes and the gentle way they could roam over her face for another day.

"I don't like him," Olivia said, now hypersensitive to what her mouth was doing as she spoke the words. "And I know it's okay to move on from Jeb. I really do."

"Well, okay," Caroline said with a supportive smile. "We don't have to talk about it again. Tonight is about Micah. Right?"

"Right," Olivia said. "I have a feeling it's going to go very well."

CHAPTER NINE

A WOMAN WEARING a name tag with CeCe on it bagged up their sandwich order as Micah snapped at his mother.

"Mom," he said. "Why do you care what I bought at the office supply store?"

When Micah had met them at The Sandwich Board, he'd so obviously kept his recent purchase from Olivia's sight, carefully moving it to the side of his body farthest from her, it made her wonder. When she was a new mother, she'd loved the adage "Silence is golden, unless you have a toddler." She'd found the observation applied to teenagers as well, especially when her favorite teenager had momentarily gone silent while casually hiding a bag behind his back.

"I only asked what you bought. What's the big deal?"

"It was the *way* you asked it. Like you expected me to tell you."

Olivia caught a glimpse of CeCe. By the way she watched them, she seemed like one of those people who rubbernecked to get a good look at a traffic accident. Olivia swiped her debit card and silently waited for her receipt. She wanted to table her conversation with Micah until they could get outside, but Micah hadn't gotten her memo about discretion. He turned to Caroline.

"She always does this. She thinks she needs to know everything about my life, but it's just her being nosy."

"Micah," Olivia warned. Micah glared at her as she completed the transaction and thanked CeCe for the order.

"Have a nice evening," CeCe muttered, though her sour expression suggested they wouldn't. Olivia wanted to explain to CeCe that her son didn't usually speak to her in this way—not since recently, anyway.

"Let's sit outside," Caroline said. "It's such a lovely evening I want to feel the sunshine on my face." Even Caroline's cheerfulness did nothing to quelch Micah's irritability.

"Did you remember to get me chips this time?" he asked, a bratty edge in his voice. As they headed for the door, he jockeyed for the sandwich bag.

"I bought chips for everyone, Micah, including you," Olivia said.

"You'll probably want to count each one as

I eat," he grumbled. "It's like living with the Mommy police." Olivia bit back a sharp reply. She put so much effort into getting along with him, but his words grated on her ears.

Micah stormed ahead and pushed out the door without holding it open for them. He might be unaware how upset she felt, but she could count on Caroline to sense it in a second. Caroline stepped ahead and held open the door for her. Once outside, Caroline, always the dutiful mediator, addressed Micah.

"Micah," she said softly. "Your mother was gracious enough to buy us dinner tonight."

Micah chortled. "Sandwiches?"

"Sandwiches that you requested," Olivia said. Micah rolled his eyes. "You're being rude," she continued. "I'd like an apology and then I'd like some thanks for dinner."

As Micah settled defiantly on his feet, Olivia didn't look away, sensing they were in some sort of blinking contest for respect. Looking away or saying anything to further explain herself felt like the best way to weaken her position. She'd been giving him too many escape clauses recently, making excuses for his bad behavior. But now his bad behavior was on full display in public and in front of her friend. Perhaps Hattie had been on to something. Perhaps she had lost her

nerve and now she needed to get it back—
tonight.

After a few moments, Micah shrugged and
delivered the best sarcasm she'd ever heard.
"*Sorry* and *thank you*." He plopped onto a
chair and extended a hand, waving for her to
cough up the sandwich bag.

Olivia's jaw clenched at the awfulness of
it. His expression had gone cold, and his gesture flexed with a challenge. She knew if she
demanded something more sincere, he could
dig in his heels all night and turn their dinner
and baseball outing into an embarrassment
for them both, even if he only ever realized
it in retrospect.

Still, she held the sandwiches and the car
keys.

A slow determination began to rise in her
chest as she thought through her next move.
When she was a girl, her mother had taught
her how to play chess. They'd play on rainy
summer nights together, and when her mother
moved a chess piece, it sent Olivia's strategy
for winning in a new direction, a new line.

Micah's challenge had knocked them into
a new line, not just for their evening but for
their relationship. He'd disrespected her on
occasion before, but this time he was bolder.

And this time it felt like a line that could take them to a very dark place very quickly.

Her relationship with Micah wasn't about winning and losing. But she needed to do something intentional to knock them both back onto a new line.

"Caroline," Olivia finally said, calmly. "I'm sorry but we can't go to the baseball game with you tonight. We're going home."

She wanted to support Micah and encourage his love for baseball. She wanted him to spend time with Tyler and cheer on Gary and enjoy himself. But more than anything, she wanted to see him grow into a good and respectful man, and that was contingent on him respecting his mother.

"What?" Micah said, jumping to his feet. "Why? I said what you wanted."

"That's okay, Liv," Caroline said, chiming in with full moral support. "We'll reschedule for another night." Olivia reached out and squeezed her friend's hand, appreciative of her understanding. Micah forced himself into his mother's line of vision.

"Mom, you're being so unfair right now."

Olivia concentrated on her breathing. She knew her strategy could only work if she correctly managed her temper.

"Micah," she said, turning her attention to

her son. "I need to speak to Caroline for a minute. Meet me at the car, please."

"Mom."

"Yes?"

Micah now grappled for a response. "I'm sorry I smarted off at you. Thank you for the sandwiches. I really appreciate the fact that you bought them. What else do you want me to say?"

"I don't want to talk about this here. I'll meet you at the car."

"Why? This is so unfair!"

"Car." Olivia glared at her son from beneath hooded eyelids.

Micah screwed up his face, any number of angry retorts locked and loaded. Instead of answering, he stormed up the sidewalk. He had stormed away from her on occasion when he'd been a child, too, his stout little body trying to command the room the way he'd seen baseball pitchers command the pitching mound at games. It had been cute at five, funny because Micah had always been a sweet, even-tempered kid. But that was then and this was now, and there was nothing cute about this display.

Olivia's eyes had already begun to fill with tears when Caroline took her by the shoulders.

"Good for you," Caroline said. "You were very calm and firm. I'm proud of you."

"Do you see what I was talking about earlier?"

"Honey, I do. His attitude came out of left field."

"That's how it always is. When I think I'm making conversation, he thinks I'm being nosy. The simplest question or comment makes him so defensive."

"Hey, he's a teenager."

Olivia nodded in agreement as she wiped her eyes, but she didn't entirely agree. "I guess…"

"He needs to go home and cool off," Caroline said.

"Yeah. We both do."

"*That* I'm not so sure about."

"Huh?"

"You need to go somewhere else and cool off."

"What? No. I need to go home and talk to Micah."

Caroline dug through the sandwich bag and grabbed Micah's sandwich, chips and soda.

"Nuh-uh. I'll drive him back to the house. Hattie should be there, right?"

"Yeah, but—"

"*You* go to the game with Tyler. The evening is way too beautiful to be stuck home getting the silent treatment from your son. Besides, if no one goes to the game it'll really hurt Gary's feelings."

"Caroline, *no*." The thought of attending the baseball game now seemed ludicrous. For one thing, she didn't think she deserved a fun evening out when her son would be stuck sulking at home, furious at her. For a second thing…

Olivia brought her hands to her cheeks. Going to a baseball game with a group of people, her son included, was one thing, but going with only Tyler now felt like crossing some sort of invisible line. It wasn't a date, obviously, but still, her stomach tightened at the thought all the same.

"I know you want to be a good mother right now, but I think that means getting a breather before starting again. In the morning when you've both calmed down, you can talk to Micah about what happened here. I think he would be much more receptive. Don't you think?"

"Caroline—"

"Tyler can have my meal." Caroline handed the bag back to Olivia.

"But… I…"

Caroline smoothed the frazzled pieces of

hair off Olivia's forehead. "Don't overthink it. Explain to Tyler what happened, have fun and call me tomorrow. Okay?"

Caroline smacked a kiss to Olivia's cheek and scooted down the sidewalk. Olivia sank onto a chair in front of the shop and placed the bag of sandwiches on the table with a plop. This was a new line she hadn't anticipated at all.

"OLIVIA?"

Olivia blinked up. Tyler's broad frame stood between her and the sunshine, casting him in shadow. She'd been lost in thought, thinking about life before Jeb's death and how parenting Micah had gotten so hard ever since. She'd also been wondering what on earth she was going to say to Tyler when he showed up and found only her waiting. She'd run out of time before she could come up with the right explanation.

"Tyler. Hi." Olivia scrambled to her feet. He shifted a few steps to his side so she didn't have to squint against the sun to see him.

"Hey. Where is everyone?"

"It's only me. We don't have to go to the game, though, if you don't want to."

Tyler gave her a puzzled look. "If I don't want to." He repeated her own words back to her so slowly she couldn't help but explain in a rush.

"I think you originally agreed to go to support Micah. I really appreciate that, by the way. He needs some friends like you here in Roseley so he isn't talking to just me all the time. I know he was looking forward to tonight, but he and I got into an argument, and he copped an attitude. It happens. Teenagers, right?"

Tyler continued to watch her silently. She wondered if a million thoughts were racing through his mind the way they were racing through hers.

"Anyway," Olivia continued. "I thought it best to send him home. My mother always said parenting was a series of judgment calls and you don't know if you made the right one until your baby has grown and flown the nest. I don't know if sending him home was the right call, but there it is. Caroline drove him, and I realized I don't have your cell phone number to text you that we were leaving, so I—"

"Olivia?" Tyler's voice radiated with patience. "Are you okay?"

"Me?"

"You said you two had an argument. It

must have been ugly if you sent him home. Do you want to talk about it?"

Olivia blinked with surprise. *That* was what he'd heard from her rambling? He actually cared how she felt about the argument with her son? Truth be told, it was still running wildly on a loop in her brain, and it hadn't even been a bad fight.

Jeb had never had the patience to listen to her talk about much. Work was the most important thing to him so if she was willing to listen to him talk about his job, he was happy to talk to her all night. It wasn't until home problems escalated enough to demand his attention that he mustered the focus to try to resolve them with her. In short, when he was on the road he didn't want to be bothered with her problems. And when he was home, he didn't want to be bothered with her problems.

"I'm fine," she said. "Completely fine." It was a lie she'd told so many times she sometimes believed it. It slipped off her lips easily.

"Yeah, I can see that." Tyler sat and she followed. "I was a fourteen-year-old man once. Lay it on me."

"A man…" Olivia said. "You're right. He's turning into one right before my eyes."

"He's probably trying to remind you of it every day."

"Try every minute. This is the hard part people warned me about, I guess." She opened the food bag. "I hope you like pastrami."

Tyler unwrapped his sandwich and took a few bites.

"Perfect," he said. "Now back to the argument. You talk and I'll eat."

"You don't want to listen to me ramble on about my parenting woes."

Tyler chewed, his gaze beckoning her to continue. She found in his expression that he didn't seem overly curious like CeCe. Nor did he seem to judge her. His interest felt refreshing after years of Jeb tuning her out. At worst, he was keeping her company. At best, he genuinely cared.

"Well…" she said, opening her bottle of water. "Where to begin? He challenges me and when he isn't doing that, he's disengaged from life and everything else."

"It sounds like you moved here to inspire Micah."

"Since my husband, Jeb, died, Micah doesn't want to play baseball. He used to live and breathe the sport but now he's turned his enthusiasm toward working at the clinic. I'm happy he's happy, but I still find it all so confusing."

"That's why you stopped by the clinic the

other night. You were trying to get a better read on him?"

"Guilty. Anything you can think of to share?"

Tyler glanced down the street, a contemplative look on his face. "He briefly mentioned Dodger."

"Our neighbor's dog."

"He wished he'd been there when it had been put to sleep."

Olivia leaned away. "Really."

"He didn't seem to want to talk about it more than that. We were in the middle of something unrelated, so there also wasn't time for him to elaborate. In general, he seems really happy."

"Gee, I wish I could be around to see that. Were you a lot of trouble for your mom, too?" She wanted to know she wasn't the only mother who struggled with her child.

Tyler shifted uncomfortably on his seat. "You met my stepmom."

"Yes, but I didn't know if your mom was still…" She didn't know much about Tyler yet and hadn't meant to tread into his history if it was painful for him. Caroline had mentioned that Tyler's mother kept to herself, but as she watched him, she wasn't exactly sure what that meant. "In the picture."

"She lives in Roseley, yes."

"Do you see her?"

"On occasion."

"What does that mean?"

Tyler took a sip of water. "It means things are complicated."

Olivia sighed. "That's not how I want Micah to describe our relationship in fifteen years."

"He won't. Anyone can see you're trying so hard. That's ninety percent of it."

"Didn't your mom try?"

Tyler shrugged and reached across the table, stealing a couple of Olivia's chips. "What position did you say Micah used to play?"

"Pitcher," Olivia said, pretending not to notice that he'd intentionally changed the subject. "Jeb wanted him to follow in his footsteps. He thought it would one day make a great human-interest story if Micah went pro, too."

Tyler frowned. "Pardon?"

"Pro, like Jeb…" Tyler's face remained blank. "I assumed everyone in town knew," she said, finding his ignorance refreshing. "Jeb played catcher in the major leagues."

"You're Jeb Howard's wife?"

She laughed that he'd just put it together. "Surprised?"

Tyler studied her for a moment. "Very. No wonder you want Micah to play baseball again."

"I don't. At least not because of his father's legacy."

"No?"

"Heavens, no. I want him to play because he used to love it. He stopped cold turkey after Jeb died, and I can't help but assume he feels some sort of survivor's guilt."

Tyler hesitated before asking, "Does he meet with a counselor?"

"He had a great counselor back home, but I have to convince him to give someone here a chance."

Tyler took another bite of his sandwich and stole another chip. Olivia waited for him to ask about Jeb's career or fawn over his baseball stats. Instead, Tyler chewed, a thoughtful expression on his face.

"You know," she said. "Most men in this situation are falling over themselves to find out about Jeb's career. That's why I don't usually mention it right away."

"Most men? Have you dated a lot since he died?"

Olivia jerked back in shock. "Men in general," she said. "People, really. *People* ask about him a lot."

"Got it," Tyler said, an embarrassed smile coming over him. "The way you said that it sounded like…"

"I've dated a lot in the past two years?" Olivia laughed uncomfortably at the thought. *"No."*

Tyler cleared his throat, noticeably as apprehensive with their line of conversation as she was. His momentary awkwardness was short-lived, but it had made him seem all the more charming. "So," he said, starting again. "You don't date, you're raising a teenager on your own and you spent your summers in Roseley. Gary said he remembers your mom."

"Oh?" She perked at the mention of her mother. Most people had adored her, so it made sense Gary might remember her, too. Olivia drummed her fingers on the table as Tyler stole another chip. She had to suppress a grin as she continued, "And you're a veterinarian who runs a family clinic, has an extremely well-trained dog and steals potato chips."

"Yes," he said, feigning seriousness. "But only the kettle-cooked flavor."

"I'm glad I stocked up."

Tyler tipped a chip into the air in a toast of thanks.

"Anything else you've observed?" he said

in a playful challenge. Olivia thought for a moment, hesitant to say what was really on her mind.

"You don't like your stepmom."

Tyler's face fell. "Sadly accurate."

"Family in general is a tender subject for you." His eyes flashed as he crunched down hard on a chip. It spurred her to quickly smooth it over. "And you don't get out much."

He held out his arms, motioning to either side of the sidewalk. "What do you call this?"

"Um…a guy who needs to eat?" She grinned.

"Yes. Thanks for the sandwich, Olivia."

She'd like to give him the entire sandwich shop if it led to him saying her name so sincerely again. "Any time," she said.

The door to the sandwich shop swung open and CeCe emerged.

"Dr. Elderman," she said, her eyes all aglow. "I didn't see you come in."

"CeCe, the pastrami was delicious."

CeCe clasped her hands at her chest. "Thank you. We added it to the menu after my niece suggested it. You know, she's been talking about moving here and helping us. *I'm* fit as a fiddle." CeCe held up a hand and whispered, "But Angelo is slowing down. Don't tell him I said so."

"Where is your niece now?" Tyler asked.

"She took a job in Europe for the summer. Wonderful opportunity, but when she makes her way to Roseley you'll have to meet her."

"I look forward to it."

"And I look forward to seeing you both here again." CeCe turned to Olivia. "How about you? Did you like your sandwich?"

Tyler moved quickly to introductions. "This is my friend Olivia. Her son just started working at the clinic."

"Oh, very good," CeCe said. "Olivia, I hope you had a nice dinner. You deserve it after… *earlier.*"

Olivia had been sure CeCe had been sizing up her mothering skills during her confrontation with Micah. Her judgmental expression had made Olivia feel like she'd been failing in front of an audience. But now CeCe's demeanor, which was almost supportive, surprised her.

"Thank you, CeCe. He's at that age."

"Oh, I know all about that age. My daughter, Tracy, went through it, too. We have got to keep on top of these young ones. From one mother to another, hang in there."

CeCe gathered their trash and flashed a wink before heading back into the sandwich shop.

Olivia turned to Tyler. "I would have

sworn that woman was mentally tearing me to shreds earlier."

"She probably was. Old habits die hard. But I think she's been trying to change."

"Then I give her credit."

"Give yourself some. Micah is a great kid," Tyler said as he checked the time on his cell phone. "We should get going."

"Do you have to get back to Ranger? I completely understand if you need to go home."

There was humor in his eyes as he said, "Are you trying to cut out on me?"

"Of course not." Truth be told, she was giving him an out.

"A friend of mine is hanging out with Ranger tonight. Come on. We want to get a good seat."

"I can't imagine the bleacher seats fill up that quickly."

Tyler waggled his eyebrows. "But we don't want just any old seats. I'll drive."

CHAPTER TEN

TYLER GLANCED AT Olivia riding in the truck beside him. When she hung her arm out the open truck window and momentarily closed her eyes in the slap of fresh air, he took a mental snapshot. He wanted to savor the moment with her, as if he shouldn't take it for granted.

He'd felt that way since he'd first met her. Once the adrenaline had worn off, he'd spent every day since their meeting just hoping he'd bump into her again. He hadn't been prepared for Micah volunteering at the clinic, but now that he was, he enjoyed working with the teen as much as he enjoyed the reality that Olivia could now drop in at any point.

Olivia pushed frazzled curls off her face, but it was as useful as building a sandcastle in high tide. He snatched his baseball cap off the back seat and handed it to her.

"Would this help?" he said.

"Couldn't hurt." She loosened the cap and

eased it over her hair. He admired how good she looked wearing it.

"I can roll the window up if it's bothering you."

"No, it feels nice," she said. "I should just pull my hair into a ponytail or something. I usually do that when I'm working."

He wanted to tell her she looked perfect just as she was, but he restrained himself. A knot in his gut formed as he tried to keep his eyes focused on the road instead of on Olivia. There was something unnerving about how he felt when she was around—intrigued but cautious. He'd agreed to attend the baseball game when it had been a group venture, but now that the group was down to just him and Olivia, he felt he had to keep some of his guard up where she was concerned.

"What do you do?" he said, giving her a side-glance.

"Art therapy. Most people aren't familiar with it. It's different than being an artist."

"But you're obviously an artist, too." Tyler motioned toward bits of paint still stuck to her fingernails.

Olivia held them up proudly. "Occupational hazard."

"Hmm," he said. "Orange, red, yellow... something autumn?"

Her mouth puckered to show she was impressed.

"You have an observant eye." The knot in Tyler's gut twinged. He'd become more observant the moment she'd come into his life, not that he would ever admit it.

Olivia picked at a fleck of orange paint.

"I know my way around a canvas, but that's not quite what I do back home. I help people, mainly children, who are struggling. Creating artwork can help them express how they feel or what they're worried or scared about."

Tyler perked up. He didn't know such a job existed. She certainly was intriguing.

"What kinds of things are they struggling with?" he asked.

"Depends on the client. Anxiety, grief, stress…all sorts of things. It helps shy children boost their self-esteem. It helps delayed children improve their social skills. It's another tool in the toolbox to help children communicate."

"Like Micah?"

Tyler hung a left toward the baseball field as Olivia managed a nod.

"It works best when the child doesn't get annoyed with the art therapist. You can imagine how much success I've had with him, huh?"

"Have you tried it with him?" Tyler could imagine the challenges of doing therapy with a parent. When he was Micah's age, he wouldn't have taken to the idea about therapy, either, although anything would have been better than what both of his mother figures had done. Neither of them had even attempted to talk to him after what happened with his dad. Anything would have been better than pretending the pain wasn't there.

"So," Olivia said, the cadence of her voice nervously kicking up half a notch. "What kind of baseball team does Gary play for again? You know I've watched more professional baseball games in my life than I'd ever care to count."

"I can imagine," Tyler said, surprised by the sudden change of subject. If the topics of Micah and art therapy converged again, he realized he should tread very carefully. By the way Olivia picked at the paint on her fingernails, he could tell Micah's therapy was a very tender point. "This isn't a professional game. Far from it."

She smiled at that. "In all the summers I spent here, my mother and I never attended a game. Can you believe that?"

"I can. This league is only two years old."

"Is it a senior league?"

"Nope."

"Okay, now I'm really curious."

He pulled into a gravel parking lot behind several rows of bleachers. Some people were milling about as others spread blankets on the grass. Children scampered around, some flailing silver pinwheels. Tyler hopped out of the truck and retrieved two bottles of water from his tailgate cooler. He led them around the edge of the bleachers, and when they spotted the baseball diamond, he stopped.

"Don't you love the sight of it?" he said. He'd always appreciated the twinge of excitement that took hold when he attended a baseball game. He appreciated how ingrained it was not just in American culture, but in his childhood. He and his dad had gotten in a lot of good years playing catch before the day came that divided his childhood into two distinct halves. The first half was *the before*, the second half was *the after*, and he did his best to avoid conversations that made him talk about it in any more detail than that.

Tyler drew a long, deep breath. Recently cut grass, freshly popped popcorn, sunscreen, dirt and the last rays of summer sunshine— all of it mingled in his nasal cavity at the base of his memory. All at once he was flooded not just with memories of playing Little League and spotting his dad in the bleachers, but of the life that he had experienced in *the before*.

Olivia drew her own breath and closed her eyes for a moment. "Baseball was such a big part of my marriage and Micah's childhood I can't keep from loving it. Without it now, I feel like I've been playing hooky from a part of my life for the past two years."

Tyler had never heard anyone describe their life in that way, but it made a lot of sense to him. He'd been playing hooky from plenty of things since *the after*.

For a brief moment, as she stood beside him nearly shoulder to shoulder, everyone else seemed to disappear. It was strange to feel such a connection with another person, someone whom he didn't know very well. It felt dangerous to get too settled, too comfortable with the feeling, because he didn't know where it would lead from there. In the past, just hoping for connection had led to very painful places.

Tyler looked around, eager to snap out of the moment as quickly as possible. When he spotted a young girl carrying a candy concession box, he winked at Olivia. "Wait here a second."

He jogged over to the girl and after a quick

transaction, he slipped a package into his pocket and returned.

"Getting your box of Cracker Jacks?" Olivia said.

"Even better. Come on. The best seats are this way." Tyler led Olivia toward a densely wooded hill beyond third base. "I used to come here with my buddies, back in the day."

"I wonder if I ever saw you," Olivia said. "Not here at games but around town."

"Did you go to the Fourth of July parades?"

"Every year."

"The Lollipop?"

"Of course!" Olivia said with a laugh. "It was always one of our first stops when we got into town."

As he watched her match his stride, step-by-step, he thought her the loveliest woman he'd met in a long time.

The crowd was growing by the moment and Olivia had noticed.

"The bleachers are filling up," she said. "We won't get a seat unless we hurry. Are we sitting on top of the scoreboard or something?"

"Now, that's an idea," Tyler said. "Maybe next time."

Once they'd gotten twenty yards from third base, he jetted left to the edge of the woods and up a steep, narrow path. A few grade school children dug in the dirt, but they popped up and ran back to the bleachers when they spotted him.

"You have certainly piqued my curiosity," she said. "Where on earth are we going?"

The beaten path rose steeper. Tree roots arched out of the ground, giving conveniently placed steps to help them navigate, but it was still a climb that required them to grab tree branches along the way for support.

"Are you okay?" he asked, glancing back at her. She accepted his offered hand, and when he grasped her slender fingers in his, it felt as natural as if he'd already done it a hundred times before. He pulled her up the sharpest part of the incline and couldn't help but think of the first time they'd met. Before he'd seen her face or looked into those deep, brown eyes of hers, he'd pulled her into his arms. He'd been scared witless, the gravity of the situation slamming his heart against his chest plate until he thought it would burst through. But now, without that element of danger, he could relax and enjoy the climb. He could enjoy the warmth of her hand in his as he anticipated the look on her face when she saw what was at the top of the hill. "Just a little farther now," he promised. "It'll be worth it."

She hoisted herself up to the top with him. When they'd both made it to level ground, she gave his hand a squeeze before releasing it as they both caught their breath.

"Tyler," she said, glancing around the wooded spot. "You certainly keep things interesting."

It was cool in the woods, shaded from the setting sun. The low-hanging trees felt like privacy curtains against the rest of the world, and he could tell she was considering this. Quiet murmurs of the crowd awaiting the game faded to background noise as his ears pricked to her soft breathing. Her chest rose and fell slower with each breath, as did his.

Her smile faded as she felt the weight of his stare on her face. He thought he should tear his eyes away and get on with showing her exactly what it was he'd brought her here to see, but for a moment, all he wanted to do was stand quietly with her for as long as she'd allow. The moment was the most peace he'd felt since he couldn't remember when.

Her skin had a shiny dew from the climb, and it brought out the highlights of her cheeks. For a moment he saw nothing else.

When his eyes met hers again, her lips parted. He thought she might say something, might ask why he'd brought her to this place, which had become a refuge for him in the first years of *the after*. But he didn't want to think about that now or even explain to himself why he had brought her here when she would have been perfectly content to watch the game from the bleachers.

A beat passed and then another as her lashes fluttered up at him, a bit awkward perhaps, but trusting. She had trusted him to pull her off the ledge of Falcon's Peak. And she had trusted him enough to talk about her struggles with Micah. The way she had confided in him, even if it was just a hint at times, he knew it wasn't something he should take lightly. He didn't want to do anything to break that trust.

All at once he felt unpracticed in how to behave around her, simultaneously wanting to draw her close while wanting to escape all the same. To keep the moment from stretching too long, he shuffled toward a nearby perch above a ten-foot drop.

"Best seats in the house."

She balked playfully. "You know how I am around steep ledges."

"Yes. Bold."

His comment landed exactly how he'd intended when her face broke into a grin of agreement. She sat on the matted grass and dangled her feet over the edge as he sat beside her.

Looking up at the branches arching above them, she mused, "It looks like a natural pergola."

"People used to prune these trees to make them grow this way. It's not entirely natural."

She stared up. "It's beautiful all the same. These are definitely the best seats in the house."

"You're in for one of the best games, too."

The baseball diamond was kept up well but it was old. The scoreboards at the back of the outfield hadn't been updated in decades, and the concession stand looked like a stiff wind could topple it. Still, the eager fans, who had shown up in droves, didn't seem to care. They cheered as a man around fifty years old ran onto the field.

"This is where they hold Little League games and community leagues. But the league playing tonight is…unique."

His voice taunted as her eyes followed the man. He wore a vintage, white and blue-collared uniform shirt and pants, blue knee-high socks, and a blue-and-white striped flat-top cap. He even wore a blue necktie, end tucked between the buttons on his shirt. He tossed a baseball in the air and caught it as players of various ages, dressed in matching vintage uniforms, ran out from the dugout.

Olivia hooted with glee. "Is this a historical baseball game?"

"Surprised?"

"Delighted!"

The first batter, beautifully donning the opposing team's white-and-red stripes, swung a few practice swings with an old-fashioned baseball bat. Even from a distance, the bat was noticeably longer and fatter than modern bats.

"He looks like he could crack it all the way to us with that thing," Olivia said.

"The baseball is softer than what they use today. He needs that bat to propel it."

"Are they playing by vintage rules?"

Tyler scratched his chin. "Yes, but I'm hard-pressed to remember them all. I know it's underhand pitching only with no fast balls. Runners can't lead off, and if a ball is caught on a bounce, it's an out."

"Interesting," Olivia said. "What rules are those?"

"Circa 1870, I think. Pretty cool, huh?"

"Yep." She grinned. "I have to give it to you. In all the years of watching baseball, I've never seen a historical game."

A sturdy man dressed in an umpire uniform brushed the dirt off home plate and called for the teams to play ball. The crowd cheered as the pitcher took the mound.

"Except," Olivia said, "it's a shame there aren't any women on the field."

"The women's league plays on Saturdays."

"Historical?"

"1940s."

Olivia laughed. "I love that. We'll have to bring Micah."

She said it so casually, as if planning a future outing for the three of them was a natural extension of their time together.

"When I was a kid," he said, "this place felt like my secret hideout." He stopped himself, surprised he'd blurted out something he'd never told anyone. Sure, his childhood friends had come up here with him after they had ridden their bikes to the baseball diamond to play a game. They had taken breaks from the hot sun to hide in the woods and drink Dr Pepper. But he'd come here many more times alone, after those carefree years, and every time he had come here, he hadn't told a soul where he was going. He couldn't think what had come over him to blurt out his secret just now.

"Micah has been spending a lot of time in the woods behind Hattie's cottage. I get the feeling he's making his own secret refuge out there, to escape…"

"To escape what?"

"If I'm being honest, to escape me." Her shoulders slumped a little. "I feel like the tree line between Hattie's backyard and woods represents an invisible boundary I shouldn't cross. I get the impression I shouldn't go back there, at least not until he invites me."

"That's thoughtful of you," Tyler said, impressed she had the fortitude to understand a young man's need for independence so well. "To consider that."

"Thanks. What about your secret hideout? Did you come here a lot?"

"Uh. I guess."

"Don't you know for sure?" Her lips curled and he could tell she was teasing, not pressing him to divulge any trade secrets of his past.

He shrugged and looked out at the baseball diamond to recalibrate his feelings. Sitting and talking with her felt so easy, but that didn't mean he could let his guard down. In his experience, love was a trap that blinded you to what a person was really like until things went pear-shaped. These moments were nice even if they wouldn't last.

He caught a glimpse of Olivia's perfect profile and had a hard time imagining her as anything other than what he saw. He tried to imagine her changing, showing true colors that were uglier than the rose-tinged ones he saw now.

"Being back here in Roseley…" she said. "If nostalgia isn't a powerful thing."

"It can hit you when you least expect it."

"Gosh, yes." Her face fell serious as she peeled at the label on her water bottle, fingertips scrapping over the plastic. "I can go about my day and then uncover an old note stuck in a book and…"

Whether or not she realized it, she was pulling away from him and he knew he was losing her to—

"Jeb?" he asked.

"And my mother," she said softly. "They're nowhere but they're still everywhere, too. Thinking of Jeb isn't nostalgia just yet. It's still grief."

Tyler sucked a breath, wishing he couldn't identify with Olivia's experience. They were both part of a club for which they didn't want to hold a membership.

"Does it barrel at you like a freight train?" he said, sadly recalling those first few months after he'd lost his dad.

"Hmm, no." Olivia paused for a moment before continuing slowly. "It sinks and sinks.

Most mornings I wake up and remind myself that the only way through the day is to swim hard for the surface."

"I'm sure it's been…" What? What comfort could he offer? He knew what it was like to lose a parent, especially a parent who meant the world to you. But losing a spouse had to be different. He didn't know anything about that. He wanted to comfort her, but he didn't know how to. "Is there anything I can do?" he finally said.

"You're already doing it." Her voice brightened slightly. "Micah needs a place to go to find a new version of himself. Providing that environment at the clinic will work wonders. I know it."

"He'd probably like it up here," Tyler said, looking at the baseball diamond. "He's the right age."

"For a secret hideout?" He found her smiling now, and relief washed over him that they were wandering back to safer topics, ones that didn't make his heart clench. "Most mothers are worried about the trouble their kid could get into," she continued, "but most days my wish is for him to get back out into the world and stir it up."

"He is. And on that note…"

"What?"

Tyler played with the soft register of his voice. "I think the time is finally right for…"

"For…" Olivia's body stiffened.

"My favorite part of the evening, if you think you can handle it."

CHAPTER ELEVEN

OLIVIA STARED UP at him, uncertainty in her eyes. "I need to know what it is first."

Tyler shook his head. "I think you already know what I'm talking about. From what I've gathered about you, I'd say you're the kind of woman who has been thinking about it ever since we arrived. I know I have." He fluttered his eyebrows wildly, letting her in on the fact that he was joking.

Olivia contorted her mouth and delivered a dry line. "I think your ego is severely misjudging my feelings right now."

Tyler laughed and quickly pulled something from his pocket. He hid it behind his back. After a moment, he presented her with two balled fists. When she playfully tapped on his left hand, he opened it to reveal—

"Bazooka bubblegum? I haven't had this in forever." She snatched one, unwrapped it and popped it into her mouth. "Yum. It even tastes pink."

"It's the best, right?" He popped a piece into his mouth, savoring the flavor of childhood.

Olivia giggled. "The best." She settled back on her hands as Tyler lay back in the grass and propped himself up on an elbow.

"Cheering is only fun when you're surrounded by a lot of people," she said. "The quiet is nice, though."

"Do you get much of it?"

Aside from his work at the clinic, he managed to find plenty of quiet. He felt safest, most protected, when he was all alone. Although he enjoyed this time with Olivia, he knew better than to believe it could continue. In his experience, feeling true peace with another person never lasted.

"More than I'd like, these days."

"Micah is pretty talkative at the clinic."

"Yeah?" She almost grinned like he'd just told her that Micah was the top of the class. With a sigh that mixed hope and longing she continued. "I'm glad he's talking to someone, even if it isn't me."

Tyler plucked a blade of clover and twirled it between his fingers. Of the few days Micah had been coming into the clinic, the kid had talked like he'd been stranded on a deserted island for a year and had only made company with coconuts. He dialogued every single thing that happened or popped into his mind.

Although none of what Micah had said had been substantial in the way Olivia hoped for, Tyler had gotten to know the kid very quickly. Between talking baseball and talking animals, Micah had asked him so many questions about what life was like as a veterinarian, Tyler had felt at times like he was being interviewed for a documentary. He was embarrassed to admit that Micah had talked so much earlier that day, Tyler had unintentionally zoned out a few times. He had been younger than Micah when he'd worked in the clinic, so he couldn't help but wonder if his dad had done the same thing with him from time to time. The thought brought an amused curl to his lips. "Now that I think of it, today he mentioned a camp."

"Nature's Heirs?"

"I think that's the one. He said he couldn't go this year."

"Couldn't or wouldn't?"

"Hmm," Tyler said, flicking the clover. "Not sure. Is that important?"

"He won a full scholarship but refused to go, and I still don't know why."

That sounded pretty important to him, but he couldn't remember Micah mentioning it.

They both lay stretched on the grass for a couple of minutes, nothing but the murmur of the crowd and the bristling of the tree branches to distract them. He could feel something stirring inside him, some desire to share something with her after she'd talked about Micah. He knew she didn't expect it. But the longer they lay on the grass and the stillness stretched further, he found himself wanting to offer up a small token of empathy.

"I lost someone, too," Tyler said, quietly. "I don't know exactly how you feel, losing a spouse like you did, but I understand how the grief is…" he shook his head "…sinking."

"Your dad?" Her voice was so caring he didn't feel the typical knee-jerk reaction to grab his own words back again. Instead, he continued.

"I told you before it was a long time ago but…"

As he chewed the inside of his cheek, understanding settled behind her eyes. For tonight, it was enough to share that, even if he couldn't share all of it and it was enough to help her understand that he knew some things about what she and Micah were going through.

"How old were you?" she asked.

"Sixteen. He got sick when I was Micah's age."

A soft hum of empathy vibrated in her throat, and he knew she would protect the full weight of his sorrow.

"I'm sorry. That must have been hard for you and your stepmother."

Tyler grimaced. If anything had been hard on Robin it was that she hadn't been able to get to the salon for her regularly scheduled appointments on time.

When his dad had first introduced him to Robin, he'd thought her to be beautiful. She'd been full of energy and life and for a short while he thought that she'd make his dad happy. Heck, he'd hoped she'd make him happy, too. Unfortunately, Robin had compounded their pain, his and his dad's. As much as he wanted to move past that hurt, just seeing Robin, thinking of how she'd treated him when he'd been a kid still floundering in his grief—it still stung deeply.

"What was your dad like?"

Tyler fully relaxed back on the grass, clasping his hands under his head. Olivia copied him. Being offered the opportunity to talk about his dad brought a warm smile to Tyler's face.

"He and Gary ran the clinic and the three

of us always talked about me going to veterinarian school so I could join them. Growing up I spent all my free time at the clinic working with them. He was a great dad…my best friend."

"What happened between him and your mom?"

Tyler lay silently for a few moments, the smile quickly fading. It was a fair question, but not one he ever entertained, especially from someone he didn't know well. He'd met with a counselor after his dad had died but he'd never spoken about his parents' marriage to anyone else, not even Gary.

He considered sitting up and insisting they watch the game instead of digging into their not-so-rosy pasts. But when he turned and found Olivia's gentle gaze, something in him fought the urge to escape. Instead, he drew a breath.

"They always fought," he managed. "He'd come home from work, and she'd launch into him about stupid things. It was like walking on eggshells." His mom would argue and yell and slam the bedroom door. Then the silent treatment…sometimes it would go on for days. Tyler knew that after a few days it would be a repeat performance. Wash, rinse, repeat, but do it all at home so no one else knew.

"You didn't deserve to live in that." There was sincerity in her tone.

"No one does," he agreed. At the clinic, his dad was always smiling and talking with people. To the outside world no one would have suspected how unhappy his parents were. No one really understood why his dad wanted the divorce, either, except him and Gary. "My dad got judged harshly around town when he divorced my mom," he shared grimly. "I remember that part clearly."

He rolled to his side and balanced his head in his palm, not wanting to relive the next part, the worst part.

Olivia bristled. "Getting judged in the court of public opinion is a common denominator for baseball wives."

"Is it?" he asked. It made sense.

Olivia squeezed her eyes shut. "People only see me as belonging to two categories. In the first, I'm a young widow raising a son on my own. People try to comfort me where they can. No one really knows what to say but most people try to say *something*."

"And in the second category?"

Olivia readjusted to better face him, as if getting him to understand this next part was crucial.

"I'm not just a widow. I'm *Jeb Howard's*

widow. People want to express their condolences not just because they're empathetic for how I'm surviving, but because of how they feel about him. They want to discuss his talent and his stats and his record. They feel compelled to tell me about all the games they watched, sometimes in uncanny detail." Her face looked like it could fall off from the weight of burden she was carrying. "As much as I want to understand where they're coming from and take some delight in how his legacy might last, the truth is, I don't want a play-by-play. It doesn't fill me with any comfort to hear them rattle on about Jeb's professional accomplishments, because at the end of the day, he might have been a great baseball player, but…" she lowered her eyes like the shame of admitting the next part was only hers to bear "…he wasn't a great husband."

Tyler had watched plenty of professional baseball games over the years, and he figured he'd seen her on TV at some point when the camera panned for a few seconds to show the players' wives. He wondered what it had felt like for her to have to be on camera and cheer for a husband whom she felt distanced from. "What about Micah?" Tyler said. "How does he handle it?"

"Like a champ in front of other people. He's Jeb's son, that's for sure."

Tyler hated the idea of putting on airs for show or simply because people expected it. Nothing about doing that felt easy.

"You don't have to pretend in Roseley," Tyler said. "Not with me, anyway."

Olivia's cheeks flushed. Her sudden embarrassment reminded him they were still getting to know each other. She had admitted a lot quickly and he knew how hard he worked to keep from doing similar things.

"I don't expect you to understand all that," she said, "but people are always so curious about Jeb and our marriage and, of course, the accident. Sometimes I do want to pretend. I want to pretend I'm someone else so I don't have to explain anything to anyone anymore."

"You don't have to explain or tell me anything you don't want to," he said gently.

"Thanks," she said, her voice wobbly. "That goes for you, too."

A lump formed in his throat, and he felt like no one had ever understood him so well, so quickly.

CHAPTER TWELVE

OLIVIA ESCAPED THE cottage early the next morning to get in a walk before Micah or Hattie awoke for the day. After watching the baseball game the night before, she'd returned home with a lot to process and not all of it was about Micah and their argument at The Sandwich Board.

Tyler had given her plenty to think about, too.

For the first time in a long time, she felt heard. It had been so long since someone had invested the time to talk, really talk, that she had almost forgotten what it felt like. Her mother had always been good at listening and offering gentle advice when it counted. Olivia had had girlfriends over the years who loved to talk, but no one had ever listened the way Tyler did. She'd spent so many years in a marriage where real connection was never really available, so when Tyler had leaned in to listen and watch her like she was the only interesting thing in the world, every inch of her felt nourished.

Oliva kicked a stone along the road. She reminded herself that their time at the historical baseball game didn't mean she was available for anything other than friendship with Tyler. Sure, there had been a couple of times over the evening when she'd wondered what it might be like to touch him, but she'd quickly pushed those thoughts from her mind. Tyler was shaping up to be a good support to Micah, and she didn't want to jeopardize that by imagining anything other than friendship. To hide any attraction she might feel for Tyler, she had to keep her thoughts clear of anything more. She had to stay vigilant.

Still, it was easy to notice how good-looking he was, despite the fact he wasn't classically handsome. If she had to be honest, at first glance, his facial features were average at best. Brown hair, average height and build. It was something about the way he looked at her, the way he listened, that made every nerve in her body stand up and take notice. He seemed to listen with his entire face, his entire body, like he was a gravitational pull tugging her into his atmosphere. That kind of attention was intoxicating.

Olivia stopped short and brought her fingertips to her lips. She squeezed her eyes shut, reliving the kindness she'd found in Tyler's eyes when he'd first found her at The Sandwich Board. Just the way he'd spoken her name, with such compassion and inquisitiveness, made her suck an extra half breath before continuing down the road.

She had felt such giddiness when Jeb had been chasing her. He'd spotted her out with friends at a restaurant and had pursued her with laser beam focus until she'd agreed to a date. Her girlfriends had helped her push away her hesitation and doubts about Jeb, reminding her about how lucky she was to go out with him. The early days of their relationship had felt wonderful, and he'd seemed fully intoxicated with her then, too. Talking to Tyler felt very different, more natural and more honest than how things had felt in the beginning with Jeb. Although she had been a different woman back then, and felt better in her own skin now, she still didn't feel right to trust her budding feelings for Tyler. Her feelings had deceived her once before, and she wasn't about to let them cover her eyes again.

The morning sun had crested the horizon when Olivia heard tires rumbling up the road behind her. She turned to find Tyler's truck approaching. He slowed to a stop and waited for her to cross to his window.

"I don't suppose I can offer you a ride," he said when she reached him.

Olivia turned up her nose playfully. "Can't you see I'm walking on purpose?"

"I was afraid of that."

"Why?"

"You forgot to give me back my hat."

Olivia gasped. "Did I?" It hadn't occurred to her, even when she'd gotten home and taken it off. She'd obviously been more pre-occupied with the events of the evening than she'd realized. "I'm sorry about that. Do you need it?"

"Of course, I need it."

"Right this instant?"

"It is my favorite hat." When his tone teased, Olivia puckered a smirk to show she wasn't buying it.

"*Falcon High* is your favorite hat?"

"I like what I like."

Olivia looked down the road. Another car had slowed, waiting to pass them. She looked back at Tyler, who seemed content to make them wait.

"I just started my walk, so I'm not ready to head back to the cottage. Hattie's at the house if you want it now or I can drop it by the clinic later if you…"

"I'll wait."

"Wait?"

The word was barely out of her mouth when Tyler pulled his truck onto the shoulder and parked. After the car passed them, he climbed out of his truck and joined her. In long khaki shorts and a vintage T-shirt, he looked prepared for whatever the day might bring.

"I'll keep you company," he said. "How far do you usually go?"

"Uh… I don't know." She started to walk again, watching Tyler's feet march in time with hers. "I haven't walked Hattie's road yet. Are you seriously inviting yourself along?"

He shrugged. "Why not?"

"I set a fast pace." Her words were a bit of a challenge.

"You didn't look like you were before."

"I was still warming up."

Tyler rolled his shoulders, preparing. "Okay. You set the pace."

Olivia set a stride much faster than what she wanted. Her walk had been more to clear her head, not work up a sweat. But having a walking companion—the person she'd just been thinking about no less—had kick-started a surge of adrenaline that needed expelling.

"Is this too fast?" she asked. Tyler shook his head.

"It feels good."

"It does, doesn't it?"

"I like to rock climb every morning, but ever since I met you, I haven't been able to." He held up his hand. "It's still sore."

Olivia held up her bruised arm. "If it feels as bad as my arm, you won't be rock climbing for a while longer."

"No worries. Walking works, too."

She searched for something to say to keep the conversation casual. "Have you already talked to Gary this morning?"

"We met for breakfast."

"At The Copper Kettle?"

It was common knowledge in Roseley that The Copper Kettle had the best breakfasts in town. Between the expansive menu, excellent prices and good waitstaff, it was a favorite among locals if you could get there before nine o'clock in the morning. After that, in the summer, it was a swarm of tourists.

"Where else? In fact…" Tyler pointed as they approached a long driveway that wound and disappeared into the woods. The mailbox on the street was copper and mounted on an ivy-entwined post. "Rick and Gemma Murdock, the owners, live there. Micah might fit in with their boys. If I remember correctly, one of them is around his age."

Olivia peered down the driveway as they passed. Micah had fallen away from his friends over the past two years. She'd understood, to an extent, because all of his friends had been teammates on his school and traveling teams. When he had stopped attending baseball practices and games, his teammates hadn't had much free time to just hang out, despite Olivia's best efforts to facilitate get-togethers.

Watching him detach from baseball, and naturally all his friends, was a sadness that gnawed at her every day.

"Thanks for the tip."

"Thanks for going to Gary's game. He told me he appreciated it."

"It was my pleasure."

"Mine, too," he said, a hint of smokiness in his voice.

Olivia wondered if she should take Tyler's words at face value, thinking only of the game. But something in his eyes, in the way he held her gaze for half a breath too long, made her sense something more. It was the same *something* she had been trying to avoid thinking about all night.

"I doubt he could hear us cheering from where we were sitting," she said.

"He knows I'm not big into cheering, regardless of where I'm sitting."

"Not me," Olivia said, proudly. "You should have seen me at Micah's games, back in the day. I loved to be the loudest."

"Is that a fact?"

"I used to put Jeb to shame."

"Show me."

"What?" She stopped short.

Tyler slowed, too. "Show me what you used to do."

"Oh, no. I'd feel dumb doing it here."

"Why?" he said, his voice fully sincere.

"It's eight o'clock in the morning. I'll wake the woods."

"No one's around. Look." He glanced to either side of the road. "It's just me. You're safe."

"Safe?" She knew he meant from public humiliation, but the genuineness in his eyes made her wonder if he meant something else. He didn't smile back at her but the lines around his eyes crinkled in the most reassuring way, softening to express how much he meant it. As hard as she was working to suppress her attraction to him, nothing about spending more time together felt completely safe.

She listened for anyone around them, but nothing—not a car rumbling in the distance nor a neighbor collecting the newspaper—was nearby. Only the quiet of the rural road and a few fluttering birds in the trees were around as witnesses.

Tyler dipped his hands casually into his front pockets. He was the essence of cool and collected, and he was making something inside her begin to unravel. He wasn't pressuring or cajoling her. He was extending an invitation so kindly she couldn't help but inwardly swoon.

"Micah just stole second base," he prompted. "He looks up in the stands to find you, and much to his delight he hears…"

Olivia shifted from one foot to the other. She couldn't help but stare helplessly for a moment, surprised at how easily he could draw her in.

"Okay, fine," she muttered. "If this will make you start walking again." She clasped her hands together like a cheerleading captain preparing to rouse the crowd. When her eyes locked on Tyler's, an excitement flashed over his expression, and it gave her just the right surge to prove what she could do.

She imagined it was the bottom of the ninth with both teams tied. When she looked out onto the baseball diamond, she saw her son on third base. Micah was playing not because he loved his dad, but because he loved baseball.

Olivia opened her eyes and punched her fists into the air. With a holler loud enough to wake the Murdocks she cried, "YEA! GO, MICAH! GO, MICAH! GOOOO!" She flailed her hands in the air and continued to cheer, her enthusiasm kicking Tyler back off his feet a few steps.

Olivia clapped several times—hard, loud clasps. Tyler's expression had morphed from his initial encouragement to complete amazement. She'd cheered like this before. She certainly wasn't pretending to impress him or exceed his challenge. But the raw cries from her throat, the exhilaration that came over her as she imagined Micah stealing home base, surprised the heck out of her, too. It felt great. It felt honest.

Finally, as she brought her hands to her hips to signal she was finished, Tyler's expression settled on pleased. When she'd cheered like that for Micah, Jeb had always disapproved—

at least, whenever he was in town to catch a game. In his eyes, she had appearances to uphold, and cheering wildly was putting on too much of a show. But when she ignored Jeb and cheered anyway, it had been one of the few times she'd allowed herself to be truly honest with him. She'd suffered her husband's ridicule afterward, but for a few brief moments, when she was ecstatically cheering for their son, she'd been honest.

"That," he said, eyes twinkling, "was fantastic."

"Thanks," she said, unable to suppress a giggle.

"Gary should hire you out for his games."

"I don't know if he can afford me."

"True. He'd be dealing with a pro, here." When they continued walking, Tyler shoulder-bumped her. "Micah was lucky to have you in the stands."

"Would you remind him of that fact?"

"He already knows." His assurance warmed her heart, but she tried not to linger on it.

They walked a while, though noticeably slower than before as Olivia caught her breath. A dirt path split off the main road and without thinking, they steered to follow it. It curved around a bend taking them into the woods. After a minute, they came to a small pond complete with lily pads, ducks, turtles and—

Neep! A little frog splashed into the pond as they approached. *Neep!* cried another.

"I think we interrupted their sunbathing," Olivia whispered as they made their way around the pond. Every few yards they walked, another frog cried and leaped into the water with a tiny splash. *Neep...neep...neep!*

"It's a chorus," he said.

"I wish I could get a better look at one before it jumped."

He pointed farther down along the water. "There's one camouflaged in the mud right by that small log," he said. "And there's another big, fat one at the edge of the grass line." Olivia squinted, trying to see what Tyler saw, but all she could see was his profile. All she could hear was the helpful, soft timbre of his voice.

"Micah used to love looking for toads," she said.

"These are frogs. Toads don't swim. See?" He pointed out into the pond where the morning sun was highlighting a little frog as it propelled itself beneath the surface of the water.

"I stand corrected," she said. The sun highlighted the golden stubble on Tyler's chin. His hair was a soft brown, but in the light, she could tell his beard would come in auburn if he grew it longer.

"Tyler?" she asked as they continued their stroll. "May I ask you a question?"

"Shoot."

"Did you want to become a veterinarian because of your dad?"

"Yes."

"That was quick. You didn't even have to think about it."

"Nope." He smiled.

"You seem well suited for it."

"How so?" he asked. They wandered under the shade of a weeping willow tree. Its dripping branches swayed delicately in the breeze, sheltering them in a private cocoon.

"You're calm. Animals probably appreciate that about you. I know people do."

"Like Micah?"

"Yes."

"Like you?" he asked, earnestly.

Olivia could nearly feel the positive ions on his skin summoning the negative ones on hers, lifting each delicate hair along her arm to be closer to him. She appreciated a lot about him and marveled at how she'd grown to care about him in such a short time.

But Tyler was also a good influence on Micah. He was a healthy role model who couldn't have come along at a better time if he'd shown up gift wrapped on her front doorstep. How could she entertain any attraction she had for him when she couldn't see it through? As a widow who needed to be solely focused on helping her son, she couldn't start something with Tyler that she didn't see going somewhere. If it went south, it would be Micah who would suffer most. He'd lose someone again and she couldn't let that happen.

"I appreciate your friendship, Tyler," she said, wanting to cringe at how empty it sounded. She searched for a sign he understood all that she meant and all that she felt. If circumstances were different, she could answer him in an entirely different way.

Tyler gathered a long, hanging weeping willow branch and carefully ran his fingers along it without disturbing a single tiny leaf.

"May I ask you a question now?" he said.

She raised her eyebrows, grateful for any change of subject. "Shoot."

"Did you use to cheer at your husband's games?"

"Cheer?"

"The way you did at Micah's?"

"Oh, no," Olivia said. "Never." She shuffled toward the large tree trunk and leaned against it, letting the jagged bark imprint against her shoulder. "Jeb would have hated that. He didn't like big displays of emotion. He'd have accused me of making a scene, which on network television was a big no-no." She kept her tone light, despite that it still hurt a little.

"That must have been exhausting."

Olivia shrugged. It had all been exhausting. Right before Jeb died, she'd felt more than just tired. She'd felt weary from putting on a facade for so many years.

"I did my best to be a good wife..." She thought of the compromise she'd finally made with herself the year before Jeb died. After so many failed attempts to turn things around with him, she'd realized she could only control how she behaved, how she reacted. If Jeb didn't want to invest himself in her or their son, she couldn't force him or convince him or plead with him any longer. She could only focus on doing her best to raise Micah. "I did my best to be a good mother."

"You *are* a good mother." The earnestness in his face melted her. "I see it not just in how you talk to Micah but how you talk *about* him. It tells me everything I'd ever need to know about your heart."

Olivia's face went emollient. No one had ever spoken about her heart before.

Tyler moved closer as his stare deepened. Close enough to touch, his eyes looked dark green. Gold flecks splintered from the irises like tines of a rime snowflake. A woman could lose herself in eyes as beckoning as his. She could let herself be coaxed into his embrace if he continued to look at her in such a way and lace his words with such kindness.

"You don't know me well enough to say that, Tyler. If you knew how many mistakes I've made…"

"It's your intention I'm talking about. Mistakes don't change how you love your son."

Her throat tightened, and she tried to fight the tears that welled in her eyes. "But it's so hard."

"Maybe it's hard because of how much you care about him. If it was easy you probably wouldn't be a very good mom."

But she didn't feel like a good mom. She tried so hard, but admitting her insecurities as a mother to a man she still didn't know very well felt risky. What if he agreed with the worst things she already thought about herself? What if he offered solutions for her to improve instead of just listening?

"You sound like Hattie." The tears finally broke free and ran down her cheeks, the beginning of her worst admission almost breaching her lips. Tyler furrowed his brow, noticeably distressed at having made her cry. "I—I always feel like I'm failing," she said.

"Be kinder to yourself, Olivia."

His words were rich like a baritone humming softly in her ear. She dropped her head, wanting to hear him say those words again, if only to have his voice wrap around her like a warm blanket on a chilly night. She wanted to let the moment draw out slowly like the last note of a sonata you didn't want to hear end.

Tyler leaned against the tree trunk beside her. He maneuvered closer so effortlessly to bring his body just inches from hers as he continued to gaze at her. He was waiting for her. The intimacy between them ballooned as neither wavered or broke focus. It rose in exponential growth so quickly she thought she might burst out of her skin.

When his fingertips found hers, exploring every crevice of her hand, a hot current skittered up her arm. The breeze that had been blowing only a moment ago seemed to disappear. Everything around her stilled and all she could see was his hand touching her skin. He caressed the delicate spot along the inside of her wrist. She swallowed, reminding herself to blink, to breathe, and she wondered if he could tell how hard her pulse was racing. With each second his hand warmed along her skin, trailing slowly up her arm, she thought the blood coursing through her veins increased its pressure.

She shuddered with him so close, the tension she'd been carrying for so long having no other place to go but out. She'd carried such stress for so long she'd hardly noticed it—until now. Goose bumps pricked all over her body. She expected Tyler to smirk or make some reference, but he didn't. He was too focused on skimming a hand over the rounded slope of her shoulder.

The sensation was so divine she couldn't keep her eyelashes from falling closed. Her hearing heightened to the shuffling sound he made as he leaned his body close and brought his face near hers. Her heart pounded. She was about to be kissed by a man who wasn't her husband.

Tyler was trying to control himself, too; she could tell. His rhythmic breathing awakened her senses to all of him. She wanted to stay suspended in the anticipation of what was coming for just a moment longer. What she wouldn't give for a few more seconds to forget she was a mother who had to be responsible or a widow still mending a broken heart. It might have broken long before her husband died, but in the years since, she hadn't been able to cement the pieces back together again. How could she offer Tyler a basket of broken pieces when she didn't know the first thing about what to do with them herself?

"Tyler?" she said, her own voice snapping her back to her senses. She knew she wasn't ready for this, and there was nothing in his delicious kiss that could hurry her to be ready now. "Wait."

She opened her eyes as he shifted, landing his cheek against her cheek instead. His stubble tickled, his breath so warm against the nape of her neck.

Words jumbled in her brain, and she couldn't pick out the important ones fast enough to explain her hesitancy.

Just then, the sound of children's giggles came bouncing from up the path.

"Don't look now," he said, leaning away. "But I think we've got company."

Olivia released a nervous laugh as rustling tree branches and emphatic little whispers grew louder. All at once, three children between the ages of three and five emerged from the path. Two women, each slung with a baby on her chest, followed. The children scampered toward the pond, each holding a slice of bread.

The spell over her and Tyler had been broken, little giggles and cries interrupting the privacy they'd shared under the weeping willow tree. The sun was climbing higher, and the humidity signaled that it was time to go.

Tyler thoughtfully stroked a lock of hair off Olivia's face. She thought he might misread her gaze, see an invitation in it. Truth be told, she felt something deeper even if she couldn't act on it. His sun-kissed cheeks, strong jaw and furrowed brow were features that exuded strength and an intensity she hadn't seen on him before. The mere sight of him was all it took to make her heart skitter.

Olivia pressed a hand to the smooth plane of his chest. She wanted to hold him and, at the same time, she knew she shouldn't. Tyler seemed to recognize her debate. For all she knew, he was reeling with the same thoughts himself.

The hard lines and edges of his features softened. His expression flickered from searching to understanding.

"We should head back," he said. He waved to the children before leading her back to the path. Leaving the ethereal, they trotted back to reality.

CHAPTER THIRTEEN

TYLER ARRIVED BACK at the clinic Monday morning just as Olivia and Micah pulled up in front of it. Olivia waved brightly as Micah jumped out and hurried to beat her to the door.

"I don't need you to walk me in, Mom," he called before disappearing inside. Olivia ignored his orders and met Tyler on the sidewalk instead.

"I think I was supposed to stay in the car."

"I'm glad you didn't," Tyler said.

"Miss me, did ya?" she asked lightly.

Tyler did his best to sidestep her question by sipping his coffee. He didn't want to reveal that he had thought of almost nothing else but her for the last two days. "Last night I performed an emergency cesarean on a golden retriever. You can come inside and see the puppies," he said instead.

Performing the surgery had almost felt like a sterile break from the beautiful imagery that swirled every time he thought of their walk to the pond. Only when he recalled it, he imagined pulling her into his arms and making their almost-kiss a real kiss.

For a few brief moments when he'd stroked a lock of hair out of her face and her eyes had drifted to meet his, he'd lost all sense of time. He couldn't accurately gauge how long they had stood there under the shade of the tree before she'd pressed a hand to his chest and conveyed that they were moving too fast. What he had realized afterward was that Olivia had been right.

He'd almost stumbled into something dangerous. Any reminders he needed for why romance was a losing game were already living in town—and their names were Sandy and Robin. He'd been young and naive when they'd hurt him, so it was easy to blame them for his pain. But he was older and wiser now, and he'd decided a long time ago that he'd never play the fool again. If he trusted someone again, no matter how much he wanted to, and they hurt him, he'd have no one to blame but himself. He'd no sooner open his heart to possible attack than he'd handle a poisonous Texas coral snake for kicks.

Entertaining his growing feelings for Olivia felt no safer than closing his eyes and picking up a venomous creature. He was not the "cross your fingers and hope for the best" type of guy.

"Whose dog had puppies?" she asked. Tyler held open the clinic door for her and followed her inside.

"Are you familiar with the Behrs?"

Olivia snickered. "Who isn't?"

Tex and Bianca Behr were two of Roseley's most distinguished residents. They had called him shortly after his walk with Olivia and given him a much-appreciated distraction. Arizona, their champion golden retriever who had dabbled in dog show circuits, had gone into labor, but when it stopped and stalled several times, they'd called Tyler in a panic. After a quick visit and emergency transport to the clinic, Tyler had made the call to take the puppies by cesarean. As it sometimes happened, his weekend plans had sort of made themselves. But once all the puppies had been delivered and deemed healthy, he'd felt, as he always did after helping animals, fully satisfied that his time had been well spent.

Tyler led Olivia to the back room, where Julia and Micah were quietly squatting near the whelping box. The lights were dimmed. Arizona barely cracked open an eyelid when they entered.

"Oh, heavens," Olivia said. "She looks exhausted. When does she go home?"

"She should have gone home this morning, but the Behrs have an event in the city," Tyler explained. "We agreed to keep these cuties until they get back."

"They look like they're doing fine," Micah said, looking up at him. Tyler regretted that Micah didn't know what had developed between him and Olivia, but it also wasn't appropriate to disclose anything about their *almost*-kiss. The fact was, they hadn't done anything that warranted an update to their relationship status.

Eight puppies squirmed against their mother as if they were one living organism with eight moving parts. Their eyes were sealed shut, and their little bodies barely coordinated enough to suckle. Some were happily latched and nursing, while others fumbled around, getting lost in the process.

"Dr. Elderman," Micah said. "May I hold one?"

"The less interaction we have with the puppies right now the better," he said gently. "We don't want to stress out Arizona. That said, you're on puppy duty for the next few hours."

Micah exchanged a look with Julia. She

seemed just as eager to get her own paws on a pup, but it wasn't her job.

Julia checked the time and climbed to her feet. They were set to open in twenty minutes, and Tyler knew they were scheduled with back-to-back appointments all day.

"Geesh. Newborn puppies will be here all day and I have to manage the desk." Julia patted Micah on the shoulder. "At least they'll be in good hands."

A little pup let out a cry. He had been maneuvering to eat but had taken a clumsy tumble farther away from his mother.

"When they cry," Tyler said, "it means they're distraught in some way."

"Cold? Hungry?" Micah said.

"Something. Arizona is a seasoned mother. She already knows what to do and has been attentive in the past. Mostly she needs quiet and privacy.

"She's also never had a cesarean section before and it's major surgery," Tyler continued. "She might roll or wedge against the pups when she moves to help them. I need you to watch to make sure everyone, including Arizona, is doing okay. We don't want anyone to get pinched."

Micah nodded. "I can do that."

"That little guy looks like he's struggling a

bit," Tyler said, squatting down beside Micah. Arizona had been roused awake by her puppy's cries, but she still looked as if she were contemplating what to do. "Let's give her a hand with this one. See if you can help him get latched."

Micah cupped a hand under the puppy like he was relocating a hair-trigger explosive. He carefully latched it nearest Arizona's heart.

"You have good instincts," Tyler said as the puppy began to nurse. Micah didn't react, his focus solely on the puppy, but Tyler knew he'd still heard it. He'd heard the same words from his dad when he'd been a kid helping at the clinic. An aspiring veterinarian didn't forget such things easily.

With the puppy happily nursing, Arizona rested her head again, satisfied she could nap for another few minutes.

Julia poked her head around the doorway. "Dr. Elderman," she said. "Your mom is outside. Should I let her in?"

Tyler frowned. His stepmother had a penchant for dropping by unexpectedly, usually at the most inconvenient time. But it was unusual for his mother to do so. In fact, he couldn't think of the last time she'd come to the clinic. If he was pressed, he couldn't remember her visiting since he'd first returned to Roseley to help Gary run the place.

"I'll walk you out," Tyler said to Olivia as they followed Julia to the front desk. Sure enough, his mother was standing outside fiddling with her cell phone.

"Hi, Sandy," he said once they'd joined her on the sidewalk.

"I didn't mean to bother you at work," his mother said, her eyes straining to make sense of Olivia.

"You're not bothering me." As it wasn't the first time he'd told her this, he hoped she knew that he meant it. "This is my friend Olivia. Her son, Micah, volunteers here." Tyler motioned toward his mother. "This is my mother, Sandy."

Sandy was wearing long tan shorts, sneakers and her Willoughby Nursery work shirt. Her butter-blond hair had grayed even more since the beginning of the summer, but she always kept it polished and pretty.

"Nice to meet you," Olivia said.

"You, too, honey," Sandy said. She clasped her hands in front of her. "How old is your son?"

"Fourteen."

"That's a difficult age."

"Is it?" Olivia said.

Over the last few days, Olivia had offered insight into her struggles with Micah, but her friendly response now to Sandy hinted at none of them. Whether she was protecting Micah from judgment or keeping the conversation light, he thought more of her for it.

Sandy jerked a thumb toward Tyler. "This one certainly had his moments," she said. "I thought the teenage years would never end."

Tyler clenched his teeth, steeling himself from taking the bait and saying anything in his defense. His mother had a knack for recalling the past in a way that laid no fault on her shoulders. She had held him to the standard of an adult before he finished middle school, and when he'd floundered, she hadn't let him forget it.

"And your son wants to work here, huh?" Sandy continued.

Tyler's gut tightened. Sandy had sounded polite enough, but to his trained ear, he knew she was inwardly judging.

"He loves it." Olivia put her hands into her front pockets and glanced at his mother's shirt. "When did Roseley get a nursery?"

Sandy's face crinkled into a mass of wrinkles as if trying to recall. "About four years ago, I think. The Hardware Shop isn't the only game in town anymore. They get pretty flowers into their garden center, but there was still an ample market for Willoughby's to move in. I've been working there since they opened."

"I'll have to pop by," Olivia said. "I'm staying with my aunt, and she's always working on something in the yard."

"Who's your aunt?"

"Hattie Pike. She has a cottage over off—"

"I know Hattie." She grinned. "I sold her some peony bushes last year. Did they take off this spring?"

"I assume so. I just arrived to town."

"You're new to Roseley? How did your son connect with Tyler so quickly?"

Tyler cleared his throat. "We needed a volunteer to help around the clinic. It was a matter of perfect timing when Micah stopped by."

"Oh, I see," Sandy said, though her expression led him to believe she didn't. "How nice of you to take on a teenager. I'm sure he'll learn a lot."

Tyler could hear a subtle shrill in his mother's voice. She'd never liked the clinic or the time he'd spent there when his father had been alive. "What can I do for you, Sandy? We're about to open."

"I need some help at the house." His mother shifted a quarter turn away from Olivia. Sandy was a deeply private woman, and he knew better than to ask her to elaborate in front of anyone.

"Well," Tyler said, "I should be done by three o'clock today…" His mother's face fell in disappointment. That was not the answer she had been hoping for, but considering she'd only asked for help as his workday was beginning, he wondered what on earth she had expected. "Unless it's pressing," he said. "If it's some sort of emergency—"

"No emergency. Three o'clock will be fine. I'll make you a sandwich."

"You don't have to make me anything—"

"I just bought those pretzel chips you like. I have some lunchmeat I must use up today or toss. If you want to come over at lunchtime instead, that would be fine."

"I can't come over for lunch. I have back-to-back appointments all day."

"Then don't worry about it at all," she grumbled. "I'll get the neighbor kid to help me."

"Now, listen," Tyler said, trying for calm. He didn't have any idea what his mother needed help with or how long it was going to take. She had a way of asking for a favor and if you couldn't deliver on her timetable, she'd log it in her record book as another example of you failing her. "I'm happy to come over after work. If you can just wait eight hours—"

"Never mind. I'll figure it out."

"I should go," Olivia said, inching toward her car. "I'll be by to pick up Micah in a few hours."

Tyler watched Olivia bolt to her car. He appreciated getting the opportunity to talk to his mom privately and could only assume Sandy felt the same. Once Olivia had begun turning her car onto the road, Sandy narrowed her eyes on him.

"Is there something going on between you and her?"

"Something?"

"Mothers can sense these sorts of things. She's all legs and eyelashes…heaven help you."

Tyler balked at the comment. Olivia was stunning and it wasn't just because of her physical appearance. She was genuine and kind, and just being around her made things in his life start to make sense. "She's a *friend*."

"I wouldn't mind getting some grandchildren before I'm too old to play with them."

Tyler grabbed the back of his neck out of sheer annoyance. He couldn't remember his mother ever playing with him as a kid, so her request for grandkids seemed as reasonable as Ranger's desire to drive his truck. "Why don't you tell me what you need help with?"

Sandy stared at her cell phone and began scrolling. At first, he thought she was searching for a photograph to show him, perhaps to better explain what she needed. After a minute, however, she tucked it into her purse and heaved a sigh.

"There are some things in the basement I need carried upstairs."

"I can do that," he said calmly. "What else?"

"That's it for the most part."

"Okay. Can it wait until after three?"

"If it must."

Sandy fumbled on her feet as if she was going to hug him goodbye. She hadn't been affectionate when he was younger, and after what had happened with his dad, he couldn't remember the last time he'd hugged her, really hugged her.

Before he could decide whether or not to extend an arm, she shuffled toward her car. Without a word she climbed in and pulled away, tossing an unenthusiastic wave goodbye. Tyler didn't know why his interactions with his mother still surprised him. She hadn't changed in the last fifteen years, but maybe something in him had—maybe even recently.

A familiar voice called out to him. "Tyler, is everything okay?"

Tyler turned to find Gary leaning out the doorway of the clinic. Though he wished his mom would change, one look at Gary's bushy gray eyebrows arched in genuine concern made him grateful his uncle hadn't.

"Gary," he said. "I have to make sure I'm out of here by three o'clock, no matter what."

CHAPTER FOURTEEN

OLIVIA ARRIVED AT The Midnight Pumpkin, the local pottery studio, just as Hattie addressed a group of people congregated at the back. Among the crowd was Caroline, who hurried to greet her.

"Ladies and gentlemen," Hattie said. "Willoughby's was kind enough to donate all of these trellises, but we need to make the most of them and have them decorated and assembled by end of day tomorrow. Here are the setup plans. As you already know, we're going with the painfully simple theme of—"

"Fall!" CeCe Makes hollered from the back of the group.

Hattie threw up her hands, pleased that others were ready to commiserate with her about the boring theme.

"That's what the committee voted on, so that's what we're doing. It doesn't mean we can't get creative inside that little box, though. Red, orange and yellow are the colors for the festival, but we can play with textures and dimensions. Remember that."

Caroline gave Olivia a side hug as Hattie continued directing the group in all things decorating for the Fall Festival. "I'm glad you made it, Liv."

"What can I help with?"

"Well," Caroline said, "if Hattie hasn't already assigned you, I could use help with my display. Sheila has a vision that involves aged shiplap and tulle."

Olivia admired the studio. "I haven't been here in ages."

"It's a great space to work since it's so close to where the festival will be. We can store the decorations here and won't have to transport them far."

Olivia brushed her fingers over a wooden high-top table that had been painted to resemble Vincent van Gogh's *Starry Night* painting.

Caroline continued. "How did things go with Micah the other day?"

"Hmm?"

"When he didn't go to the baseball game. I drove him home, remember?"

Olivia recalled the conversation she'd initiated with Micah over the weekend. Her almost-kiss with Tyler had only been an hour cold when she'd returned to the cottage to find Micah on his way to the woods. She'd stopped him to discuss his behavior at the sandwich shop and had found him so congenial he'd even divulged that he was building a fort for himself in the woods. The conversation hadn't lasted very long since Micah had easily accepted responsibility for his rude behavior and then quickly apologized. The entire interaction hadn't lasted more than a minute and had ended with Micah happily trotting off with Boomer hurrying to keep up.

"It was easy—too easy."

"Oh," Caroline said. "That's good, right?"

Olivia watched an employee inventory bottles of glaze on a nearby shelf.

Nothing about her conversation with Micah felt like it had gotten to the root of any problem. If he'd wanted to get her off his back as quickly as possible, he'd said everything needed to do that. He'd been pleasant and polite without a hint of attitude, but it had still left her feeling unsettled. He had come alive at the clinic, working with the puppies, but she never saw that same kind of light in his eyes when he was home...or with her.

"How was the game?" Caroline asked.

The game. Olivia remembered how much had developed between her and Tyler since the last time she'd spoken to Caroline.

"Fine."

"Did Gary's team win?"

"Mmm-hmm," Olivia hummed, hoping it was the truth. She hated to admit she couldn't remember who had won. She'd done a lot of talking and a lot of *not* watching the baseball game. "It was a nice evening, Caroline. I appreciated you driving Micah home. Thanks for that."

"It was my pleasure. Has Micah taken to his job at the clinic?"

"He loves it. Working with Tyler doesn't hurt."

Talking to Tyler was so easy. He seemed to understand more than just what she'd conveyed in words. There was an intuitive way about him that made her feel at peace, and she had to imagine Micah appreciated that trait in him, too.

"Tyler's a good guy," Caroline said. "I'm sure he's a good influence on Micah."

"Yeah."

"And as his mother, *you're* a good influence, too. Did you try again with your art therapy?"

Not exactly. She'd booked him an appointment with a counselor, though.

"The Midnight Pumpkin," a woman's voice sang. Olivia watched the woman at the counter on the phone as an idea came to her. "Yes, ma'am, we're open till nine o'clock tonight."

"Yes," Olivia said with a smile. "I'm going to try again."

TYLER HAD DARTED out of the clinic without more than a wave to Julia and Gary. He'd promised his mom he'd arrive shortly after three o'clock, but when an appointment with a senior dog went long, he found himself speeding to her house after four o'clock.

When his cell phone rang, he assumed it was her calling to say that his apology via text message was not enough. He punched the gas and answered without checking to see who it was first.

"Hi, I'll be there in two minutes," he said.

"Tyler?"

Tyler pulled onto Front Street as he realigned his response. "Olivia?"

"I'm sorry to bother you since you're probably at your mom's—"

"It's okay. What's up?"

"It's a little late notice but Micah and I are heading to The Midnight Pumpkin Pottery Studio tonight and want to invite you to join us."

"Pottery?"

"Yeah. It's half-priced tonight, and I thought

it would be a good activity to do while I talk to Micah."

"Art therapy?"

"More like Mom therapy. I know he'd love it if you came."

"Uh…" Tyler checked the time as he pulled into his mother's driveway. Just as he'd expected, she was standing on the front stoop glaring at him. "I'm not sure how long things with my mom are going to take."

"Of course. I didn't want to press you. I sold the pottery idea to Micah by saying we could invite you, but we can catch up with you another night."

"Did I help you sweeten the deal?"

There was a pause on the other end of the line. "Maybe," she said softly.

Tyler parked and cut the engine. He held up a finger to show his mother that he was wrapping up a phone conversation. Agreeing to hire Micah on at the clinic was one thing. Agreeing to attend a baseball game in a group was low risk, as well. But once he'd lost his wits completely and had almost given in to his desire to kiss Olivia, he knew his choices were charting a new course. An outing with Micah *and* Olivia meant heading into unknown territory. On the surface, going to the pottery studio with them seemed like a pleasant, safe option. However, he knew saying yes was a dangerous move for a guy like him…

"What time were you thinking?" he said.

"We'll be there at six o'clock. Just drop by if you can make it."

Tyler agreed and ended the call with Olivia. By the time he'd climbed the porch steps, Sandy looked like a hen rearing to peck.

"Who was that on the phone?" she said.

"Pardon?"

"Is that why you're late?"

"I'm late because I got tied up at work. It happens sometimes."

Tyler had heard his dad try to explain that concept to his mother a hundred times in a hundred different ways. Animals didn't know the clinic was about to close for the night when they got sick or hurt. When a person showed up to the door at closing time with a wounded pet in his arms, was his dad supposed to point to the clinic hours displayed in the front window and suggest they return the next morning at 7:00 a.m.?

After listening to all of his parents' arguments, Tyler had at least learned not to repeat the past and defend himself to his mother's needling.

Instead of a reply, he opened the front

screen door and entered the house. Everything inside was meticulously clean and kept in place, as always. Eight-inch-tall figurines of men and women in eighteenth-century European costumes adorned the many shelves lining the entryway. To the right of the entrance was the sitting room, where no one ever sat. To the left of the entrance was the dining room, where no one ever dined. The same silver-framed photograph of him as a three-year-old sat on an end table near the entryway. It was the only photograph in the room, perhaps in the house.

Sandy led him to the top of the basement steps.

"There's a fan I want to put in the kitchen." As they descended, each wooden stair creaked like they were playing notes on a scale. At the bottom step she pointed across the room to the far corner.

Tyler eyed the heavy metal fan. The entire basement was free of dust, including the tall, oscillating fan. He knew his mother had painstakingly dusted every inch of the house before he'd arrived.

"This thing looks like it was made fifty years ago," he said.

"It probably was. It's good for airing out my kitchen when I bake."

Tyler heaved the metal fan up by the base. It weighed a ton, certainly too much for Sandy to manage. He was relieved she hadn't tried hauling it up the basement steps on her own, as she would have certainly hurt herself.

"That was all I needed," Sandy said once he'd placed it in the kitchen. She plugged it into a nearby outlet and scowled as she refamiliarized herself with the settings.

"Are you sure?" Tyler said, wandering around the kitchen. "If I'm here, you might as well put me to work."

"If I think of something, I'll call you."

Tyler peeked into the living room. The front windows were bare. "What happened to your drapes?"

"I'm washing them."

"You're right on schedule." Like clockwork, his mother liked to wash everything before buttoning up the house for the fall.

Right on cue, the dryer alarm sounded in the basement.

"You can carry them up for me if you want. I have to hang them immediately so they don't wrinkle," Sandy said. They worked silently, Sandy pulling the drapes from the dryer and piling them into Tyler's waiting arms. When she'd finished, he followed her up to the living room. Sandy smoothed a warm drape panel before handing it to Tyler. He worked quickly to run it on the curtain rod. When they had finished both windows, Sandy stood back and stared at them.

"Take them down. I need to press them."

Tyler stared at the drapes. They were dated and had fallen out of fashion long ago, but they looked fine to him and would probably fall smooth after hanging awhile. However, he recognized this wasn't his house anymore, so if his mother wanted perfectly pressed drapes that no one would ever see but her, she could have them.

Tyler carefully took down all the drape panels and laid them over the arm of the couch.

"I'll press them in the morning," she mumbled. They both stood staring at the drapes when Sandy perked and made her way to the back door. "Come see my firethorn."

They made their way outside to a fence along the back of the quarter acre lot where his mother's firethorn plant grew. The evergreen shrub had climbed along the fence and bloomed its tiny red fruits.

"It looks healthy," he said, admiring it.

Sandy plucked at the tiny red bulbs. "It makes a nice privacy fence between me and the Hannigans. If those kids kick their ball over this fence one more time so help me…"

"Have the deer been eating off your apple tree?"

"It's those Hannigan kids. They keep climbing it and knocking the apples off."

The mention of apples made Tyler's stomach growl. He'd worked through lunch, and as he had been promised a sandwich, he was ready to make good on it.

"I'm starving," he said, turning back toward the house. "Let's eat."

"Eat what?"

"You said you had sandwich fixings—"

"I already ate," she said testily. "At three. I'm not hungry now."

A knot at the base of Tyler's neck began to tighten. All at once his arteries felt hot; blood pulsed in his ears. In his mother's typical fashion, she had promised him a dinky sandwich and now acted as if making one was too much effort. Gary was always warning him to manage his expectations where Sandy was involved, because whenever he let his guard down, he always ended up feeling duped.

Tyler's jaw felt tight as he bit out a reply. "I wouldn't want you to trouble yourself."

"I guess if you really want something…"

"I'll grab something on the way home."

Sandy wafted a hand of dismissal into the air. "You always were one for taking care of yourself."

"I don't know about that."

"It's true," Sandy said with a snort. "You've always been self-sufficient. I raised you to pull your own weight. That's what your father never understood."

"Is that what we're calling it? Pulling my own weight?"

"Of course," Sandy said. "You're nobody's fool, because I didn't coddle you."

"And what about Dad?" Tyler knew better than to challenge his mother when it came to life in the past, but the urge to say something was too strong.

"Your father made his bed a long time before I stopped taking care of him."

"Taking care of him? Wow." Tyler grasped the back of his neck, wanting to relieve the intense pressure he felt there. Nothing he could do now could stop the heat rising in his face or the vise tightening in his gut.

"Wow what?" Sandy said.

"You're rewriting history...*again*."

She scoffed. "The ink on the divorce papers was barely dry before he moved that floozy into an apartment with him."

"By 'barely dry' you mean two years. You didn't take care of him when you two were married—"

"He didn't take care of *me*!"

"And then you cut him loose when he needed you."

"He *divorced* me. He wanted me to spoon-feed him when he had a younger, hotter wife to do it?"

"But she didn't—"

"Not my fault."

"So *I* had to."

"You were grown by then."

"I was *fourteen*."

She shrugged jerkily. "There was a time in history when fourteen was considered an adult."

"I was barely out of middle school," he said, exasperated. "I should have had someone taking care of me, not the other way around."

Sandy threw up her hands and waved them madly to bat the truth away. Finally, with a resolute arm jerk, as if she could command Tyler to stop talking like a conductor silencing an orchestra, she glared at him. "The past is the past. I never want to relive it. I don't know why you do."

She disappeared into the house, much in

the same way she had disappeared on him when he had needed her most. He certainly didn't want to relive the past, either, but sometimes the past wouldn't stay settled.

CHAPTER FIFTEEN

OLIVIA HAD JUST finished setting up her selected paints when she spotted Tyler at the front door of The Midnight Pumpkin.

"Hey, stranger," she called. "We're glad you made it."

"Yeah?"

"Of course."

Tyler moseyed to their table, a blue-and-red splotched design that resembled a Jackson Pollock painting. Micah had already selected a garden gnome that Olivia could only assume was meant to be a gift for Hattie.

"Dr. Elderman," Micah said, brightening. "Do you paint pottery?"

"I thought I'd check it out," Tyler said, his eyes shifting around the room. Olivia watched him for a moment as he cracked his knuckles and then rolled out his shoulders. He seemed on edge, like he'd just consumed eight cups of coffee in one sitting.

"Come pick out a pottery piece," Olivia said, eager to get him alone for a moment.

Tyler followed her to the wall of pottery pieces priced from low to high. He seemed to look at the selection without actually seeing any of it.

"This is it, huh?" he said. "I just pick one?"

"Yes," Olivia said. "Then you pick your paint—"

"I thought you could throw pottery here."

"Sure, if you want. Have you ever done that before?"

"No, but there's a time for everything, right? That's what I'm gonna do."

Olivia turned back to Micah, grateful he hadn't begun painting yet.

"Micah, would you rather throw clay?"

Micah slid off his seat and made his way to his mother. "Obviously, I'd rather throw clay."

Tyler slapped Micah on the shoulder and the two grinned at each other.

"I guess we're throwing clay," Olivia said.

JASMINE, THE WOMAN working the shop for the evening, had quickly gotten everyone set up. Fortunately, it was slow for a weekday, so changing plans hadn't been a problem at all.

"Have you done this before?" Tyler said, starting his pottery wheel.

"All through college," Olivia said. "I loved it."

"I'm going to make a vase," Micah said as Olivia dropped a chunk of clay on his wheel.

"Not yet," she said. "This is your first time so tonight is more about *experiencing* the clay." Olivia dropped clay on Tyler's wheel, too. "Play with it, feel it, see how far you can push its limits."

"I think I need more clay than that," Tyler said, frowning.

"You need about a pound and a half or the size of a small grapefruit." Olivia sat at her own pottery wheel. "There are two main rules for pottery—"

"Only two?" Tyler said as he squeezed his clay.

"Only two you need to remember tonight. Keep the clay wet and keep the clay spinning."

"Easy enough."

"Yeah," Micah said. He dipped his hands into the water bowl and smoothed it over the clay.

Olivia took several minutes to teach them how to first center the clay. Her hands made quick work of it, coning it up and down as if no time had passed since she'd last thrown. Both Tyler and Micah watched her, trying to mimic the smooth transitions she made.

She let them experiment for several minutes, trying to guide instead of instruct. Tonight was about talking and sharing, not creating anything recognizable.

"What do you think, Micah?" she said.

"What do *you* think?" he said as a lop-sided tower he had created began to cave in from the side before collapsing completely. "Timber!"

Olivia winked before turning her attention to Tyler. He stared at the clay with ferocity. "Tyler?"

"I can't get this heap to do anything."

"That's okay. You don't need to. Just find its limits."

Tyler wet his hands and continued to smooth the clay. Olivia drew a breath to ask Micah a question when Tyler grumbled something she couldn't quite decipher.

"What did you say?" she asked.

"Figurines," Tyler repeated. "My mother has a million of these stupid figurines all over her house. Powder-faced men and women in wigs and stockings and fancy garb. They're waltzing or flirting or promenading..."

"Promenading?" she asked.

"Yeah, how dumb is that? Why on earth would you want figurines of people promenading all over your house?"

Olivia smoothed her clay as she watched Tyler. Whatever was bothering him about the promenading figurines, he was certainly taking it out on his clay. He pushed and pulled at it, wiggling it out of center before pushing it to the middle again. Micah had also taken note of Tyler and was quick to commiserate.

"My dad used to have a baseball from every state he ever played in."

"Oh, yeah?" Tyler said without looking up.

"He displayed them in a big case in our TV room."

"*My* mom," Tyler said as if upping the ante, "has tiny thimbles from each state. She didn't visit each state, but she sent away for them."

"Did she hang them up in the kitchen?" Micah asked.

"Bingo," Tyler said, his eyes dark. "They're right where everyone can see them when they visit, not that anyone ever visits…or ever did."

"My dad didn't spend enough time in the TV room to even admire his baseballs. I don't get it."

"Me, neither."

Olivia pretended to focus on her clay as Tyler and Micah lobbed experiences back and forth as methodically as a ping-pong match.

"Did your dad collect stuff, too?" Micah asked.

"Nah," Tyler said, centering all his clay on the wheel again. "He liked animals, obviously, but he wasn't a collector. He liked people."

"My dad liked baseball more than people," Micah grumbled as his hands slowed on his clay. "Did your dad ever teach you how to play baseball?"

Tyler shrugged as if answering on autopilot. "Yeah, we threw the ball around sometimes until he got sick."

Micah glanced at him. "How sick?"

Tyler pressed into the center of his clay, forming a wobbly bowl before pushing to ruin it again. "He had a stroke and couldn't…you know…"

Micah stopped and sat back from his wheel. "Couldn't what?"

Tyler squeezed the clay between his hands and sucked a breath. "Do anything. He was paralyzed from the neck down for two years before he died."

Olivia stopped short. She didn't mean to stare, but it felt completely out of her power to focus on anything but Tyler. His face had grown red, noticeably uncomfortable with the direction the conversation had taken.

"Did he live in a hospital?" Micah asked. Olivia wanted to tell Micah not to ask such a personal question, but Tyler continued on quickly.

"It was all a strange matter of timing, buddy." Tyler gathered all the clay in his hands, eyes still focused on it as he spoke. "See, my parents fought all the time, and my mom was really mean to my dad. He wanted to stay married because of me—something about keeping the family together for my sake. I overheard him telling my uncle Gary about it when I was almost twelve. One day when he and I were working in the clinic I confronted him about it. I told him I didn't want him to stay married because of me. I thought my mom was really mean to him, and I wanted him to be free and happy." His words ran together like one long stream of consciousness.

"What did he say?" Micah asked.

Tyler shrugged. "He cried."

"Did you cry, too?"

"Yeah, buddy. When your dad cries in front of you for the first time in your life, you cry, too."

Micah nodded in agreement. "Of course."

Tyler cleared his throat and continued. "My dad met with a lawyer about how to get custody of me. It was a tricky business, I guess, but when I said I wanted to live with my dad, my mom got really mad but agreed to it. She warned me, however, I would regret my decision someday." He sighed.

"About two years after the divorce my dad met my stepmom, Robin. She was pretty and fun and laughed at all my dad's dumb jokes. He seemed happy enough with her. I mean, she didn't fight with him like my mom had.

"Robin wanted to get married and have kids of her own, so they got married quickly." He hesitated for a moment. "Six weeks after the wedding, my dad had his stroke. It really showed Robin's true colors. It showed a lot of people's true colors, like my mom's. Under the circumstances, I thought she'd soften and, you know, help me or at the least give me someone to lean on." Tyler clicked his tongue in disgust. "Nope. I think she found my situation fitting given her warning."

"Tyler," Olivia said slowly, the lump in her throat almost keeping her from uttering his name. She'd listened to people share many personal things over the years as they painted or drew or crafted together. But Tyler's story hit a little too close to home. Perhaps it was because he'd been a similar age to Micah, and she couldn't imagine leaving Micah to fend for himself after Jeb had passed away. Perhaps it was because she'd begun to care deeply for Tyler, and learning that he'd suffered some sort of abandonment from his mother shook Olivia's nurturing instincts to the core. Whatever the reasons, his story crashed against her and urged her to say something to comfort him. As she watched him scowl at the clay like he was blaming it for his admission, all she could manage was, "That must have been painful."

"Yeah," Micah said. "Moms shouldn't do that. Moms are the ones who jump in to help in a crisis."

Olivia tore her gaze from Tyler to look at Micah. If he believed that, was it because he knew she had always done that for him? She eased back on her chair, wondering if Micah's words were a glimmer of hope that he knew she was still there for him.

"Do you talk to your mom anymore?" Micah continued, oblivious to Olivia's revelation.

"Eh. Not really."

"You help her," Olivia offered gently. "Didn't you help her tonight?"

Tyler slowed his pottery wheel. He let his dirty hands hang lifelessly at his sides. Olivia could see his jaw muscles flexing as he worked out what to say or maybe what to do. Finally, he lifted his face. It looked so long she thought she should catch it before it drooped all the way to the floor.

"Thanks for inviting me to join you, but I think I need to call it a night," he said. His voice conveyed an apology for disappointing her. She wished she could help him understand that he hadn't.

"Of course. I'll clean up here," Olivia said. She and Micah sat quietly as Tyler washed his hands and exited the pottery studio. Once he'd left, Micah turned to her.

"A mom should never act like that," he said quietly. "You would never do that to me."

Olivia met her son's eyes and offered him a wistful smile. Things between them had been so strained that Micah's observation was the sweetest thing he'd said to her in a very long time. What else could she say to convey that she loved him and wanted to help? As she stared back at Micah, she wondered if perhaps her actions had already been conveying just that.

"Do you want to stay a little longer?" she asked.

"Yeah," he said. "But is it okay if we don't talk?"

"Sure, kiddo," Olivia said. "Whatever you want."

ANY EXPECTATIONS OLIVIA had had for their excursion to the pottery studio had gone up like flames to paper, but by the time they had driven home, she'd decided that was okay. Perhaps Micah listening to Tyler talk about his past was all the evening was meant for. They had returned home to discover Hattie stoking a small campfire.

"Howdy, my loves," Hattie called when they'd followed the smell of burning wood to the backyard. Twelve solar garden lights— blown glass balls the size of apples and each a different color—gleamed brilliantly. They caught every color of the spectrum.

That morning Olivia had watched Hattie stake the lights, staggering them between three lawn chairs facing the firepit. She hadn't thought much of it at the time, but now she realized Hattie had been preparing a little backyard therapy of her own. Olivia appreciated it. It was nice to have someone looking out for her for a change.

"This looks magical," Olivia said. "You certainly know how to set a scene, Hattie."

Hattie poked the fire with a long wooden stick. "Who wants a s'more?" she said. "I've already eaten two and could use some help roasting marshmallows."

Olivia looked hopefully at Micah. She felt

like she'd been dealt a second chance to connect with her son that night.

"How about it, kiddo?" Olivia said. "I hear a s'more calling my name." If the beautiful lights and smell of campfire didn't lure Micah in, the promise of chocolatey goodness might.

Micah accepted the bag of marshmallows from Hattie.

"How was The Midnight Pumpkin?" she asked him.

"Decent."

"Did you paint me anything?"

"We threw clay, but I didn't make anything worth firing."

"Your mother used to be a pottery pro, Micah. She made me a set of dessert bowls that I still use."

Micah soured a face at Olivia. "Why don't you do that anymore, Mom?"

Olivia shrugged. The time to explore different art mediums hadn't lasted very long in college. Once she met Jeb and had become a young bride, she'd hurried to finish her degree so she could narrow her world to supporting his dreams. "I haven't had the time."

"You have time now. You should *make* stuff instead of just talking to people about stuff."

After the brief connection they'd shared at

The Midnight Pumpkin, the rest of the pottery session and the ride home had been silent. Micah's prodding was certainly a change.

"Maybe I will, kiddo."

"We could set you up with a pottery wheel in the shed if you'd like," Hattie said.

Olivia appreciated the offer, but it felt like a loaded one since she didn't know how long they'd stay in Roseley. For now she was happy at the cottage, and Micah seemed more than happy working in the clinic with the animals...with Tyler.

Olivia wondered how Tyler was doing. Before the pottery session, something had to have happened to cause him to ramble. It had seemed out of character for him, but then again, there was something about expressing yourself in art that helped unleash built-up thoughts and feelings. She had seen it happen so many times over the years. She usually worked with children, encouraging them along as they worked, but people of any age could benefit. It was the process of creating that was important, not the end result. Olivia saw her role as merely a conductor or guide, not as any type of teacher or cheerleader. If she could create a space that was free of judgment, whether good or bad, she was doing her job well. The point of art therapy was to create and share. Tyler had done that, and it was exactly the sort of thing she wanted for Micah, too.

"Both my loves are creative *and* caring," Hattie said. "My niece is an artist who loves animals, and my grandnephew is an animal lover who does art. Both of those passions feed the soul."

"How do you know I do art?" Micah said with a hint of suspicion. "I never told you that. Just because Mom does it doesn't necessarily mean I do, too."

Hattie threaded a fresh marshmallow on her roasting stick. "I saw the paintings you started for the festival."

Micah watched Hattie as if he were about to place a bet but didn't trust her insider tip. Hattie and Olivia exchanged a confused look.

"Micah," Olivia said. "Is something the matter?"

"No," he grumbled. "I'm fine. Just hungry, I guess."

Olivia wanted to believe him, but his shift in demeanor, even if it was a subtle one that only she would notice, made her wonder.

"We only have one decent roasting stick," Hattie continued, her chipper voice noticeably trying to lighten the mood. "But I know for a fact it is free of poison ivy. Care to give it a try?"

Micah accepted the stick and slumped onto a lawn chair. "Sure. Thanks, Hattie."

"I ran into Dr. Gary Elderman at The Lollipop tonight," Hattie said. "He had some things to say about you, Micah."

"Oh?" Olivia said. "What did he say?"

"He was pleased with how Micah helped with the puppies this morning."

Micah rolled his eyes. "There was nothing to do except sit and watch them."

"That's not how he told it. He said Tex and Bianca Behr were pleased to hear your report."

"I only said that Arizona and the puppies were all doing well," Micah said. "The puppies were all eating fine."

"That's the kind of report you want to hear when you're worried about your dog," Hattie said, reaching down to scratch Boomer behind the ears.

"I agree," Olivia said. "I'm sure they appreciated you."

"I dunno," Micah said. "Maybe."

Maybe was such a simple, noncommittal word, but after the evening they'd had at the pottery studio, Olivia was hopeful it had a more optimistic attitude behind it.

Micah had been so hard to read for such a long time. His eagerness to throw all of his energy into working at the clinic had certainly surprised her. She might not have understood his initial desire to work with animals, but in a short time he seemed happier. He wasn't confiding in her at all, but he was at least talking to Tyler and doing something he loved again.

"How's Boomer?" Olivia said.

"He seems like he's back to his normal self. I can't ask for anything more," Hattie said.

Micah turned his stick, carefully hovering the marshmallow several inches above the flames.

"Tyler showed up tonight," he said.

"Oh?" Hattie asked, turning to Olivia.

"He threw clay with us." Olivia didn't think it was appropriate to mention that Tyler had seemed distraught, and she hoped Micah would keep mum about it, too.

"Well, that's a treat. How did he like it?"

"He talked a lot," Micah said, his eyes focused intently on the marshmallow. Olivia could see Micah working something out in his mind, but she didn't know if it was something about Tyler or something about himself. She wanted to protect Tyler's privacy and not mention anything about—

"His mom sounds like a piece of work," Micah said.

Sandy.

She didn't want Micah to speak about Tyler's problems in front of anyone, even if it was just Hattie. She knew how much Tyler respected his privacy and she also suspected that the things he had shared were things about his past that he didn't share lightly.

"*Micah,*" Olivia said. "We don't know Tyler's mother and you may not speak about her like that."

"Why not? Tyler is a great guy, and he didn't deserve how she treated him."

"That's not your business to discuss."

"Oh." Micah flicked his marshmallow into the fire. "I just didn't like any of it, that's all."

"Me, neither," she said gently.

"He didn't have a dad when he needed one. I get where he's coming from, you know. Having a dad right about now would have its advantages."

Olivia's heart sank. "Yeah, I know kiddo…"

"I'm not a kiddo," he said, letting out a harrumph. "I'm fourteen, Mom. I can do stuff."

"I know that."

"No, you don't. I mean like *real* stuff. Dad let me do stuff you never let me do."

Olivia racked her brain to remember. Jeb

was never around long enough to invest in an activity that drew out longer than an afternoon. At least, in retrospect, that was how she remembered it. Certainly, he and Micah had done fun things together, but why could she not remember now?

"Like what?" she said.

"Like stuff. *Adult* stuff."

Olivia knew her face was drawing as much of a blank as her memory, and Micah certainly wasn't giving her any hints. He was opening up to her, even if he didn't realize that was what he was doing. She grappled with something to say to keep the conversation going. "Dad loved doing stuff with you."

Micah poked at the fire, jamming his stick into the bright embers. "I guess."

It was as noncommittal a response as his *maybe* from earlier, but it was something.

"You know," Olivia said. "If he could see you now working at the clinic, I'm sure he would be completely amazed."

"Who knows what Dad would think," Micah said, standing. "He's not here to tell us." He trudged off toward the woods.

"Micah," she called. He continued walking, making no indication he would stop. *"Micah."*

He turned, the firelight catching an indignant expression that reminded her so much of Jeb the night she told him she wanted a divorce. He'd been so shocked she thought he had staggered back a step. When the aftershock wore off, he'd made the same face Micah had just now.

Jeb had been killed less than a week later. No one had known they'd talked about divorce or that she'd been the one to first bring it up. She hadn't told anyone, and knowing Jeb, she knew he hadn't, either. He would no sooner admit that he had been failing in some aspect of his life than he would throw a World Series game. Once he was gone, she promised herself she'd never tell another living soul about wanting the divorce—ever.

"What?" Micah spat in a mix of impatience and anger.

"It's too dark for the woods." It was. She had no idea how far back from the tree line Micah liked to go, but as he wouldn't be able to see much farther than a footstep ahead of him once he left the firelight of the backyard, she didn't want him venturing off on his own now.

"I gotta get out of here for a little while," Micah said, a plead registering. "Can't you understand that?"

She could. Maybe it was because that same

feeling was what had propelled her to leave town and move them to Roseley. In some ways she struggled to recognize him anymore and in other ways, in this moment, she saw how similar they were.

"If you're going out there," Hattie said, hurrying over to him, "at least take my flashlight. Wave it around so the coyotes don't get you."

Micah begrudgingly accepted the flashlight. Within a few moments he and the bobbing orb had disappeared into the tree line. The snap of branches under his feet got softer the farther into the woods he walked.

"He'll be fine," Hattie said. "The fort isn't that far, and I haven't heard coyotes out there in ages. I'm sitting out here for a little while, so I'll keep an ear out."

"That makes two of us."

Hattie looked at Olivia as if she'd just bubbled in the wrong answer on a test. "Since you two got into town, Micah has had his guard up around me. But after witnessing that—"

"What?"

"Let's just say I have a better idea of what you're talking about now."

"Are you going to give me that 'he knows I

can handle it' talk again?" She could hear the exhaustion in her words as she said it.

"You already know you can, so no need," Hattie said without missing a beat. "What I was going to say is that you can also get out for a while if you need to."

"Where? It's late."

Hattie crinkled a smile and tipped her s'more in the air like a toast. "I think the right place will come to you."

CHAPTER SIXTEEN

WHEN OLIVIA HAD let her mind wander and go to a peaceful place, she couldn't help but see Tyler's face. That was how she had found herself driving to his house before she could think better of it. He'd given her all his contact information when Micah started volunteering at the clinic. She wasn't sure what she wanted to say to him or what she hoped he'd say in response. All she knew was that she wanted to see him. Since her mother had died, she'd felt like she'd been fighting for a life that was recognizable to her. Something about being near him helped right her ship, which had been storm-tossed for years now.

Olivia rapped on Tyler's front door. The little house stood farther off the road than the neighboring houses, shrouding the front walk and porch in darkness.

She wasn't sure what to say to Tyler when he opened the front door, other than to ask if he was okay. Her evening with Micah still weighed heavily on her.

Olivia rapped on the front door a second time. She could see the glow of his television flickering from behind the front curtains, but the sound was too low to hear. She pulled out her cell phone and texted him.

Still awake? I'm at the front door.

After a few moments she heard him call her name, but he wasn't calling from inside the house. He was calling from somewhere around back.

Olivia walked around the house and continued farther up the driveway to a detached garage at the back of the half-acre lot. The garage door was open. A dark figure stood in the shadows. Even if he hadn't just called her name, she would have instantly recognized his silhouette. Whether it was his stance, his frame or the cool, confident way he swaggered a few steps to meet her, she knew she would recognize him anywhere.

"Hey," he said. "What are you doing here?"

"Checking on you, I guess."

Olivia wandered closer until she was in the threshold of the garage. Without the help of pale moonlight to illuminate his face, her eyes adjusted to see the rough contours of his jawline and forehead. She wished to see something there that conveyed he was happy she'd dropped by.

"I hope it's okay that I'm…here," she said, the last word getting stuck in her throat.

He shifted closer, a sort of delicate hesitation that might happen before dance partners were assigned. She caught a sense of his concern. His tenderness was matched by no one she had ever met before, and though she couldn't see it in his expression, she could feel it emanating off him.

"By the sound of it," he said, "I should be the one checking in on you."

"My evening with Micah didn't go well."

"About that." Tyler ran a hand over his face. "I'm sorry about earlier. I had this thing happen before I got to the pottery studio—"

"With your mom?"

"Yeah. I don't usually let my mouth run away from me like that. I know you wanted Micah to do the talking and instead of helping, I ruined it."

"No," she said, stepping closer. "You didn't."

How could she let him apologize when he'd been the best thing in recent memory to happen to Micah? The best thing to happen to her?

"I'm not great at saying sorry, Olivia, but I'd like to get this off my chest."

"You don't need to, Tyler. You don't need to feel bad. You opened up in front of Micah tonight, and I think it can help point us in the right direction."

He hitched his shoulders. "I don't see how."

"From what I heard tonight, I think it had the potential to help you both. He saw an example of how to share, and because of all the things you said, I think I understand you better."

Tyler groaned in concession. "That makes one of us."

"I know Micah was all ears tonight," Olivia continued. "He took it all in, and he's processing it on his own, in his own way." Olivia released a heavy sigh. She had to believe that. It wasn't how she wished Micah would process things, absent of her, but she wanted to try to respect it all the same. "It was a start, Tyler."

"It was dumb."

"It was honest. I've grown to appreciate that about you."

They stood for a moment, and she could tell he didn't know quite what to say. She chose to let him off the hook.

"What are you doing out here in the dark?" she asked.

He led her to a back part of the garage. "This is where I keep my lions and tigers."

On the floor lay a rickety old porch swing. He hoisted one end before she hurried to lift the other.

"Some tiger," she said.

"Wait until you see it in action."

They walked the swing out of the garage and to the front porch. Tyler quickly set about hanging it to the ceiling hardware already mounted.

"It looks old," Olivia said. "Where did you get it?"

"I stole it from Gary."

"Poor Gary. Is he looking around for it right about now?"

"Probably."

Olivia was about to protest at such a naughty deed until she caught the mischievous tone in Tyler's voice.

Tyler pushed the swing back and forth a few times. It made a series of sad, wailing creaks. He retrieved a can of WD-40 from his back pocket.

"It needs a little tune-up," he said, shaking the can. "Also compliments of Gary."

After he'd sprayed the hinges, they noticed Ranger watching them through the front window.

"Aw," Olivia said. "I think he feels left out."

"Do you want to come inside for a minute?"

Olivia wavered on her feet as Tyler cracked open the front door. He stared back at her, the light from inside the house brightening the side of his face. He looked just as handsome as she remembered. Not textbook handsome, a thing of magazine spreads or Hollywood photo shoots, but everyday, regular guy handsome. Wide, confident gait with one hand dipped effortlessly into the front pocket of his blue jeans, he was the kind of man you might not notice on the street until he smiled at you and turned everything in your body to jelly.

"I should get home to Micah," she said, wondering if her lie was as obvious to his ears as it was to hers.

"And disappoint Ranger? Poor guy."

"I wasn't planning on staying long."

"You just came by to…" His eyes drifted to her mouth, instantly making her feel flush.

She hurried to complete his sentence. "Check on you."

"Thank you."

"You're okay, then?"

"I am." He hesitated at the door. "But you should come in for a minute or Ranger will never let me hear the end of it."

Once he went inside, Olivia gathered the

jelly circulating throughout her body and followed him through the door.

TYLER STRODE TO the kitchen to wash the last bit of wood filings from his hands. He had promised Gary he would sand and repaint his porch swing for him. After a long day at the clinic, Gary liked to relax on his swing. Unfortunately, Gary's swing had seen better days. His uncle rarely asked for anything, so whenever Tyler spotted an opportunity to do something for him, he jumped at it.

Tyler peeked into the front room where Olivia was scratching Ranger on the head. When she'd shown up unexpectedly, he appreciated having his uncle's swing at his disposal.

Ranger licked Olivia's hand before flopping to his side and glancing up at her. He was a beggar for belly scratches.

"You're coming on too strong, buddy," Tyler whispered to himself. "You have to relax." The comment was meant for Ranger, but he couldn't help recognizing that he felt exactly the same way about his interactions with Olivia.

When he'd been working in the garage, he had thought nothing of the headlights brightening his street. He'd been too focused on sanding the swing. When his phone had chimed with her text message, the sound might as well have been the clink of steel meeting flint. When he'd called out for her, not yet believing she'd really dropped by, the sparks from that flint had set to tinder. And when he had seen her emerge from around the side of the house, he'd jolted to his feet as if his body had been packed with kindling. What a challenge she posed, sauntering up to him so casually when something inside him sizzled alert. It was all he could do to get a grip of himself.

He had returned home from the pottery studio that night in a funk. He'd spent the rest of the evening sanding the porch swing and savoring the scent of powdered cedar on his hands.

Working in the garage always felt like a bit of a refuge for him, perhaps because it had always been his dad's place to retreat to whenever things with Sandy went south. Among his dad's old tools and workbench and second-hand furniture he fixed up on rainy Sunday afternoons, the aroma of faint mildew and lumber and empty gasoline cans accompanied all the good conversations he and his dad had shared before the stroke. Tyler had recreated his garage to somewhat resemble his dad's and, luckily, the familiar smells lingered here, too. They brought him some comfort as he'd grappled with how to apologize to Olivia for his behavior at the pottery studio.

He had picked up his phone at least half a dozen times that night, trying to think of how to word an apology text to her. The point of the pottery session was to get Micah talking, and he had been invited to support that cause, not hijack it. He'd just resigned himself to the fact that he needed to apologize to Olivia in person when she'd appeared in his driveway.

Tyler dried his hands and returned to the living room to discover Olivia and Ranger at the far corner of the room beside the bookshelf. Olivia stared at a piece of artwork displayed in it.

"Did you make this?"

Tyler shook his head. "My dad did."

The large metallic artwork, about the size of two basketballs side-by-side, was a soldered compilation of various hardware. They had been odds and ends of scrap materials his dad hadn't used over the years and had instead thrown into a giant scrap bin at the back of the garage. Occasionally, as a child, Tyler had gone hunting through the bin, digging his fingers through the assortment of bolts and screws, hinges and mending plates. A month before the stroke, his dad had finished soldering the metal gutters and had gone about soldering the scrap pieces of metal together for fun. His dad had even let him try out the welding gun.

"It's an interesting piece," Olivia said.

"Heavier than a ton, too."

Ranger yawned and leaned against Olivia's leg.

"Don't look now," she said. "But I think your dog likes me."

"He must. He only ever does that with me."

"Jealous?" She playfully flicked up an eyebrow. He knew what she meant, of course. Was he jealous of her? But he looked at Ranger and thought the dog the lucky one.

"Extremely."

"Yeah?"

If she knew what he was really referring to, she didn't let on. She plucked a framed picture off the bookshelf. It was a photograph of a baby goat standing on an adult goat standing on a donkey.

"Is this real?"

"I snapped it myself."

"Where?"

"Texas. In college I spent a summer on a dude ranch working with livestock animals. I saw goats in some pretty funny places."

"How do they manage it?"

"Fierce determination, I think."

Olivia rose and made her way around the room, but there wasn't much to see, as she'd already admired his two favorite decorations. When she strode by the couch and continued to the front door, he could see she clearly had no intention of staying but wasn't ready to leave yet. It made him grateful for the swing.

Tyler opened the front door but motioned for Olivia to wait at the threshold with him.

"Don't go out there just yet," he said. "We'll want all the lights out for this next part." Her eyes widened ever so slightly, and he could feel her unease as he flipped off the living room light, shrouding the three of them in complete darkness.

"Mosquitoes," he explained quickly. "I don't turn my porch light on until I come in for the night."

"I see." She hesitated on her feet as his eyes adjusted to the dark. "I guess I'll see you tomorrow, huh?"

"You're going to leave and make me test this swing by myself?" Tyler pulled the front door shut behind them and slowly sat. After a few swings, he stretched an arm over the back and relaxed fully onto it.

"Care to join me?" he said. "Just a few minutes?"

Olivia stared up at the ceiling brackets. "Will it hold?"

Tyler brought the swing to a stop. "Of course."

Even in the dark he could see she was hesitant. She gingerly sat beside him, not fully giving her trust over. Her mouth twisted again at the corner like it had when she'd lingered at the doorway. It appeared to be a subconscious tick to hide what she was really feeling or thinking. Still, it was just his theory. He'd have to put it to the test.

"This is...nice." Her spine was as rigid as a fence post.

"Comfortable?" he said, his voice laced with amusement.

"Nope."

"You'll be fine. This swing has held Gary, me *and* Ranger a time or two."

At his name, Ranger sat at attention in front of them, tongue wagging as he awaited Tyler's invitation to leap up.

"Oh, no," she said. "Ranger, I love you, but you can't come up here with us."

"He's fine at our feet." Tyler changed the pitch of his voice, something he reserved for Ranger's commands. "Lie down," he said.

Ranger stretched out on the floor and exhaled loudly.

"Does he always listen to you?"

"Yep. We're a good team."

As Olivia watched Ranger, Tyler let his eyes fall over the angelic line of her profile. He knew he should manage his expectations where Olivia was concerned, and not let his desire run away with him. It seemed easy enough as he was good at practicing restraint. The fear of getting hurt was enough of a reason to slam the brakes, but he also couldn't ignore how nice it felt to spend time with her. Just when he'd thought the day had been a complete bust, she'd strolled up the driveway and had caught him completely, and delightfully, off guard. In fact, that had been his experience since the day he'd first met her.

"You can trust this," he said softly. He had meant the swing, but when she turned to look at him, he caught a gleam in her eye.

He wished he could believe his own words—believe he could trust what had been transpiring between them since he'd first rescued her on Falcon's Peak. He wanted to give in to his feelings and trust Olivia as much as he trusted the rickety old swing. But he'd never been able to do that before, and he didn't know the rules of how to manage it now.

Gradually, Olivia settled, nestled. She sank against his body, tucking herself into the negative space under his shoulder that he had created for her. He'd offered it like an invitation and once she'd accepted it, getting comfortable like a cat preparing its bed, her scent floated around him. He caught the faintest hint of coconut, like he had fallen asleep on the beach and an island breeze, skimming across the ocean, had roused him awake. It teased at his senses, making him want to draw closer to capture every ounce of her.

He reminded himself to be careful, not just to protect her, a grieving widow with a teenage son, but to protect himself. In his experience, women were not the soft place to fall after a long, hard day. They were the raging lion at the door ready to take a swipe at you when you were already too tired to fight.

One night after his dad had returned home from the clinic, tired and heartbroken after failing to save a wounded Labrador, Tyler had witnessed just what his mom's swipes could do. The kitchen had smelled of a freshly baked, savory casserole, and Tyler had watched his dad close his eyes to relish the smell as he dropped his coat on the kitchen chair. His mother, however, had baked the casserole for a sick friend. She'd told his dad that she didn't bother cooking him anything since she figured he'd be late anyway. She'd left the house in a huff, taking along with her the delicious casserole, and any inkling of empathy for his long day.

Tyler had realized that his mom's absence would have been better to come home to. He'd learned something that day about marriage and all the pain it could bring if you opened yourself up to it and began to hope for a return on love.

Olivia's curly tendrils grazed over his arm, tickling his skin to send a shiver throughout his body. As soft as she seemed, he knew that it was best to not put himself in a vulnerable position. As much as he enjoyed their time together, he needed to keep her at an arm's distance. He needed to keep from hoping for anything more…yet his desire for more had led him to this very swing with her.

"Are you cold?" she asked.

"No. You?"

"A little."

It was all the confession he needed to maneuver closer. With his arm stretched around her shoulders, he smoothed a hand to cover her arm, rubbing quickly to warm her bare skin. He wanted his touch to feel dutiful, protective, like he would do the same to help anyone.

But she wasn't just anyone. She was becoming someone so much more treasured.

When she murmured something of a thank-you, he slowed but kept his palm there like a protective blanket, his longing to be near acting as a heat conductor.

"It's quiet here," she said. The street was completely still, no car or person present. Even the wind didn't bristle. It was exactly how he liked it.

"What do you think?" he said. "Do you like it?"

"It's different. The houses in California are bigger and spaced farther apart. But when it's quiet at night, it doesn't feel peaceful like it does here. The silence there is very different, sinking."

They swung. Each pushed their feet lightly against the ground, holding up an unspoken bargain to keep the swing moving.

"What was life like for you?" he asked.

"Before Jeb died or after?"

"Either."

Olivia ran her hands down the tops of her thighs. If she had secrets to share, he was more than willing to listen.

"Hectic when Jeb was home and quiet

when he wasn't. Before Jeb died, Micah and I were buddies. He always wanted to show me things and tell me things and confide in me. But since the accident we've been floundering to find our footing as a family of two. Instead of feeling like we're in this thing together, I always sense Micah distancing himself from me. I look for ways to offer him support but it's been difficult."

A note of empathy reverberated in Tyler's throat, humming encouragement for Olivia to keep going. He knew it wasn't enough to convey all he felt for her and her pain, but he hoped she would trust that his willingness to listen was sincere.

"His counselor helped a lot," she said. "But we still have a long way to go."

"How did Micah hear the news about Jeb's accident?"

Olivia stared at her hands. "Few people know about that. It's not something…"

"You don't have to share anything you don't want to," he said. "I didn't mean to pry."

"I want to," she said, shifting to better see him. He followed her lead and readjusted his body to bring his hands to his lap.

"All right," he said softly. "I'm all ears."

"I didn't have to tell Micah about Jeb's accident," she said carefully. "Micah was *in* the accident."

The confession socked Tyler hard in the gut.

"No one knows that except Hattie and our counselor and, of course, the first responders. Because Micah didn't get injured, the hospital discharged him before the media found out. I worked to keep it that way so it wouldn't be splashed across SportsCenter for the whole world to discuss. I was at work when I got the call."

Olivia pressed her fingertips to her mouth but continued.

"Jeb had taken Micah out for the afternoon. I don't know what they were doing outside the city or where they were heading. Micah has only ever said they had gone for a drive. Jeb liked to speed on long highways just to get a rise out of me and a laugh out of Micah, but the police said speed wasn't a factor that day. For some reason Jeb clipped a mailbox and…it threw them off. Jeb wasn't wearing a seat belt so when they crashed, he hit his head in just the right way—or more like the wrong way."

Her tears glistened in the very distant light from his neighbor's porch. He wanted to stroke a hand over her cheek and smooth the hurt away. Instead, he rested a hand over hers. It was a small sign that he cared deeply and that he would listen and bear witness to whatever details of the story were still left to share.

Olivia squeezed her eyes shut. Tyler searched for words to comfort her, but he didn't have the best examples to fall back on. Many folks had said things that dripped with empty, uplifting advice after his dad died. He wouldn't dare offer her anything like that now.

"Olivia?" he said.

"Yes?"

She'd shared something about her past that she hadn't told everyone else. He would protect that confidence, protect that pain. If she had presented him with clasped hands and had slowly peeled open fingers to reveal an injured baby bird, he would react just as protectively. If he could only comfort with his words and his presence, he would do so wholeheartedly.

He drew a breath and said the first thing he could muster. "Thank you for trusting me with that. I can't imagine it was easy for you to do."

"I feel the same way about the things you've shared, too."

He didn't want to think about his things to share. His wounds preferred the sealed enclosure of his hands awhile longer.

His mind cried out to remember his restraint. He'd promised himself he would never fall victim to the kind of love that his dad had embraced. His dad had been young and naive and didn't see the warning signs when he'd married Tyler's mother. He could only imagine it was loneliness and longing that had made his dad try again and marry Robin. Both of those choices had caused his dad so much unhappiness. He'd been shucked to the curb when he should have been cared for, and Tyler had been shucked right along with him. It was enough to make a man swear off love completely.

But the sincerity in Olivia's voice, her confidence in him, chipped away at his promise to stay guarded. Her words had felt like the realization of his deepest desire, one he'd been hiding away for so long.

Before he could think better of it, he brought a hand to cup Olivia's face and contemplated how rough his hands might feel to her. Where his calloused fingers had been sanding the wooden swing, scouring the coarse edges, now he felt them mold like velvet as he ran them down the smooth flesh of her throat.

His eyes collided with hers and he remembered how beautiful she was inside and out. All he might do, if he gave in to temptation and crossed the line from friendship into something more, was hurt her like he'd ruined the clay and abandoned it to the potter's wheel. She wanted someone who could love and trust easily, and he already knew he wasn't that person. As much as he wanted to hold himself accountable and suggest they call it a night, just like she'd suggested they not cross the line by the duck pond, he couldn't. All he could do was offer up a simple question and let her—and fate—be his guide.

"May I kiss you?" he asked. He stared at her mouth, watching for it to twist and contort, a subtle sign that she wanted to say no. But instead, her full mouth parted, a mix of surprise and yearning registering on her face. With lips that looked as soft as silk, he wished they would speak and somehow abrade his senses. Maybe then she would snap him out of this spell, like a thunderclap sounding above his head.

A slow shiver rippled down her entire body, but it wasn't enough consent for him to proceed. He was already scared he was racing into something he couldn't control, as keeping his distance from Olivia took more strength than he had left for the day. All he wanted to do now was kiss her, but only if she wanted him to, only if she gave some sign that she wanted him just as much.

Olivia scooted close and balled her hands into the neck of his T-shirt. She moved deliberately and confidently, with a grace reserved for dancers or queens. It was a move more assertive than he had been prepared for, the act electrifying every nerve across his chest. His hands found the dip at the small of her back. Her mouth hovered dangerously close to his.

She grazed the tip of her lips against his and hummed with satisfaction. He'd never been so aware before of how sensitive the lightest vibration against his mouth could feel. He moistened his lower lip and tasted a sheen of her sugary lip gloss, which would only take a moment to kiss off.

As he pulled her up against him and covered her mouth with his, something inside him shattered, and he knew it could never be perfectly pieced together ever again.

CHAPTER SEVENTEEN

OLIVIA ROLLED OVER the next morning, squinting against the sunshine. Hattie was right; if she forgot to close the drapes before she went to bed at night, her wakeup call would be earlier than she wanted.

She slung an arm over her eyes, not wanting to wake up from what still felt like a dream. Her first kiss with Tyler had shaken her, not just because it was fantastic, but because it had been her *first* first kiss since she'd been twenty years old.

In many ways, she had still felt like a girl when Jeb swept her off her feet. He'd already been brought up to the majors and was making the kind of money that could wine and dine her in ways she had never imagined for herself. She'd been lovestruck, young and naive. When it came to dating Jeb, Olivia's mother had warned her to take it slow. Instead, Olivia waited only a few months before marrying Jeb and trying for a baby. Mom had died before Micah turned six and hadn't been around to see just how cold things between her and Jeb had gotten, but when it came down to sage warnings, Mom's had turned out to be right.

Kissing Tyler, however, had felt different. He'd been the first man she'd seen, really seen, as a woman. Even though remembering the evening made her stomach go topsy-turvy, she also believed she had two feet on the ground this time. This time she would approach a budding romance with heart *and* mind, feeling *and* logic. This time she would be smart enough to not get hurt.

"Where *were* you last night?"

It was Micah who snapped her back to reality.

Olivia peeked out from under her arm to find her son propped up on his bed glaring at her. She recounted the events from the night before. After her kiss with Tyler, he and Ranger had walked her to her car, and she'd gotten home before eleven o'clock. Micah had been zoned out in the living room in front of the television and hadn't made so much as a mumble of acknowledgement when she'd kissed him on the forehead and said goodnight.

But by his sullen expression now, she could

tell she'd done something very wrong by his standards.

"I went out for a little while," she said. "Did you stay in the woods long?"

"No."

"Oh."

She wondered what had happened after she'd left. Hattie had been sitting at the bonfire, practically encouraging her to take some time for herself, but perhaps going out had been a mistake. What if Micah had quickly returned, finally wanting to talk to her, and she'd been gone?

"Did you want to do something with me today?" she said, hopefully. "Anything you want."

"I have to work at the clinic and then... *you know.*"

Olivia inwardly groaned, not wanting Micah to realize she'd forgotten. He had his first appointment with the new counselor.

"Tonight, then. We could take a drive or do some of those things Hattie mentioned. I'm not into cliff jumping, but you know I like kayaking or—"

"Dad wanted to take me kayaking. Do you remember that?"

Olivia fumbled. "Oh, I'm sorry. I don't."

"Remember that vacation we took to Lake

Superior? The rental place was closed, so we hung out on the beach instead." Micah rolled to face away from her. "I'm gonna go back to sleep. I don't need to get up for another hour."

When he didn't move, indicating he might have really gone back to sleep, she slipped out of her bed, got dressed for the day and went downstairs. Hattie was already awake and standing over her printer. She sipped a cup of coffee as Olivia joined her.

"Hungry?" Hattie said as Olivia stole a piece of toast from Hattie's plate. "Thief."

"I'll make you more, if you want."

"I'd rather you tell me about last night. Where'd ya go? Who'd ya see?"

"Who says I saw anyone?"

Hattie peeked at Olivia over the top of her bifocals and sniggered before opening the cartridge tray on her printer and giving it a little jostle. She punched at the buttons and when an error message flashed on the screen, she muttered some unsavory words under her breath. "This thing cannot be out of toner already. I just refilled it last week."

"I can pick some up for you today."

"Thanks, I'll need it. Is Micah working at the clinic?"

"Mmm-hmm." Olivia took another bite of

toast and mused. "I think he was looking for me last night."

"He was. By his demeanor, I got the sense he had a change of heart about leaving you at the bonfire."

"He wanted to talk?"

"He alluded to it."

"Was he mad I was gone?"

"I don't know. Does it matter?"

Olivia thought it mattered a lot. She'd taken somewhat of a plunge the night before, kissing Tyler and enjoying every delicious second of it. But she'd moved to Roseley to better connect with Micah, not the handsome hometown veterinarian. She had to keep her eye on the priority—Micah. If entertaining her feelings for Tyler jeopardized things with Micah, she'd have to make a choice. Micah's happiness was the only thing that mattered.

TYLER AND MICAH wandered to the front desk to wave goodbye to Miss Jenkins and her new kitten, Antiquity. Micah had been Tyler's shadow all morning, watching as Tyler delivered vaccinations, prescribed medication and set bones.

"Want a soda?" Tyler asked, heading for the refrigerator. Micah followed and gratefully accepted a purple can. They cracked open their drinks and leaned against the counters on opposite sides of the kitchenette.

Micah picked up a stuffed koala as he drank. "Does working here make you want to adopt every animal?" he said.

"Sometimes."

"But you only have Ranger."

"Ranger is all I can handle."

Micah snorted. "You're a vet. You could handle an entire houseful of pets."

"I like it quiet without a lot of…" He paused and took a swig of cola.

"Responsibility?" Micah said.

"Distraction."

"Distraction from what?"

"Work, hobbies, life."

Micah seemed to accept this answer as Julia called back to him. When they reached the front desk, she held the phone receiver out to Tyler, her hand covering the mouthpiece.

"It's Mrs. Elderman," she said. "Your mom."

"Why?" Tyler sputtered. Julia lifted a brow. "I mean," he said as he hoisted up his manners. "Why is she calling me at the office?" He checked his cell phone but no call from his mother had come in.

Julia shrugged and wielded the phone in

front of him like a fencer instigating a match until he accepted it and pressed it to his ear.

"Sandy?"

"Tyler. Are you busy?"

Tyler wasn't sure what she meant since she *had* just called him at work. "Is something wrong?"

"No, but you need to come over now."

Tyler pinched the bridge of his nose. How many times had he needed his mother to drop everything and come help him when he'd been too young to handle things himself? How many times had she found any number of excuses not to?

"I get off work today at five o'clock—"

"If you can't do it, you can't do it."

"Can't do *what*?" He fought for patience. "Where are you?"

"Home. Where do you think?"

Tyler shook his head in confusion. "You called me at the clinic instead of on my cell phone."

"I misplaced my cell. I can't remember your number."

Now, *that* was something that finally made sense. Sandy no doubt still had the clinic phone number memorized even after all these years. For all the times he'd heard her call to deliver a tongue-lashing over the phone to his dad, she could probably dial the clinic number in her sleep.

"If you need me to come over now, I can get away for a few minutes—"

"That's fine." His mother hung up the phone in lieu of a goodbye.

After checking in with Gary and grabbing his truck keys, Tyler had just thrown his truck into gear when Micah came running out, waving. Without a word the teen jumped into the front seat.

"Where do you think you're going?" Tyler asked, suppressing a surprised smile.

"Gary is heading into surgery, and I'm not allowed in there. What else am I gonna do?"

Tyler had never had a wingman before, but Micah's reasoning was sound. That was how Tyler found himself walking into his mom's house a little while later with Micah trailing behind him.

"Sandy?" Tyler called. He wandered around the first floor before Micah called to him from the stairs.

"I think she's up there," Micah said, leaning on the banister to peer up to the second floor. "I can hear water running."

"Sandy?" Tyler called again.

"In here!" his mother cried, her voice muffled behind the bathroom door. Tyler took the stairs two at a time. He threw open the bath-room door and surveyed the damage. Water sprayed from a busted-off bathtub faucet, though thankfully, most of the water trajectory was hitting the inside of the bathtub and running down the drain.

"What happened?" Tyler asked.

"Look at this mess!" she cried. "It's been spraying for a half hour."

"Why didn't you turn the water off?"

"It's stuck."

"Do you have a wrench?"

Sandy wiped her eyes. "I dunno."

Tyler turned to Micah, who'd followed him upstairs. "Would you grab my toolbox out of the bed of my truck?"

As Micah sprinted off on his errand, Sandy stood and wiped perspiration off her forehead. He wasn't sure what on earth she had been doing for the last half hour to solve her broken faucet problem, but whatever it had been, it had upset her.

"Are you okay?" he asked, noticing the hammer on the ground for the first time.

"Just peachy."

"Why didn't you tell me the faucet broke off?"

"It wasn't broken then. I didn't think you'd really show, so I tried fixing it and…"

She kicked the side of the bathtub. She had most likely stripped the threading on the dial and had then taken out her frustration by hitting it too hard with the hammer.

Micah returned with the toolbox and Tyler quickly shut off the water at the valve. He examined the damage. He could replace the faucet and solve her problem for now. The house was old and everything would need to be replaced in its own time.

"Can you fix it?" she asked.

Tyler recalled how Sandy had certainly never felt the tug of obligation to help where he and his dad had been concerned. If she had harbored any maternal instincts toward him, she had never showed them. When he'd left Roseley to go to college, he'd been happy to put some distance between them. He'd hoped having Sandy out of sight would help keep her, and the old hurts, out of mind. It hadn't worked, though.

In the end, she was still his mother, so once he returned to Roseley to put down permanent roots, he knew that life in the small town would include not just seeing her but helping her. If there was any way forward for the both of them, he had to be the one to set the better example. He had to do for her what she had never properly done for him. Didn't he?

Tyler was still struggling to find a response that was representative of the better person he *wanted* to be when his mother powered on. "I'll call a guy. I have some other things for him to look at anyway."

Tyler tossed the broken faucet into his tool-box. She didn't have the money for a plumber and they both knew it. The project would be quick anyway and he could pick up a new faucet and threading kit at the hardware store faster than she could get a plumber lined up.

"Don't take the faucet." His mother scowled. "The plumber is going to need it—"

"I'll get you a new faucet. We can look at the other things you need help with after I finish at the clinic."

"Tyler..." Her voice was a warning, but Tyler matched her with his own.

"Sandy..."

"Wow, you guys are funny," Micah said. Tyler and Sandy looked at him. "You're argu-ing over who gets to do the work. Shouldn't it be the opposite?"

"No," Tyler said. "That's not what family does." He'd said it out of a place of honesty, an inner struggle to be the kind of son that would make his father proud, but after his re-cent argument with Sandy about the past, he wondered if she read a double meaning in his words. For all he knew, he'd subconsciously laced it into what he'd said.

Tyler and Micah left the house and got back into the truck. He started the engine, and as he drove back toward the clinic, he replayed the events at his mother's house over in his mind. After a few minutes, he noticed Micah had a contemplative look on his face.

"So that was my mom," Tyler said, realizing he had not thought to make introductions.

"She didn't seem very happy to see you."

"Ah, that's typical."

"Why?"

"I don't know."

Micah drummed his fingers on the truck door. "You call your mom Sandy?"

"It's her name."

"Yeah, but for you?"

"I haven't thought of her as a mother in a long time. She's Sandy to me."

Micah nodded. "My old counselor would call her a difficult person. Some people are just like that, I guess."

Tyler rested his arm on top of the steering wheel. His mother had been a difficult person his entire life, so he had gotten used to it. Sort of.

He recalled how the old hurts bubbled up

too quickly to control sometimes. There never seemed to be any getting used to that.

"My dad was difficult," Micah continued. "Geesh, was he hard to read. I could never get a sense of if he wanted to hang out with me or not. I think most of the time it was a big, fat *not*."

Tyler stole a glance at Micah. The teen's brow was furrowed into a scowl. If Tyler was going to offer some sort of encouragement or wisdom, it couldn't sound cliché. He had to speak from the heart the way his dad always had, or the way his uncle still did.

"You're turning into one of my favorite people, Micah," he said. "If your dad was a difficult person, I think it had nothing to do with you. Chances are, you were the greatest son. I know your mom always speaks highly of you."

"She talks about me?" he asked quietly.

"Sometimes."

"What does she say?"

"Mom stuff."

Micah grimaced. "*Mushy* stuff."

Tyler wondered if he should share any of the sentiment he'd heard Olivia express when talking about Micah. Her dedication and devotion showed her deep capacity for loving, and it touched Tyler. Still, what Olivia had told him about Micah was done in confidence. It wasn't really his place to speak up for her where Micah was concerned. He knew Micah was a bright kid and could connect some dots when it came to clearly seeing his mom, especially when he saw how other moms, like Sandy, behaved with their sons.

"It's nice the way she talks about you," Tyler managed.

It was. He just wasn't sure if that changed anything for Tyler where he and Olivia were concerned. If his own mother hadn't felt any desire to stick by Tyler's side, why would anyone else? Even someone like Olivia?

As Tyler pulled up in front of the clinic, he spotted Olivia waiting for them.

"What's she already doing here?" Micah said.

Tyler wasn't sure, but he was anxious to find out.

CHAPTER EIGHTEEN

OLIVIA PUSHED OUT onto the sidewalk as soon as she spotted Tyler's truck pulling up in front of the clinic. She'd been surprised to drop by and discover neither Tyler nor Micah was there. But when Julia had explained that Tyler's mother had needed help, she'd been happy to know that Micah had tagged along.

"Hiya, strangers," she said as the two men made their way to her.

Micah put his fists on his hips. "Mom, you're early."

"Can't I visit you at work?"

Her eyes flicked to Tyler for a second. His face was relaxed and conveyed that he knew she'd come to visit him, too.

"I don't get done for another hour," Micah said. He'd taken to volunteering longer hours on Fridays.

"I brought you both some lunch. The festival volunteers ordered pizza and they had leftovers."

"Works for me," Micah said.

Olivia turned to Tyler. "Does it work for you, too?"

He nodded. "Perfect. Thanks."

"My pleasure."

She wanted to ask him how he felt after their kiss, because she hadn't been able to think of much else all morning. But if she did, he might ask her how *she* felt and she wasn't sure how to answer. As wonderful as it had been, the nagging feeling that it should be their last had been growing all morning. Compounding all the doubts she'd already had about getting involved with Tyler was the fact that she hadn't been available to Micah when he'd needed her. That had been the entire point of moving to Roseley, so if she was wavering in her motherly duties because of their relationship, she had to course-correct now.

Micah's stomach growled loud enough for the three of them to hear. "Whoa. I didn't realize I was so hungry."

"You're always hungry," Tyler said, feigning annoyance. "And thirsty. Some volunteer you're turning out to be. You're going to cost me a fortune in soda."

Micah beamed with pride. "It's the price you gotta pay, unless you want to actually start paying me."

"You're hitting me up for hourly now?" Tyler slugged Micah playfully in the arm, making the teen laugh and swat him back.

"I wouldn't charge you *that* much," Micah said.

Olivia hadn't seen her son this happy, this playful, in a very long time. It made the heaviness on her heart lighten—momentarily.

"You just stick to being my wingman and don't get any crazy ideas about money, huh."

"Any time," Micah said. "Mom, I'm helping set up the clinic booth this afternoon. Do I still have to go to…you know?"

Olivia understood. Micah didn't want to explicitly talk about his first appointment with Dr. Scott in front of Tyler. She'd honor that. "Your appointment is at two. But I thought you were helping Caroline and me."

"Gary and I could use his help," Tyler said quickly. "If that's okay with you."

"I guess I don't mind." She glanced at her son. "Micah, is that what you want to do?"

"Yep. They need me."

"It's true," Tyler said, making Micah beam. While Olivia had hoped to spend the day with Micah, one look at his face told her he was already planning to have a great time at the festival. Just seeing the light in his eyes, something that had been missing for so long, helped manage her disappointment.

"I'm gonna grab pizza," Micah said, already looking lighter on his feet with the matter settled.

As he disappeared into the clinic, Olivia shuffled to the curb and fiddled with the fabric of her sundress. Tyler moseyed closer, following her.

"Was there another reason you stopped by?" he said.

"Not really."

"Liar."

"What?" Olivia frowned.

Tyler moved closer and skimmed a finger to the dimple at her mouth. Her face went hot, not just at his touch, which reminded her of the night before, but because her aunt had been right. She had a poker tell she was unaware of, and Tyler had learned it.

She lowered her eyes, not wanting him to see how much she still wanted him.

Tyler shifted his weight back on his heels and moved back a few steps as if instinctively suspecting he'd done something wrong. While Olivia appreciated the space, a deep sinking feeling came over her as she recognized she might never move into Tyler's personal space again. Once she said what she needed to say, their orbits wouldn't cross paths the way they had the night before.

"Do you and Caroline need help with the festival?" he said. "I know we poached Micah, but we can—"

"I'm glad Micah is helping. I think he's looking for ways to prove himself to you."

"Good," Tyler said. "We'll give him all the heavy lifting."

Olivia ran a hand along her hairline, fussing with stray hairs. His eyes beckoned, as if wanting to draw out every wisp of her soul. Part of her wanted to swoon into his strong arms and pull his face toward hers the way she had in the darkness of his front porch. But nothing about her life was easy now.

She began slowly, "Tyler, I wanted to see you..."

"I wanted to see you, too."

"You did?"

Tyler grabbed the back of his neck. "Uh-oh," he said. "Surprised? Last night must not have gone as well as I thought, huh?"

His voice teased, but it only made her next words harder to eke out. Their evening on the porch, wrapped in each other's arms, had been one of the most beautiful experiences she'd had in recent history. Even though the timing had felt right last night, in the early morning hours she'd been filled with the sense that it had happened too fast. Maybe it shouldn't have happened at all.

"I'm happy we shared that," she said. "It'll stay with me for a long time."

The softness in Tyler's eyes faded as if preparing for the second shoe to drop. "But?" he prompted.

"I'm glad I met you, *we* met you. You have no idea what you mean to me, Tyler."

A clarity came over his expression. "But you're glad we're friends, *just* friends. Is that it?"

"Working for more than that right now doesn't feel right."

"No? How so?"

She wavered on her feet, not expecting she'd have to fully support her statement. "I'm taking Micah to a new counselor this afternoon—"

"Good. Glad to hear it."

"And between his schooling and getting him settled in Roseley, I think it's best if we don't…"

"Come on," Tyler said, softly. "Don't do that. You don't have to make Micah the fall guy here. If you don't have feelings for me, it's okay, Olivia. It really is."

His response, so matter-of-fact and casual,

slugged something hard in her gut. For him to brush off what they'd shared so easily, as if she'd just told a waiter she didn't want a second cup of coffee, made her insides churn. She didn't think his reaction broke her heart, but standing in the wake of it, he'd certainly bruised it.

"I care a lot about you," she started again. "What's going on in my life doesn't change my feelings for you."

"I'm glad we're friends. No worries, okay?"

"No worries? What does that mean?"

"It means, it's fine. Really. Don't worry about me." He flashed her a fleeting smile before turning toward the clinic door. "I gotta get back to work, though. Thanks for the pizza."

"Y-you're welcome?" she said. "This wasn't what I—"

"Olivia," he said, turning. "It's okay. Completely okay."

"Okay," she managed, as he darted inside, but nothing about that word felt right.

TYLER STOOD ON the bed of his truck and passed the end of a folding table down to Micah, who was waiting on the ground.

"Easy, now," Tyler said. "Don't hurt yourself."

"This is easy," Micah said. He repositioned his grip to carry the table to their designated spot on Main Street. The police had blocked off the road earlier that day, detouring traffic so a two-block stretch of the road was protected for the Fall Festival. Tyler appreciated that this year, the committee—notably CeCe—had assigned them a spot close to the town square and gazebo. Dog owners tended to drift toward the gazebo to lounge on the grass with their dogs, so the nearby foot traffic was good for business.

Gary slid two folding chairs off the bed of the truck and waited for Micah to return. The teen did so at a jog, eager for more things to haul. When Gary winked at Tyler, he knew his uncle was preparing to razz the kid a bit.

"Hey, Tyler," Gary said once Micah was in earshot. "I like this. We delegate and Micah hustles."

"Don't say that too loudly, Gary," Tyler said. "Or he'll be hitting us up for a paycheck. He already tried it on me earlier."

"Dr. Elderman," Micah said. "I didn't say you had to pay me—"

"He's cutthroat, Gary. As ruthless as they come."

"In it for the money, eh?" Gary said, winking at Micah. Micah rolled his eyes and took the chairs.

They teased all in good fun, but the truth was, he and Gary had already decided they would pay Micah for his time helping with the festival. His help for the next two days was certainly outside the scope of typical volunteer hours. He was a great kid and a good worker, and they were looking forward to surprising him with compensation.

Once the truck was unloaded and Micah had finished carrying the last of the supplies, Tyler jumped down from the bed of the truck.

"You could have parked closer," Micah said, wiping perspiration off his brow.

Tyler patted him affectionately on the back. "What for? We have you."

"You're killing me!" Micah cried, but he beamed with pride all the same.

"Thirsty?"

"Do you even have to ask?"

Tyler reached into his pocket, counted out some cash and handed it to Micah.

"Go see if they're making fresh lemonade yet. Grab three, if they are."

"And elephant ears," Gary said, rubbing his belly. "All that heavy lifting made me work up an appetite."

"I was the one who did everything!" Micah cried, dramatically snatching the cash.

"I've never worked so hard in my life," Gary continued. "Elephant ears, Micah. Stat!"

As Micah trotted off to fetch snacks, Gary gave Tyler an elbow in his side. "He's a great kid. I love that we can mess with him."

"You like anyone you can joke with."

"That's why I always liked you." Gary leaned back against the truck tailgate and studied his nephew. "What's going on with his mom?"

"What do you mean?"

"You know what I mean. I drove by your house this morning and saw you hung up my swing. I kind of figured…"

"You figured what?"

Gary flashed a wily smile. "I figured you were putting it to good use."

"I need to repaint it. That's how you paint a swing."

"Riiight."

"We're just friends." He felt a twinge in his chest even as he added levelly, "She made that clear earlier this afternoon."

Olivia hadn't said much but it had still pierced him. He felt like a fool for letting his guard down for even a moment. He hadn't just kissed her; he'd opened up to her and had begun to feel comfortable for the first time in a very long time.

"Oh. I'm sorry to hear that," Gary said gently.

"No need to be." Tyler crossed his arms over his chest and watched the crowd setting up for the festival. "After losing her husband, Olivia doesn't want to get involved with anyone. It's for the best because I'm not interested in getting involved with anyone anyway."

It felt true, didn't it? He'd been happy before he'd met Olivia and without her, he would surely be happy again—right?

"Still? Now that you're settled in town and into your house and the clinic, I thought you'd be ready to find a lovely lady and—"

"Nah. I was already thinking along the same lines as Olivia—friendship, I mean. If she hadn't said anything, I would have."

Tyler repositioned his arms tighter across his chest as he reminded himself that the words he'd just spoken were true. Sure, he felt disappointed that she'd rejected him just when he had begun to open himself up to her, but she'd given him a gift, too. She'd reminded him that taking a risk on love was never worth it. She might not have gift wrapped it, but that reminder was all he needed to keep his distance in the future.

"Is that really what you want?"

Tyler knew he didn't want to convince Olivia to be with him. He also knew he didn't want to get hurt. Falling for someone as smart and kind and all-around great as Olivia Howard nearly guaranteed that he would. He was lucky to cut ties before he was wounded any deeper.

A deep hum of disagreement resonated in Gary. "Gosh, I thought this woman was the one."

"The one? There is no such thing."

"Of course, there is."

"Where's yours, then?"

"I haven't found her yet. I'm playing the long game." Gary winked. "But you...you don't need to wait. Olivia is fantastic."

"She is fantastic *as a friend*. Gary, there is no 'the one' for me. You sound like a hopeless romantic like Dad."

Gary tipped his head back, recalling. "Ah, he really was hopeless, wasn't he?"

"Yeah, and look where that got him."

"It got him you." His uncle smiled at him. "You were the best thing that ever happened to him. He said so more times than I could count."

Tyler worked his jaw even as he kept his composure.

"Some consolation prize I was." He huffed in his best cool-guy impression. "I couldn't take care of him the way he needed."

"You were a kid, and you did your best. We both did. He loved you for trying so hard."

Gary waved to Micah as he made his way back through the crowd, empty-handed. He stopped to talk at Caroline's booth, several spaces away. When Olivia emerged from behind a large heart display and caught Tyler's eye, her brows lifted.

At the sight of her, Tyler's unrequited feelings coiled inside him. They yearned for an escape that he knew wouldn't come, no matter how hard he tried to pretend that he was fine. He forced his friendliest, "I'm fine, we're just friends" wave. Olivia returned it before turning to talk to Caroline.

"You deserve someone like Olivia," Gary said.

"Thanks, but I'm fine the way things are."

"Yeah, you look fine," Gary said, his jovial demeanor now darkening to sarcasm. "Just swell."

"Look," Tyler said, running a hand down his face. "Olivia is a gem, but she doesn't want to be with me."

"But you want to be with her."

Tyler let out an exasperated laugh. "I didn't say that."

"You kind of did."

"Are you reading into everything I say now?"

Gary grasped Tyler hard on the shoulder and gave him a shake. "Of course. I'm your best friend, aren't I?"

"You and Ranger are neck and neck."

Micah returned and gloomily held out the money to Tyler. "They said they're still setting up."

"Keep it," Tyler said. "You can buy the first round of snacks tomorrow."

Micah shoved the wad of cash into his pocket. His smile burned brighter with a new willingness to help. "Is there anything else you need? Your wish is my command."

"Really?" Gary said, brightening. Micah held up a hand, realizing his poor choice of words.

"Don't get any crazy ideas."

"Let's take a walk and check out the other booths," Gary suggested.

Tyler shook his head. "I'm fine here."

"You're missing out," Gary said, his voice something of a taunt. He led Micah along the booths, wandering to say hello to Caroline and Olivia. Tyler waited for Olivia to glance his way again, but after a moment, he wondered what the heck he was doing. Would it satisfy something in him to think she really did have feelings for him but was choosing to not get involved?

Tyler hopped in his truck and pulled into a nearby parking lot. There *was* something—or more like some*one*—he needed, but unless she needed him, too, he didn't want to spend any more energy wishing for it. He'd spent years wishing for people to care for him more than they did, and wishing had never gotten him anywhere. It was time to move on and consider his time spent with Olivia just another tough lesson learned.

CHAPTER NINETEEN

THE FALL FESTIVAL had been in full swing for several hours Saturday when Olivia arrived with coffee, croissants and a willingness to keep her friend company for the day. She couldn't decide if the fact that Caroline's booth was also less than twenty yards from Tyler's booth was an added perk or torture.

Olivia dropped heart-shaped chocolates into the waiting hands of several children who had already collected candy twenty minutes earlier. When they scampered off, she turned to Caroline.

"At this rate, you're going to run out of candy."

"It wasn't my idea. You know how I feel about all the mushy, lovey-dovey wedding stuff. If this were my business..." Caroline checked on either side of her as she lowered her voice "...I'd focus on the big events, not weddings."

"Like what?"

"When corporations need to plan a fund-

292 HER VETERINARIAN HERO

raiser or throw a huge bash, they would call me. I'd make galas my specialty."

"Why don't you do that? Get out from under Sheila's thumb and—"

"Ladies!"

Caroline's eyes flashed. Her boss had almost overheard them talking.

Sheila, a fifty-year-old woman with big hair and a big smile, hurried over to them. "Ladies," she said. "You're supposed to be inviting people to take a photograph in our fabulous backdrop and then share on their social media. Olivia, make sure you hand out flyers with those chocolates."

"Olivia doesn't work for you, Sheila," Caroline said.

"I know that. Thank you, Liv, dear, for volunteering. But if a person's hand is already opened to get a candy, you can stick a flyer in there, too, can't you?"

"Sure," Olivia said.

Sheila winked at her. "That's a dear. Caroline, you have lovely friends. I'm going to work the crowd."

Caroline waited until Sheila was several booths away before groaning. "That's all she does when we work a wedding, too. She should have been a professional wedding crasher."

"How does she stay in business?"

Caroline opened her arms in a ta-da movement. "Yours truly."

"All the more reason to strike out on your own."

"In this town? As much as I can't stand Sheila, I wouldn't want to hurt her or her business by competing."

"She can do the weddings since we know how you feel about them." Caroline made a fake gag to agree. "*You* can specialize in big things like...what did you call them?"

"Galas."

"Right, galas. There's room in town for you both."

Caroline shrugged. "Yeah, maybe."

"Yeah, *yes*. If you're working this booth next fall for Sheila, I am going to shake you silly."

"Speaking of silly," Caroline said, shifting her eyes toward the clinic's booth before landing back on Olivia again. "What's going on with you and Ty? We've been over here all morning and he hasn't looked at you once."

"No?" Olivia plucked a candy out of her bag and unwrapped it. She'd noticed that, too, but it was because she couldn't stop stealing glances at him. "We decided to be just friends."

"You *both* decided?"

"Mmm-hmm."

"*Impossible.* If a couple decides to be just friends, there's always one person who wants to be friends and another person who wants to be more. Which one are you?"

Olivia bit the inside of her cheek as she recalled just how nice Tyler had been during their talk. So nice. Too nice. He hadn't seemed distraught at all. In contrast, she hadn't been able to sleep from tossing and turning and thinking about how much she already missed him.

If Caroline was right, Tyler must have been the one who had really wanted to be friends all along. She was the one who initiated the conversation, true, but that didn't stop her from longing for a time when they could be more.

"It's not a good time for us," Olivia said, popping the candy in her mouth. "I'm getting Micah adjusted and I need to focus on him. That's what I came to Roseley for and that's what I'm going to do."

Caroline squinted in confusion and pointed a finger toward the crowd. "Isn't that Micah, now?"

Micah was drinking a lemonade and laughing with Gary. "What's your point?" Olivia asked.

"He seems like he's adjusting just fine."

"It seems that way on the surface," Olivia said. "But back at the cottage he won't talk. He gets cross with me, and he retreats to his fort every chance he gets." Olivia bit down hard on her candy, remembering how many sleepless nights she'd spent worrying about Micah and praying she was parenting him well. As a single mom the last couple years, she hadn't had anyone around as a daily witness to how hard things had been, and that loneliness had only added to her worry and uncertainty. "Right now, the laughing is the exception. Grumpy, irritable, hiding-his-feelings Micah is the rule."

"What about his counseling?"

"He said his first session went fine."

Dr. Scott had been lovely. She hadn't shared much about her first session with Micah, except to explain that it took time to build trust and rapport with a new client. Micah, as usual, hadn't shared any details except to say that Dr. Scott had really cool throw pillows on her chairs.

"What about *your* counseling?"

Olivia stiffened. "I'll book something soon."

Caroline clicked her tongue in disapproval.

"I will," Olivia said. "Now that Micah's sessions are scheduled, I'll schedule mine next."

"How is tutoring with Maggie Joyce going?"

"They hit it off." Olivia was grateful that at least Micah wasn't falling behind in school.

"Okay…"

"What?"

Caroline scooted closer to her friend. "Micah has a job, but you don't yet. Micah is seeing his counselor, but you haven't scheduled your appointment. Micah is doing his schoolwork, but you don't know what to do in Roseley aside from help him. Do you see a pattern?"

Olivia fumbled for the chocolates, furiously unwrapping another one as she explained. "I've been the common denominator for his success," Olivia said, her voice breaking. "That's what a mother does. She takes care of things."

"And you've done a great job, Liv." Caroline laid a hand over Olivia's fidgety fingers. "Look at your boy."

Olivia watched Micah stroll off through the crowd with Tyler, the two most likely going to look at all the other booths. She wanted to be the one Micah turned to and spent time with, but she felt grateful that he had at least found a friend in Tyler.

"Maybe it's time to start taking care of things for yourself," Caroline pressed.

"I am. I'm here, aren't I?"

"True…" Caroline said, stealing a candy from Olivia's bag. "But I think there's someone else you'd like to have here with you."

TYLER WANDERED AROUND the festival booths with Micah, giving as much focus to the different displays as he could muster. No matter where they walked, he always felt painfully aware of where Olivia was in proximity to him. If she wanted space from him, from what had been developing between them, then he'd respect that. He figured space was a good thing before they tried their hand at being friends again.

After their kiss, his favorite kiss on record, his mind had been whirling. Yet at the same time, he reminded himself that their conversation had been for the best. It was always best to get out before anyone, especially him, got hurt. In the past, whenever he'd tried to lean on his mother or stepmother, they'd dropped him cold and made him feel like the rejection had been his fault. Plus, losing his dad, the one person Tyler thought would always be there, was enough to make anyone trigger-shy about love. Olivia had at least been kind and straightforward about rejecting him. Plus, she wasn't dropping him completely. She wanted to stay in his life—sort of.

The sun was making its descent, cuing an afternoon of contests, giveaways, music and dancing. From the gazebo, the Hometown Jamboree had struck up their first set. Their star fiddler player wailed on the strings, making everyone within a block radius stop and take notice. Children skipped around the small dance area and adults lounged on the grass watching them. Tyler sat down on a patch of grass near the gazebo as Micah devoured a hot dog.

"Are you eating your way through the festival?" Tyler asked.

Micah puffed out his chest. "Sure, why not? I'm going to try the deep-fried Twinkies next."

Tyler laughed. "When I was a kid, my friends and I waited all year to binge on deep-fried Twinkies. My dad would give me money to buy them for all my friends."

Micah's brow creased. "Didn't your dad die when you were my age?"

"He got sick when I was your age. I used

to ride my bike all over town because I didn't like being at home."

"Before my dad died, I thought about mowing lawns to make money so I could buy a new bike," Micah said.

"Oh, yeah?"

"Yeah. He used to have a fifty-four-inch zero-turn riding mower with smart speed. It was like riding on a cloud."

Tyler could only guess how many times Micah had heard his dad list off the lawn mower's description to still remember it years later. He smiled fondly at the satisfied look on Micah's face to talk about it now.

"My dad used to pull me on his lap when he cut the grass, too," Tyler said, the familiarity of their exchange bringing up memories with his own dad... As he admired Micah, a boy on the cusp of adulthood, he wondered if the nostalgic sentiments he felt now were the same ones his dad had felt when he'd been Micah's age. For the first time he began to see his memories with his dad from a new perspective. While he'd only had the recollections of a kid looking up to his dad, now he looked back and saw his innocence and inexperience through an adult lens, the way his dad must have viewed him all along.

"Oh, no," Micah huffed. "He never did that,

at least not that I remember. My dad wanted me to drive it."

"On your own?" Tyler chuckled in disbelief.

He'd never met Jeb. He wasn't about to pass judgment on someone he didn't know, especially when he'd never had to parent a child himself. But what Micah said didn't sound right. If Jeb died two years ago when Micah was twelve, anyone that age or younger seemed way too young to have full control of such a powerful machine. It sounded irresponsible, at least in his opinion.

"Yep," Micah said. "He and my mom used to fight about it. He said he did way more dangerous stuff at my age, so sometimes when she wasn't home, he'd let me take it for a spin."

"Is that right?"

"Just as long as I made nice, clean swipes in the grass."

Tyler rasped a hand over his chin. He was beginning to get a better idea of Jeb and the dynamic between him and Olivia. Before he could ask Micah what other things Jeb let him do, Micah continued, "What happened with your mom? Did you fix that faucet yet?"

"This morning."

Tyler had felt grateful Sandy hadn't been

home when he'd dropped by with the replacement parts. He wondered if she'd be disappointed to learn he'd fixed the faucet while she was away, because after he'd finished and left her house, he couldn't help feeling disappointed himself. As lovely as it was to work in peace, he'd also felt working without her there had been something of a missed opportunity. He could always predict how their interactions would go, but it didn't keep him from hoping, at least secretly, that they could be better. They didn't have the kind of mother-son relationship he wanted, but he didn't know what to do to change that. At best he tried to be cordial and help her whenever she asked.

"That's good," Micah said. "But I could tell you wanted out of there the other day."

"It's probably hard for you to understand since your mom is so great."

Micah nodded. "She's a good mom most of the time."

"And the other times?"

Micah tipped back a swig of soda. "For starters she still thinks I'm a little kid. My dad had me doing stuff at twelve that some adults don't know how to do. He wasn't around a lot, but when he was, he made sure I knew how to do stuff."

Tyler leaned forward and rested his elbows on his knees, curious. "Like what?"

"Well, not babysitting puppies." Micah's sarcasm dripped as heavy as maple syrup and Tyler could tell he was trying for a laugh.

"Are you trying to start something?" Tyler said, grabbing Micah around the neck in a headlock. The teen flailed against him, but Tyler had already dug a grip into his rib cage and tickled hard the way his own dad had done to him numerous times. The scuffle only lasted a few seconds, as Tyler didn't want to embarrass him, but when Micah caught his breath, he didn't seem like he cared about that. "I thought you liked watching the puppies."

"I did. I'm kidding about that, but I can do more at the clinic, too, you know," Micah said.

"Yeah?" Tyler said, laughing. "Should I put you on surgery rotation?"

Micah smirked. "I could probably figure it out."

Hattie Pike strolled over. She stopped shortly in front of them and placed her hands proudly on her hips.

"Well, boys," she said. "What do you think of my festival?"

"You'd better not say that too loudly," Tyler said. "CeCe will have your head."

"Eh, it's *our* festival—the lot of us. The dance floor was my idea, though." She pulled Micah to his feet. "You should go ask someone to dance."

"You've got to be kidding," Micah said, as if the suggestion was more appalling than scrubbing out the long row of porta potties.

"Someday you might want to, kid," Tyler said.

"Guys don't ask girls to dance anymore. It's old-fashioned," the teen insisted.

"Dancing is never old-fashioned," Hattie said. She swayed her hips back and forth, letting the loose material of her long, red paisley skirt move freely around her ankles. Her bangle bracelets jingled, her eyes twinkled and everything about her signaled her readiness to join in. "Micah, would you do me the honor?"

"No way." Micah backed away from her. "I'm getting another hot dog."

"Oh, you're no fun!" Hattie called as he raced off through the crowd. Hattie puckered her bottom lip in a pout. "I've been working on this festival for months and now I'm ready to cut loose."

Tyler scrambled to his feet and held out

the crook of his elbow. A woman like Hattie didn't belong on the sidelines. "Let's show them how to do it," he said.

Hattie's face brightened before looping her arm in his. "I knew I liked you, Dr. Elderman."

Tyler led Hattie to the dance floor. Within seconds, his dance partner was clapping and moving to the beat. He wasn't usually one to dance; in fact he couldn't remember the last time he had, but Hattie's energy rubbed off on him.

Hattie looped her arm in Tyler's again and swung them in a full circle before stopping and reversing direction. After they had made a beautiful spectacle of themselves, Hattie pulled Tyler close and whispered in his ear. "Let's get this party started, love. On the count of three, go grab another partner."

Over the music, Tyler had barely heard her. But before he could clarify what she had meant, Hattie had abandoned him to drag Chief Marley off his seat and onto the dance floor. The police chief was dressed in plain clothes and had been enjoying a drink with his wife, but that hadn't stopped Hattie. She had him to his feet while his wife laughed and egged him on.

Tyler scanned the crowd, searching for a

partner. His instinct was to find Olivia, if only for an excuse to hold her again. But as hard as he tried, he couldn't see her anywhere. Because he'd known exactly where she was only moments before, the irony jabbed.

He did, however, spot former Falcon High alums Emily Peaches and Samantha McTully whispering and making eyes at him. Emily was adorable with strawberry blond hair and the prettiest rosy cheeks. But Samantha was like an injection of loud, bold fun. He needed a partner who was more than willing to join him and then keep the dance partner swap going. That meant Samantha.

"Come on, Sam!" Tyler called above the music. "I know you've got the moves!"

Samantha dramatically fluffed her hair and sprang onto the dance floor to join him, making Emily hoot encouragements from the sidelines.

"You haven't lost your touch, Doc," she said before he spun her around. After a minute, Hattie danced by with Uncle Gary while Chief Marley danced with Dolores Mitchell, the owner of The Cutest Little Tea Shop. Her violet-gray perm was difficult to miss.

The dance floor had quickly begun filling up, but Tyler's mind was on something else.

If both he and Gary were on the dance floor, who on earth was running their booth?

When Samantha pulled Dash Callahan onto the dance floor and into her arms, Tyler darted off to find out. Zipping in and out between folks, he finally felt the crowd part so he could see his booth, and Olivia standing behind it.

"Hey," he said, jogging up. He didn't know if they could find the easiness they'd shared not two days ago. At the very least he was grateful for an excuse to talk to her when all he'd been doing all day was thinking about her. He grabbed the back of his neck and tried for casual. "Did Gary rope you into this?"

"I offered."

He waited for more of an explanation, but when she rifled into her candy bag, he knew he'd have to settle for a chocolate instead. She handed him one.

"Thanks. Your aunt sure is persuasive."

"You should have seen the look on Gary's face. He didn't need much persuading." She smiled, then looked around. "Where's my son? Isn't he supposed to be helping you?"

"Hot dog run. How's Caroline's booth doing?"

"Lots of interest. Many folks are planning weddings for next summer."

"I always liked outdoor summer weddings." The words were out of his mouth in such a flash, he felt compelled to clarify. "As a guest."

"Really?" she said. "Have you given a lot of thought to them?"

He figured she really wanted to know whether he had given thought to marriage. He had, in fact, and had decided many years ago that it wasn't for him. After watching how unhappy his dad had been with Sandy and then again with Robin, he had decided he didn't want to walk down any aisle.

Tyler shrugged. "Did you and Jeb have a summer wedding?"

"Yes," she said wistfully. "It was like something out of a fairy tale."

He tried to picture Olivia as a blushing bride. Had her hair been pinned up or had it spiraled down around her shoulders? Had she worn a veil to hide those mystical eyes, or had she donned a tiara? She deserved the fairy tale, even if he couldn't be the one to provide it for her.

Olivia wavered on her feet, as if deciding what to do next. He wanted to pull her into his arms and onto the dance floor. He wanted to tell her that just being friends was the stupidest thing he'd ever agreed to, but he didn't.

Instead, he stole another chocolate from her candy bag.

"They're not bad," he said.

"It's no Bazooka bubblegum," she said with a hint of a smile. "But I'm good at sharing."

"Friends are always good at sharing."

"Yeah," she said, softly. She stared at him, but her mind looked like it had drifted a thousand miles away. "Friends."

CHAPTER TWENTY

THE AFTERNOON HAD inched closer to sunset and the large crowd from earlier was slowly dwindling as Tyler and Gary worked to disassemble their booth. They had cut Micah loose a couple hours earlier, encouraging him to explore the festival with Ricky Murdock Jr., who was slightly younger but fast on his feet. Once Tyler had paid Micah for his help with working the festival, the two boys had run to blow the money on games and festival food, including a mixture of ten different slushy flavors they proudly dubbed "the cannonball."

Tyler checked his cell phone and found a text message from Sandy.

Faucet working fine. Thanks.

"It was a pretty good festival," Gary said, breaking down their table. "I'll have to tell Hattie."

Tyler shoved his cell phone in his pocket. "You two were getting friendly."

"What? Oh, no. We've known each other for years."

"I saw you dancing out there. You gave the walking club plenty to talk about tomorrow morning."

"Oh, shut up," Gary said, though he was grinning from ear to ear. "When a woman asks you to dance, you always say yes. At least, that's what Hattie said."

Tyler quirked a brow. "I doubt you needed much persuading. Just the same, I'm glad you had fun."

"I sure did, but I don't think *she* is." Gary elbowed Tyler in the side while staring at the dance floor. "Don't look now but your girl-friend needs you."

Dex Randall, who had always been a hard-edged brute of a guy, was trying to persuade Olivia to join him on the dance floor.

"She's not my girlfriend."

"That's unfortunate."

It certainly was.

The burnt orange sky was quickly darken-ing to dusk as a jaunty tune filled the gazebo and dance floor. Many folks had congregated to cheer on the fiddler, who had gone off-page and played harder and faster the more people clapped and cheered. The resurgence of excitement had only continued when thousands of twinkle lights, which had been strung over the dance floor, powered on. People finished clapping for the fiddler and then looked up in awed delight. That was probably how Olivia had found herself milling close to the dance floor and directly in Dex's sights.

From afar, Dex looked like he was exhausting all of his persuasive tactics. He hadn't reached for her, but Tyler thought he was standing just a little too close. His eyes had narrowed on her just a little too intensely. Regardless of what Dex was saying, he gave Tyler the impression he would pursue Olivia until she agreed to dance.

The adrenaline coursed so hard, so fast, that Tyler shoved the box he'd been holding into Gary's waiting arms with a thud.

"Ugh," Gary groaned. "I'll take that."

He knew Olivia could handle herself, even with a guy as assertive as Dex. Still, he felt compelled to help her. Every fiber of his body sprang alert, ready to jump in and do…something.

Tyler muttered, his eyes fixed on Olivia. "She needs…"

"Yep," Gary said.

"I gotta go and…"

"Yep."

"Give me a minute," Tyler said. He cut a straight line to Olivia and Dex.

He was at Olivia's side, reaching to take her hand, before Dex could manage another word. Her eyes flooded with relief when she saw him.

"Olivia," he said. "You promised me a dance."

Dex scowled. "Wait a second, Doc. We were in the middle of something."

"Not anymore."

Olivia threw Dex an apologetic smile and clasped Tyler's hand tightly. "I'm so sorry... Dex, was it? I have to go home soon, and I did promise him."

Dex's expression darkened. He pursed his lips as Tyler pulled Olivia to the dance floor.

"You're just in time," she breathed. "Again."

"Again?"

"You have a habit of saving me."

"Dancing with Dex *is* worse than falling off a cliff."

Olivia muffled a laugh. "I got that impression, too. Thanks."

"That's what friends are for."

Tyler led Olivia to a clearing in the center of the dance floor. A group of teenagers had formed a small circle. They cheered as each one took a turn solo dancing inside the ring.

Children and their parents continued to mill around the space.

Tyler knew people would see them; people would talk. He imagined Caroline and Hattie and Gary winking at each other in that sly, knowing way adults sometimes did. CeCe would probably add them to her list of gossip topics for the next day, giving the walking club plenty of fodder.

If Micah spotted them, Tyler wondered if he would be shocked at the development. His mother was dancing with a man who wasn't his father. Could something like that shake a kid up? It had felt very strange when his dad had started dating Robin, but his dad had been so unhappy for such a long time, Tyler had forced himself to feel better about the match sooner than later. As it turned out, his dad's happiness had been very, *very* short-lived.

One song, Tyler told himself. Friends could dance to one upbeat tempo song without causing a stir.

Olivia wore a blue dress that in the sunshine looked cobalt. The light of dusk now played with the shade. As she sashayed her hips, he marveled at the way her body moved with the music, the cotton fabric shifting over her curves like dark waves on the ocean.

"We should stay out here for a while," he said. "At least until Dex leaves."

"Whatever you think."

He thought it was fascinating the way her face caught the twinkle lights. Just as soon as he thought about touching her cheek to remember how soft it was, fate dealt him an opportunity. The up-tempo song ended and a new song, a dangerously slow one, began.

OLIVIA HAD ALWAYS loved the way a man looked when offering his hand to a woman. As a young girl she had seen the scenario dozens of times in television shows or movies. Whether he was helping her step down off a train or greeting her at a ball, the man's eyes usually looked so warm and inviting.

But when Olivia accepted Tyler's extended hand, it wasn't his eyes that overtook her. It was the way he invited her into his space, his closeness.

"Do we dare?" he said. His voice hinted that they were breaking some sort of rule.

She supposed they should stay on the dance floor a little longer. After all, she didn't want to return to the booth and get cornered by Dex again.

Olivia took Tyler's hand and maneuvered closer. He positioned his arms to frame her body, like a craftsman sizing up a portrait. His broad body was perhaps as sturdy and protective as a break wall shielding her from nature's fury, or at least the jitters wriggling throughout her body. In this moment, with him, she didn't have to be strong. She didn't have to make any more judgment calls or second-guess any decision. For as long as the song played, she could just be with Tyler.

The warmth of the day had cooled to night. Tyler slipped his hand more snugly around her lower back like setting the canvas in the frame. With his other hand, he guided her palm to his chest just over his heart. He traced a fingertip over her knuckles, tracing something she couldn't decipher but understood all the same.

"Is this okay?" he said, the tenderness in his voice eclipsing her hesitation. She wanted to say that it was more than okay. She wanted to say that all day she'd reviewed the reasons they should stay friends, but just then, as his touch tickled, she couldn't remember any of them. Swaying in time to the music, wrapped in Tyler's embrace, she couldn't clear her mind long enough to remember what she had been thinking.

He covered her hand with his own. Between the slow-tempo guitar strum and the *thu-thump* of his heartbeat under her palm, she didn't have to know the choreography of their steps. The beat of his heart was as steady as a metronome, guiding her, leading her. She could set her feet to it and to the melody drifting all around them.

Their feet shuffled, mere centimeters at a time, rotating them slightly in a circle. The Roseley firmament had settled, sealing them off from the rest of the world, but she surrendered to it willingly and gratefully.

Carefully, she lay her head against his warm chest and relaxed on her feet. Tyler lowered his head to nuzzle his face closer to hers. His whiskers scratched against the collar of his shirt. It was a sound so simple yet dripping with masculinity. It resonated in her ear and sent tickly shivers down the back of her neck like sparks falling from flint.

"I like this song," she murmured.

"Me, too."

She closed her eyes and let her other senses take over. Tyler's controlled breath blew faintly on her eyelashes. His hand shifted at her back, adjusting to keep her pressed against him. They moved as one, a pair of bookends that had come together for one song only.

"Olivia."

"Hmm?" she hummed.

"Olivia." His voice caught an edge that felt out of place.

"Wh-what?" She blinked, confused. The song hadn't ended, and she felt cheated. "Tyler," she said, staring up at him. His face had sobered in a flash. "What is it?"

"Micah."

On his word, Tyler bolted from the dance floor. Olivia had no idea where he was going or what was wrong. All she knew was that her son had been the cause. That fact instantly flooded her veins with fear.

Olivia followed as Tyler ran behind the clinic's booth and over a large stretch of grassy hill that butted up to the closest parking lot. The jerky flash of Tyler's truck brake lights was all she could focus on as Tyler reached the pavement and called to the driver.

The truck jolted backward.

"Put it in Park!" Tyler cried.

Olivia raced to catch up. Most people had begun to clear out for the night, but out of the corner of her eye, she spotted Hattie and Gary running toward them.

Once the truck had come to a complete stop, the driver's-side door creaked open.

"Is it in Park?" Tyler said, holding his forehead as he caught his breath. "Are you okay?"

Micah sheepishly slid out from behind the

steering wheel. "Yeah," he muttered. "I didn't drive it far. Just from the far side of that lot."

"Micah," Olivia said, her sheer exasperation keeping her from saying anything but her child's name. She couldn't say she was angry—yet. More than feeling worried or scared or furious, she was completely shocked at her son's behavior. He might have been a challenge on occasion over the last two years, but he'd never attempted something like this. She stared at him, mouth agape.

"Gary wanted to finish breaking down the booth," Micah explained hurriedly. "He gave me the keys so I could unlock the truck tailgate and start loading. But it made more sense to pull the truck closer. Work smart, not hard, right?"

"If something had happened, I would have been liable, Micah," Tyler said. "It's my truck."

"Nothing happened, though."

"I don't care," Tyler returned. "You don't have a driver's license—far from it."

"Micah," Hattie said, finally reaching them. "Are you okay?"

"Fine."

"Heavens, child. You could have hurt yourself or someone else."

Micah's eyes flashed, hot with anger. *"I'm not a child."*

"Micah," Olivia said. "Is that all you heard? You could have hurt somebody."

"I didn't hurt anybody!" Micah held out his arms to prove it. "Do you see anyone hurt? It's not that big a deal."

"Not that big a deal?" Olivia repeated.

She might believe Micah had had a momentary lapse in good judgment, but to not acknowledge he'd done something wrong infuriated her. She didn't recognize the boy standing in front of her. His thick, curly hair was dewy with sweat just like it used to get when he had spent an entire summer day playing baseball. She'd wrap her arms around him at the end of the day and bury her nose into the top of his head. He smelled sour, the fragrance of summertime lived to its fullest.

But with his sulky expression and dismissive response, he also looked so much like Jeb when he was shaking off any wrongdoing, like he always had when they'd been together. Jeb had wanted to live marriage by his own rules. She'd seen the same look on Jeb's face the night she'd told him she was tired of being second, sometimes even third, to his career. When she'd dropped the word *divorce*, he had at first mocked her, treating her like she was completely out of touch with reality. How could she have known that that night of arguing would be the last time they would have a conversation that lasted longer than twelve seconds. She'd argued with him that night out of anger and hurt and rejection. She didn't want to speak out of anger again and say something she might later regret.

Micah's face was still round, his body still lean, the build of a boy who hadn't yet done hard work or gotten dirt and life under his nails. He wanted so much to be a man, and she struggled with what to say to him. He was floundering to find his way, trying to punch the gas into adulthood without knowing how to shift gears safely.

"Micah," she began, reminding herself to breathe.

"Mom, I don't want to hear it."

Olivia made a noise she had never heard herself make before. It was an assertive scoff that cued her son into their new reality. *"Excuse me?"* she burst. Micah's eyes rounded, preparing for impact. "Micah Joseph Howard," she said, her voice turning gravelly. "You will hear every single thing I want to say to you because I am your mother."

Micah turned to Tyler, most likely looking for support, but his boss backed away.

"We'll give you two a minute," Tyler said. He motioned for Hattie and Gary to follow him back to the booths. As he walked past Olivia, he gave her a quick, supportive wink. She had no idea what she was going to do next with Micah, but she appreciated the fact that Tyler had her back.

"Aunt Hattie," Micah called. "Can you drive me home?"

His request dissipated into the evening air as Hattie had already begun walking away. It was just the two of them now.

"Go get in the car, Micah," Olivia said.

"Are you going to ground me?"

Olivia wasn't sure what she was going to do, but she had to think quick to figure it out.

CHAPTER TWENTY-ONE

TYLER SAT BEHIND the wheel of his truck. He'd gotten to the clinic at the usual time, a few minutes before the walking club arrived, but he wasn't ready to go inside yet. He was curious if Gary would act any differently this morning, seeing as his dance with Hattie had overshadowed gossip about anything else— even Tyler's dance with Olivia.

After the events of the weekend, Tyler had had a hard time believing life could get back on schedule so quickly. As much as he wanted to get back to normal, things felt different. *He* felt different. He'd spent the entire night tossing and turning, trying to piece together why. He'd gotten out of bed that morning sleep-deprived and without any answers.

He'd texted Olivia before heading to bed Saturday night, to ask how it'd gone with Micah. He'd told himself that a friend would follow up to check on her, and considering Micah was his employee and he had grown to be quite fond of the kid, he had all the more reason to check in.

Olivia had texted back to explain that she'd taken Micah home, had had a one-sided conversation where she did the talking and he did the mumbling, and then she'd sent him to bed, grounded. He figured she hadn't slept very well, either.

Tyler spotted Dolores's violet-gray perm from a long way down the sidewalk. It was the first sign that she, and the rest of the walking club, were back in action. The ladies marched up the sidewalk, heads forward and arms swinging. CeCe, as usual, had taken the point.

Tyler counted down slowly to himself, watching for Gary's cue.

"Five…four… Gary…" he muttered. "Two…"

Just then, Gary swung open the clinic door and jostled his keys. He always made a big show of unlocking the doors and then pretending to notice the ladies.

Tyler couldn't say for sure which woman in the walking club Gary liked the best. As a general rule, however, he enjoyed their attention just before seven o'clock every morning.

Just as Tyler leaned back to watch the daily exchange, his uncle spotted him in his truck and waved him over.

"I was giving you some privacy, big guy," Tyler muttered before stepping out.

"Dr. Elderman!" CeCe called as he approached. "What was your favorite part of the festival?"

Tyler knew holding Olivia in his arms had been the highlight, but he figured CeCe was looking for something a little more festival related.

"Does he have to pick just one?" Gary said. The women giggled. Once they'd finished chatting, Gary waved the ladies down the sidewalk as Tyler slugged his uncle in the arm.

"Do you live for this every day?" he said.

"It's a perk of working on this street, yes."

"Which one do you like?"

"All of them."

"CeCe is married but several of the others are single. Do you ever want to ask one to dinner?" Tyler pressed.

"I don't know. I like things the way they are."

Gary opened the clinic door and went inside. He flipped on the lights and wandered to the back kitchen to start the coffee maker.

"Joan Baskins is sweet on you," Tyler said, following him.

"Is she?"

"And Dolores, I think."

Gary swept a hand around the clinic in a grand gesture. "Everything I need is right here. I have my work, which I love. I have my hobbies." Gary released a satisfied sigh and studied his nephew. "Anyway, are you sure we're talking about setting *me* up?"

Tyler frowned. "As far as I checked."

"What about Olivia?"

"What about her?"

"I saw you two Saturday, stealing glances at each other for hours before you ended up on the dance floor."

"I was saving her from Dex. We're just friends."

Gary harrumphed in disagreement.

"Hey," Tyler said. "She made it perfectly clear she didn't want more."

"Change her mind."

"*No.* I'm not going to…to…"

Tyler's cell phone vibrated in his back pocket. He fumbled for it, hoping it was Olivia.

Tyler sighed when he saw the text message. It was from Sandy. The faucet wasn't working again.

"Is everything okay?" his uncle asked.

When it came to his mother, things were never okay. She only seemed to reach out when she needed him to do something for her. Once, just once, he wished she'd reach out just to say hello.

"Fine," Tyler said, shoving the phone back into his pocket. With his mind still on Sandy, he asked in an absentminded way, "What were you saying?"

"I was going to accuse you of not putting yourself out there, because you're afraid of getting hurt."

Tyler jerked alert.

"Whoa, whoa, whoa. I wouldn't put it *that* way. The only cautionary tale I need, though, is Dad. He was a risk-taker in love and look where that got him." Tyler held up a hand in a stop motion. "Don't say it got him me. I've heard that before."

"That's the thing about the truth. It keeps bubbling to the surface. Face it, kid. You were the love of his life."

Tyler's gut slammed to the floor. He'd never heard it put that way before. But when he thought about all the good times he and his father had spent together—laughing, talking, working in the garage or the clinic—they *had* been each other's favorite person.

"I think that title is usually reserved for a romantic partner," Tyler said, making quickly for the door. He didn't want Gary to see how his comment had gotten to him, made him miss his dad so much it hurt.

"Well," Gary said. "I think you have a shot at that, too."

TYLER LET HIMSELF into his mother's house without knocking. She'd left the front door wide open with only the screen door latched.

"Hello?" Tyler called. He went upstairs and poked his head into a couple of bedrooms until he found his mother in the guest bedroom that no one ever slept in. She was sitting on the bed surrounded by old boxes.

"What are you doing in here?" he asked.

Sandy held up a paper gold star with three macaroni noodles stuck to it. "Remember this?"

"No."

"Preschool." She flipped the gold star around. A tiny photograph of Tyler was glued to the back.

Tyler soured a face. "I hated that haircut."

"It was your own fault for taking scissors to your hairline when I wasn't looking."

Sandy scrounged in the box and pulled out a soda can with the top cut off. It had been painted and decorated with fuzzy stickers.

"How about this?" she said, holding it up.

Tyler shook his head. It didn't look familiar

in the slightest. Sandy tipped the can to read the date scribbled on the bottom.

"Mother's Day. Third grade. You said it was a flower vase."

"Look," Tyler said, confused. "I have a few minutes if you want me to look at the faucet." He felt uncomfortable watching his mother hold up things from his childhood when he didn't recall her ever caring about them. He didn't know she'd saved them and it unnerved him to see the things now, especially when he couldn't remember any of them.

"Okay," Sandy said. She tucked the pieces back into the box before yanking out a soap bar pressed in the shape of a rose. "I'm sure you recognize this one."

"I don't know what it is," Tyler said, even though something about the soap looked vaguely familiar.

"This," Sandy said, "was the first thing you bought with your own money."

Tyler could feel the memory trying to flag his attention. It was nearly there, hiding just outside the recesses of his mind.

"Oh, come on," Sandy said, noticeably annoyed he didn't remember. "You were helping your dad at the clinic every Saturday and your dad told me he wanted to pay you. I didn't like the idea, but your father insisted.

He said you needed some money of your own so you could learn how to budget wisely."

Sandy held the soap to her nose and smelled it. "I've always loved the smell of roses." She sighed.

"I did buy you that," Tyler said, now remembering. The details of the purchase were slowly brightening his foggy mind like pinpricks of sunshine squeezing through a threadbare curtain. He'd wanted to make her happy, even though some part of him knew she never would be. No matter what he did, or what Dad did, she was who she was. He better understood that truth now, but back then, at his tender age, he had still been trying to change her.

"It was for no reason at all," she said, putting it back into the box.

"You told me it was a waste of money."

"It was," Sandy said, doubling down on her opinion from so many years ago. "I said you should have saved it for my birthday or something. Who gives a gift for no reason?"

"I gave it to you because you love roses. I had it gift wrapped and everything."

"Yes. I saved that, too."

Sandy pulled out the small box and perfectly pressed tissue paper. A lump formed in Tyler's throat. He'd had no idea she'd saved the soap, let alone the wrappings. He'd checked her bathroom sink for weeks, waiting for her to use the soap, but once he'd given it to her he'd never seen it again. She'd never mentioned it. If hard-pressed, he couldn't remember if she'd even said thank-you.

"I have to get back to the clinic," he said, a salty mix of old hurt and present confusion clouding his thoughts. "If there's a problem with the water shutoff…" He made his way to the bathroom and got to work checking the faucet. Something deep inside him ached. It was a place he'd been covering up for so long that the surprise at touching it again, and right out of the blue, felt jarring.

Sandy wandered into the bathroom as he turned the water on and off again a few times.

"It's fine," he mumbled. "It's all just fine." He meant the faucet, but he uttered the words out loud a few times to help soothe himself, too.

"It was leaking this morning."

"It's fine now." Tyler stood as Sandy elbowed her way to test the faucet herself.

"If you turn the water on and leave it running for a while…"

"That's what I did," Tyler said.

"No. Watch it a second. Please."

Tyler drew and released a deep breath as

Sandy straightened and stood next to him. The water poured from the faucet as the two of them stood silently watching. It poured and poured—clean, fresh water splashing and running and gurgling down the drain as a total waste.

Tyler had never been one for deep symbolism or making mystical connections between things. But something about watching the water falling and the way his mother sneaked peeks at him, most likely checking to see how long he'd willingly stand there with her, made him draw some correlations that were long overdue.

Had she kept all those old things because she actually cared about him? If so, she'd had a terrible way of showing it over the years.

"I don't want you to leave before seeing it," she muttered. He knew she meant that the faucet would eventually start leaking again, but something in her insistence made him wonder if there was something else he was supposed to see. Every time she asked him to come over and fix something, was she trying to show him…what? That she wanted to connect but didn't have the faintest idea how?

"I can wait."

"You don't mind?"

Tyler shook his head. Another minute

passed and then another. It felt like the longest minutes of his life, but also the longest he and his mother had ever been in each other's presence peacefully. She'd hurt him so deeply he didn't know how to connect with her, either. He didn't think they ever could unless she acknowledged, at least in some way, that she'd hurt him.

Finally, with a disappointed sigh, Sandy turned off the faucet. "Figures. It'll probably leak as soon as you leave."

"Then I'll come back."

Sandy's eyes glinted up at him, discerning if he meant it.

"I have to get the newspaper," she said, briskly leading him out of the bathroom and down the stairs. He followed her outside and down the front walk. As Sandy checked her mailbox, Tyler pulled her trash can up the driveway to her garage.

"Martin never gets his trash can," Sandy said, glancing at her neighbor's bin, the irritability in her voice resurfacing. "Last week it sat on the street for two days. Does he think the whole neighborhood wants to stare at it?"

"I gotta go, Sandy," he said.

"I'll call you if the faucet…you know."

"It's a plan."

Tyler climbed into his truck and started the

engine. When Sandy shuffled to his window, he lowered it. "Was there something else?" he said.

"Tyler," she said, her face contorting. He prepared himself for another complaint, another comment about what was wrong in her world. "You were always a good son," she said. On the surface the words would be touching, but she hadn't landed them easily like a compliment. "Even if…"

"What?"

"I wasn't a good mother."

Tyler worked his jaw. His mother lowered her eyes, her head, her shoulders, as if the shame of the statement might drag her to the earth.

He didn't feel like lying or reassuring her that she had been a good mother. She hadn't been. She'd abandoned him emotionally, and he wasn't prepared just then to talk about it. He had deserved more from her.

Still, her acknowledgement, the first one he'd ever heard from her, felt like a slight tightening of the faucet. The water was still flowing and wasting down the drain, but perhaps at a slightly slower rate.

"I'll come back if the faucet starts to leak again," Tyler offered. "Okay?"

His mother stepped back from the truck and waved him to go. "Okay."

Things didn't feel okay just then, but Tyler wondered if one day, things might start to feel a little closer to it.

CHAPTER TWENTY-TWO

OLIVIA CHOPPED FURIOUSLY at a green bell pepper as Hattie moved the caramelized onions around the pan on the stove. The garlic sizzled.

"The garlic is speaking, love," Hattie said. "Are you sure you don't want any help cutting those veggies?"

Olivia knew she needed help, but it felt good to wield the knife and pretend she was a sous-chef under pressure to deliver a gourmet meal in mere minutes. The food she could control. Things with Micah were another story.

She scraped the pepper into the pan and delighted in the fragrant steam that instantly billowed.

"You've got something in your head," Hattie said, turning the heat on the stove down a notch. "It might help if you let me in on it."

"We're going to have a nice sit-down dinner together," Olivia said. She was still reeling at the contentious evening she'd had with

Micah the other night after he'd driven Tyler's truck. She had wanted him to explain what the heck he'd been thinking, but as much as she tried to connect the dots for him, Micah couldn't make the connection that what he'd done had been dangerous and reckless.

She'd told him he'd acted irresponsibly, and he'd told her she was overreacting. She'd asked him to acknowledge that he'd done something wrong by driving Tyler's truck, but all he'd said was that she didn't understand him. He'd grumbled several things under his breath, exited the car before she had brought it to a complete stop and slammed every door he could on his way from the car to his bedroom.

Since she'd told him he was grounded, and that included from working at the clinic, she hadn't seen him since. He'd refused to come close to any room she occupied. He was quieter than a mouse and had most likely memorized, and avoided, which floorboards on the stairs creaked under pressure.

"Have you talked to him today?" Hattie asked, popping a hip to lean against the counter. Hattie had graciously driven Micah to tutoring but said he hadn't spoken a peep to her. Olivia cored a red pepper and sliced it.

"I needed time to gather my thoughts."

"You mean when the adrenaline and anger weren't flowing?"

"Right. I'm not going to raise a son who doesn't know the consequences of his actions. He won't talk to me and now he's progressed to felonies."

"Felonies?" Hattie howled. "Ha! Olivia, I don't think you've calmed down enough to have any follow-up conversation with Micah."

"I'm calm," Olivia said, the mere memory of seeing Micah behind the wheel of the truck angering her all over again. She scraped the red pepper into the pan and slammed the cutting board and knife into the sink with a clank.

"Yes, I can see that."

Olivia faced her aunt. "I want to be a good mother."

"You are. That's what I've been telling you, child. Do you think you're not any good because your son did something wrong? Nonsense. I may only be a dog mom to the sweetest canine in the world, but I know a good mother when I see one. My sister was an excellent one and she raised *you.*"

Olivia's cell phone rang just as she punched her fists into the sink of soapy water.

"It's Tyler," Hattie said, picking it up off the kitchen table. "Want me to answer it?"

Before Olivia could reply, Hattie answered in a singsong voice. "Well, if it isn't my *second* favorite Dr. Elderman... She's giving hell to some peppers... Dinner is in twenty minutes. Can you make it?" Hattie pantomimed innocence when Olivia smacked her arm with a dish towel. "Okay, thanks for calling, Tyler. I'll tell her. Bye!"

Once Hattie hung up the phone, Olivia found her voice. "What did you do that for?" she cried, drying her hands.

"Tyler's turning onto our road. He'll be here in twenty seconds."

Olivia hung the towel, bit her fingernail and hurried to the front door. She waved when she spotted Tyler's truck pulling up the driveway. Talking to him was the only thing she wanted to do now, but that made the "just being friends" thing much more complicated. If Micah's escapade with the festival had taught her anything, it was that she could not get distracted by dating right now.

Once Tyler had parked and made his way up the walk, he confessed, "After what happened Saturday night, I figured I should call first."

"You're welcome any time. I'm sure Hattie can finish up dinner."

"She can," Hattie said, giving Olivia a nudge out the door and quickly pulling it closed.

"She has a way with words, doesn't she?" Tyler said. Olivia led them around the side of the house to the backyard.

Hattie's yard was still beautifully manicured and prepared for the autumn frosts. Birds still splashed in her birdbath. Her woodpile was evenly stacked with the precision of an engineer. It hinted at the many cold winter nights Hattie could spend reading in front of her stone hearth, warming her toes by a crackling fire. The trees were changing, too. The branches swayed, casting colorful leaves to the ground by handfuls.

"I'm sorry if Micah didn't call you about not coming into work today."

"He did," Tyler said. "He also apologized again for taking the truck. I accepted his apology and said he could return to the clinic when he was done being grounded."

"Oh. Good to hear." Olivia felt pleasantly surprised to learn her son had done the right thing. Maybe her emotions *were* shooting her way off the mark where Micah was concerned. "I'm talking to him tonight."

"Didn't you already do that?"

"To ground him, yes. I think there's something more going on, and I want to get to the bottom of it."

"Someday he'll appreciate your perseverance, and I should know." He sucked a breath. "Today my mom admitted she hasn't been a good mother."

"Wow. That's a big step for her, huh?"

"I'll say. I always knew that she wasn't supportive when my dad was sick, but all this time I've felt like I was the one who did something wrong." Olivia winced. It must have been a painful burden for Tyler to carry, believing his mother's coldness was all his fault. She wished he could see what a wonderful person he was, despite his mother's influence.

"If I had been a better kid," Tyler continued, "maybe she would have felt more of an instinct to help me. I think I've been backing away from people ever since my dad died."

She laced her tone with compassion as she said, "Don't you know that people want to support you now?"

"That's not so easy to understand. Losing my dad was the hardest thing I've ever had to go through, so I've been trying to avoid any situations that might lead me to feel that again."

"I'm sorry that happened to you, Tyler. I'm glad, at the least, that you had Gary."

"Me, too." He smiled slightly. "He's probably the only reason I have any roots at all. Without him and a desire to run the clinic as a family business, *my* family's business, I might be a wandering vagabond."

He said it as a joke, but she sensed he was being truthful.

"Maybe your conversation with Sandy will help you heal a little, huh?" Her supportive smile sobered when Tyler reached for her. When he found the tender spot on her arm where he'd squeezed to save her life, he caressed it sweetly.

"It has brought some other things in my life into sharper view."

She knew he was going to ask her something to which he wouldn't like her answer. He had just admitted that he'd pulled away from people for years, and as much as she didn't want to be another person in his life who did that, she worried that anything more than friendship right now would distract her from her own son.

Tyler's eyes searched hers as if deciphering a map legend.

"Olivia." The timbre of his voice had never captured her name so fully. Rolling off his lips, it sounded like an impassioned plea. "These last few days have had my head spinning in a cyclone. Meeting you has made me question my purpose here in Roseley, at the clinic. What's the point of building a life I sure do like a lot, if I know that a better life is possible?" When he cupped her face and stroked a thumb over the dimple at her mouth, she could feel him pushing all of his chips to the center of the table.

"Tyler..." she began but he shook his head as if he could shake away her hesitancy. He was trying to read her, trying to see if she was holding back her feelings from him. His touch almost made her forget her promise to herself to put Micah first and above all else in her life. Almost.

"Since you came into my life—"

"Please don't say anything more," Olivia whispered. She couldn't stand to hear him confess his feelings for her. It would be torture for her to have to withhold hers.

"But I have to. I've been driving around town for hours imagining what the future could hold if I wasn't afraid anymore."

"You've been afraid?" she said, peering up at him. She wasn't the only one who felt so lost and uncertain on where to go from here?

"Terrified. I've never trusted anyone the way I've trusted you."

His confession rang true with her own sentiment. But restraint made her next words feel empty. "Friends should trust each other."

"Can't you see what I'm trying to say?" he said. "I don't want to be just friends. I can't help but think, at least I'm seriously hoping, that you want to be more, too."

Olivia's eyes glistened with tears. His words were like uncovering a golden treasure in the sand, but at the same time, she felt the prize was too rich to keep. She had to return it before she squandered both it and the progress she had made with Micah.

"Tyler," she said. "I'm so sorry, but I can't."

TYLER'S THROAT CLENCHED. On his drive to Olivia's house, he had been terrified of what she might say if he finally asked for what he wanted. Yet some part of him, maybe the hopeless romantic part that echoed some trait of his dad, made him think that she'd instantly pull him into her arms. As much as that thought still terrified him—giving himself over to another person like that—he wanted to risk it. For the first time in his life, he wanted to put everything on the line and try for the life he wanted. He wanted Olivia.

"Please, Tyler," she said. "I want you to know that I care about you more than you can imagine."

It was a sweet sentiment, but it didn't promote them out of the friends category.

"Is that all? You don't feel anything more for me than friendship?"

"What does it matter what I really feel if I can't be with you?" She pulled herself free from his hold. "I once loved Jeb, too. I wanted us to be happy, but things didn't work out in our marriage long before he died."

"That doesn't mean they wouldn't work out if you tried again, tried with me."

"This time I have another person to think about." Her gaze seemed to plead for him to understand.

"I'm thinking about Micah, too," he said, earnestly. "I care about him, Olivia."

"I know you do," she said, squeezing her eyes shut. "I see it every time I watch the two of you together. But ever since the car accident Micah hasn't been the same. What you see of him every day is not what I see, behind the scenes. Whenever I talk to him it feels like talking to the tip of a massive iceberg. I always sense he's hiding so much below dark waters. I'm willing to go deep and help him shoulder whatever burden is weighing on him, but he won't let me in and it scares me."

She peered up at him, and for the first time he saw the maddening worry behind her eyes.

"Trauma…grief…missing his dad…" Tyler said. "All of those things would weigh on him."

"Of course," Olivia said.

"Isn't that what you sense?"

"No."

"I don't understand, then," he said.

She slumped onto a bench on Hattie's porch as if defeated. Tyler had come here to confess his feelings for her, but when Olivia was obviously feeling so much turmoil with Micah, how could he win her heart without listening to it first? He followed and sat beside her, letting his presence smooth a path for his words. When she glanced at him, he continued. "I may not understand what you're talking about, but I want to."

Olivia began, "Everyone else thinks Micah's just a regular teenager dealing with those issues while pushing boundaries, but I can feel something more going on. He can fool everyone else—Hattie, Dr. Redwood, you—but I know him better than anyone, and he can't fool me. Taking your truck like he did…it's not my son, Tyler. Can you understand that?"

Tyler hated to admit that he could. He also hated to admit that loving Olivia, the way she truly needed to be loved, meant encouraging her to move closer to Micah. Even if it meant moving farther away from him. He didn't think one should exclude the other, but how could he convince her of that now when she was distraught over her son?

"Trust your instincts," Tyler said. "Keep trying. He's worth it."

Tyler thought Olivia was worth it, too. Maybe if the circumstances had been different, he could start to confess the fullness of his feelings for her, and she'd finish his own sentences for him. But things weren't like that now. Her life was too complicated for him to wade into it, and he was never one for going where he wasn't invited. The consequences could be devastating.

Suddenly, Micah's story about the riding lawn mower popped into his head. "When Jeb was alive," Tyler said, "did Micah do anything dangerous?"

"You mean like driving your truck?"

"Exactly."

"Jeb used to goad him into doing things he

wasn't ready for—reckless things. We had plenty of arguments about it, that's for sure."

Slowly, a sickening thought came to Tyler. Piecing together the conversations with Micah and all Olivia had told him, too, he couldn't shake the feeling that Micah really was hiding something important. If Tyler's instincts were right, it was something Micah would never, could never, tell his mother.

"Oh, Olivia," he said. "I think there *is* something going on with Micah." Fear flashed over her eyes. "He said Jeb used to let him race your lawn mower."

"You mean *push*. We had a push mower and a—"

"Fifty-four-inch zero-turn riding mower with smart speed?"

Olivia's face fell grave. "No… He was probably just telling you that to impress you."

"Or to see how I'd react before telling you the worst of it."

"What could be worse?"

He needed Olivia to connect the dots faster. He needed her to figure it out on her own so he wouldn't have to be the one to suggest it. How could he verbalize such an idea?

Then, all at once, the realization landed on her face like a knockout punch. She smacked a hand over her mouth to muffle a horrified gasp.

"Micah would have told me that. The paramedics, first responders, *police*...would have known the facts of the accident, wouldn't they?"

When her gaze shifted, they both turned to see Micah sauntering out of the woods and crossing toward them, unaware of what they had been discussing. When he spotted them, he cringed, most likely from getting caught red-handed out of the house when he was supposed to be grounded.

Tyler gave Olivia's hand a supportive squeeze. He wanted to do this next part *with* her, but he felt like he would be overstepping an invisible yet firmly drawn boundary circling a parent and her child.

With Olivia's hand in his, the realization dawned on him so naturally it felt like waking up from a blissful dream. He turned to admire her beautiful profile and found it cinched in anguish. This wasn't one of those magical moments conveyed in storybooks when time stands still and you fall in love with someone amidst butterflies and rainbows. This was real life and heartache and having the hard conversations because you loved someone.

As he watched Olivia wait for Micah, ready to have one of those hard conversations, Tyler realized that he had fallen completely in love with her. He could hardly believe it, as he had spent his entire adult life protecting himself from such a dangerous thing. Part of him wanted to slip away so he could come to terms with it on his own. But the other part, the stronger part, squeezed Olivia's hand again. She and Micah were at the edge of a steep precipice and he loved them both too much to leave now.

"Olivia," he said. "I think you need to ask your son a very important question."

CHAPTER TWENTY-THREE

OLIVIA BIT BACK all the emotion welling in her voice as she whispered, "It has to get worse before it gets better, right?"

"I wish someone had talked to me after my dad died. You have a chance here."

"Tyler!" Micah called as he approached them. He rolled his eyes and corrected himself. "I mean, *Dr. Elderman*. I have to call you that or Mom lays into me."

Olivia never felt like she laid into Micah about anything, even when it came down to grounding him over the truck. But if he was feeling guilt about something else, it would cloud his perception, wouldn't it? That made sense, didn't it?

An icy realization skittered down Olivia's body. What if she said the wrong thing? What if her questions sounded like accusations to Micah's ears? She wished she could put this conversation on hold and call Dr. Redwood for advice. He'd know the right thing to say, the right questions to ask. He was the doctor and she was...

Olivia straightened her shoulders and drew a deep breath.

She was the mother.

"Are you staying for dinner?" Micah asked.

"Not tonight, buddy."

"Why not?"

"You and I need to talk, Micah," Olivia began calmly. "Just you and me."

"Mom, why are you acting so weird?" Micah glanced between her and Tyler. "Have you guys started dating yet?"

"What?" Olivia and Tyler said in unison. Micah rolled his eyes at the heavens this time.

"I saw you two dancing. Everyone did, for goodness' sake." Micah playfully elbowed Tyler in the gut. "You can do a lot worse than this guy."

"We're not dating," Olivia said, suppressing a blush. She was used to the reverse situation when she said or did something to unintentionally embarrass her son. Being on the receiving end of Micah's insightfulness, especially when it made her cheeks redden, was a new experience.

"Why not?" Micah said with a retort. Tyler lifted his brows with amusement, and it spurred her to hurriedly explain.

"Dating isn't on my agenda right now. I have other things on my mind."

"Can't you walk and chew gum at the same time?" Micah looked to Tyler for some encouragement, but to Tyler's credit, he remained emotionless. At least in the way it affected Micah, he was supportive of her decision.

"I want to focus on our life together, Micah—yours and mine," Olivia said.

"What does that mean?"

"It means we've been getting adjusted to Roseley, and I need to decide if we're going to stay and put down roots or go back home."

"Do I get a say in that?"

Olivia did a double take. "I—I suppose. I'll do what I think is best for us, because I'm the mother, but I'll always listen to you."

"Always," Micah scoffed. "That's rich."

"Hey," Olivia said, unable to suppress the hurt in her voice. "What does that mean?"

"You don't take into account what I think. You never have."

"Never? Like when?"

"For a start, moving us to Roseley."

Olivia spoke as carefully as she could manage. "Drastic times called for drastic measures, Micah. I don't know if you noticed, but you and I weren't doing so well back home.

Hattie offered me her support and I latched on with both hands—for us."

"I mean, I'm happy here," Micah continued, noticeably surprised by his mother's explanation, perhaps because she'd been honest with him in a way she hadn't been before. "But you didn't run it by me first."

"That's because I thought it was the right thing to do." Olivia stopped to consider that she meant it. She'd been second-guessing herself for so long because Micah had been difficult, but now, listening to him, she knew she'd done the right thing bringing them to Roseley and she was pleased to say it.

"Well, there have been other things, too," Micah said.

"Such as?"

"Dr. Scott."

"That was the right call, too," Olivia insisted. "You have to meet with a new counselor."

"Yeah, well…"

"What?"

"Just…that's not even one of the things I'm talking about."

"Then, tell me."

"Never mind."

Micah started to make his way toward the door, but Olivia stopped him. Out of the corner of her eye she could see Tyler moving around the side of the house to give them privacy. If he was doing exactly what she'd asked him to do—give her space to focus on Micah—why did the sight of him leaving feel so wrong?

Olivia almost called out to him to stay with her, stay with them, but instead she regrouped and tugged Micah on the arm.

"Sweetheart, talk to me. What does that mean?"

Micah whipped around. "It means you didn't care about what I thought before Dad died, but now you can't stop talking about what I need with everyone else. I've heard you talking to Hattie. The air vents in this place carry the sound up to the bedroom like you're talking to someone in the same room."

Olivia's brain scrambled, trying to remember anything she might have said to Hattie that would have upset her son, when Micah suddenly tugged away and sprinted off toward the woods. She knew he was going to hide out there for the rest of the night. All this time she'd thought of the woods as a refuge for him, a sacred space she didn't want to visit unless he invited her. She sensed that if she went there otherwise, Micah would see it as trespassing, as overstepping, maybe even smothering.

But as she watched him disappear beyond the tree line, she felt her feet lifting off the ground and thudding hard to catch up with him.

"Micah!" she called. "Wait!"

When she made it to the tree line, she could see him in the distance, his red sweatshirt ducking around trees, following a beaten path he'd forged since arriving in Roseley. Olivia plowed through branches, hurrying to catch him. Twigs clawed at her face and snagged at her clothes, but she didn't really feel them. All she could think of was healing whatever was broken between her and her son.

After a minute, she came to a small clearing where three large trees stood in a circle. Their trunks were only a few feet apart, as if they had sprouted from the same root and had broken through the surface of the soil together. Four feet from their base, Micah had built a platform. He had fenced it in with walls of wooden slats, thick branches and a giant tarp he must have repurposed from Hattie's shed. A few wooden boards in one of the trees acted like holds on a rock-climbing wall. In a flash, Micah had gripped them and climbed up into his fort, leaping behind the tarp and pulling it closed behind him.

"Micah, please," Olivia called. "I want to come up. I have to talk to you."

Silence met her, yet she persisted. Navigating the wooden holds, she climbed the trunk and pulled back the tarp. She wasn't sure what she had expected to find. All she knew was that she never in her wildest dreams expected the sight that awaited her.

Olivia crawled into the fort and sat beside Micah on the scratchy wood floor. In front of them was a photo collage that stretched as tall as the fort. There were dozens of photographs and drawings of Micah and Jeb together—fishing, playing, dancing, surfing. It dawned on her as she looked at the photographs that most of them had been manipulated and photoshopped. Many were of activities Micah and Jeb had never done together, not even once.

"Wow," she breathed, staring up at it. She didn't want to pass judgment, good or bad. Creating the art wasn't about making something beautiful; it was about expressing something that words couldn't touch. Falling back on her professional experience, she whispered, "Tell me about this."

"You can see for yourself."

Olivia touched Micah's hand. "I want to see what you see."

Micah picked up a photograph he had edited to look like him and Jeb paddle boarding. He tacked it to a small white space at the top of the collage.

"I keep thinking of all these things I'll never do with Dad. When I won that camp scholarship, I kept thinking about how I wanted to do that fun stuff with *him*, not a dumb camp counselor." Micah slunk back onto the floor beside her. "Hattie had all these photographs of us just gathering dust in boxes, so I scanned them into my laptop, edited them and printed them to look like…this."

It was a magnificent sight, the images of Micah and Jeb together. The representation of all that could have been if fate had sought out a different future for them. It made a part of her heart writhe under the crushing weight of loss all over again.

But still, as she cataloged each photograph and the glimpse into Micah's soul that it symbolized, some part of her son, the part that felt like it had been drifting away for two years, now seemed to return to her all at once. He had been listening to her after all.

"Do you feel guilty Dad died?" she said.

Micah tipped his head, confused. "Guilty?"

Olivia held very still as she forced herself to ask the question that her conversation with Tyler had led her to. "Were you driving when you and Dad got into the accident? You can tell me. I won't be angry."

"No," Micah said, visibly horrified. "How could you think that?"

"It's okay if you were—"

"I promise I wasn't. Mom, please believe me."

She peered into his eyes and saw pure honesty staring back at her. She did believe him, and it sent a wash of relief through her. "I do. I believe you."

Micah relaxed, noticeably relieved, too. She clasped his hand, and when he didn't pull it away, instead adjusting it to fit more snugly in hers, she felt he had more to reveal than just the photo collage.

"There *is* something I haven't told you," he said. Her gut twinged as she felt him preparing to get something big off his chest. "I've been really mad at you."

Olivia nodded. "Do you want to tell me why?"

Micah looked at his photo collage as if pulling encouragement from it. "I knew about the divorce."

Olivia frowned, confused. No one in her life knew that she'd been considering divorce except Jeb, and she'd only told him about it days before he died. "I don't understand."

"Dad said you wanted to leave him."

Her breath caught. "Excuse me?"

"The day we went for the drive, he said he'd messed up. *I really messed up, Micah*, he kept saying. *But I'm going to fix things. I'm going to fix things with your mom.*"

Those words, that sentiment, sounded nothing like the man she'd married. She tried to imagine the words coming out of Jeb's mouth, but…nothing.

"Is it true?" Micah said. "Did you want a divorce?"

Olivia struggled to respond. Of course it was true, but how could she say that to her child?

"Your dad and I had some problems in our marriage…" Olivia began.

"Just tell me the truth," Micah said. "I deserve to know."

Olivia sighed. He wasn't the child she still wanted him to be anymore and if they were going to move forward to a healthy place, it required her being honest, too. "I was prepared to get a divorce if your dad didn't want to try anymore," she said. "But he shouldn't have told you any of that, Micah. What went wrong between your Dad and me was between us. It had nothing to do with you."

"He said that, too," Micah said quietly.

Olivia found some relief in that her husband had had the clarity of mind to explain that much.

"He said," Micah continued, "that he was going to win you back. He was going to retire from baseball and get a job in town…go to counseling. That's why we went for a drive. He was apologizing to me for not…not…" Micah's voice broke and all at once Olivia had to hold him. She lurched forward and pulled him into her arms. "Not being there," he finished.

Jeb had never really been there for them. He'd flitted in and out of their lives physically, but he'd never been there in the way they'd needed.

"I think he wanted to change, Mom," Micah said. "He said he was going to, and I believed him."

"Maybe he was, Micah," Olivia said, but what bothered her was why Jeb would tell Micah before telling her. Had he thought she wouldn't believe him? Had he not intended to tell Micah about the divorce, but it had spilled out in a moment of weakness? She wished Jeb was here to explain himself.

Micah pointed up at the photo collage. "Just when he was ready to be the dad I always wanted, he got taken away from me."

"Is that why you made this?"

Micah nodded.

"But why have you been mad at me?"

Micah pulled away from her. "I don't know. If you hadn't wanted the divorce, Dad wouldn't have been upset on the drive and then maybe he wouldn't have hit the mailbox... I don't know. The whole thing...it's not fair."

"Do you blame *me* for the accident?"

"No," Micah protested. "I... I don't blame anybody for it. It just happened. I'm just..."

Tears cascaded down Olivia's cheeks. "Sad?" she whispered.

"So sad."

"Me, too, kiddo."

If Jeb had been engrossed in a heavy conversation, searching Micah's expression to be sure his son believed he wanted to change, it was reasonable to think he could have momentarily lost control of the vehicle and caused an accident.

"Things feel better in Roseley," Micah said, burying his nose into her shoulder. "Can we stay?"

Olivia clung to her son. "I'd really like that."

CHAPTER TWENTY-FOUR

OLIVIA RAKED AT a pile of freshly fallen yellow leaves. With each little pile she accumulated, Boomer waddled through them, burying his nose in the mustiness.

"There was a time he ran into the piles," Hattie said, cutting a line from the house, a mug of hot cider in each hand. Olivia leaned on her rake and accepted the mug, letting the steam warm her nose as she sipped. "I guess we're both slowing down a wee bit, aren't we, Boomer?"

Boomer flopped to his side on the leaf pile, making the women chuckle.

"How was Dr. Scott?" Hattie asked, kneeling beside Boomer to give him a belly scratch.

"She said some good things to challenge my thinking," Olivia said.

"Interesting. Enlighten me."

Olivia handed her mug back to Hattie and returned to raking. She'd spent the last few weeks trying to get Tyler out of her head, but Dr. Scott always had a way to lead their conversation in a direction where she felt compelled to talk about him. Although, she was probably doing a lot more leading that Dr. Scott was.

"Oh, the usual," Olivia said. "She was a good find."

"I'll say." Hattie took a sip of her cider. "Especially now that you and Micah are here to stay."

Olivia had officially resigned from her job back home and was already searching for something new in Roseley. Packing up the house, selling things and moving valuables to a nearby storage unit would take a little longer to manage. Roseley had always felt like home, so making Hattie's address her permanent one, at least until she and Micah found a new place in town, felt like an easy yes.

"When is Micah due home?" Hattie asked.

Olivia shrugged. "I'm sure he's getting in as much time at the clinic as he can before he starts going to school next week."

As they were now official Roseley residents, Olivia had broken the news to Micah that he had to jump into school midsemester. She'd thought he was going to take it hard, but once she agreed to let him work at the clinic after school and on weekends, he'd gotten on board.

"I put chili in the Crock-Pot," Hattie said. "As soon as this weather starts to turn, I'm ready for hot, savory meals."

"Sounds great."

"I made plenty. Is there anyone you'd like to invite?"

Olivia wished she could just ignore her aunt's question, but silence spoke more than a lie did where Hattie was concerned. "Caroline is working late tonight," Olivia said, turning away from her.

"Love, you know that's not who I mean."

Olivia sighed. It had been weeks since she'd spoken to Tyler. She felt that seeing him again, seeing everything she felt like she couldn't have, was worse than avoiding him. Micah had started back at the clinic, but he'd caught rides with Hattie when he wasn't riding his bicycle to town. Even dropping Micah off and spotting Tyler in the window would hurt.

"I'm fine with just us three," Olivia said.

"That's hard to believe when you hang on Micah's every word after he works in the clinic. You don't have to live like this."

"Live like what? Micah has grown more in the last few weeks than in the previous two years. We're figuring things out together, as a family."

"There's always room for another when it comes to family. Didn't you already know that?"

Olivia scraped at the leaves, pretending her aunt's words didn't ring true. Then she tore off her garden gloves as Hattie stood and closed the distance between them. "Between you and Micah, I'll never hear the end of it. I'm happy, you know. I'm content with this phase of my life and I'm just...just..."

"Fine?"

"Right."

"You already said that. Except..." Hattie pressed a finger to the corner of Olivia's mouth, her eyes crinkling in a wise smile. "Blood doesn't lie, love. Same twist as your mother, bless her sweet soul."

Hattie strode back across the yard as Olivia tried to wipe off her mouth twist. She hated having a poker tell that she couldn't hide and everyone else seemed to recognize.

"I'll set the table for just three!" Hattie called before disappearing into the house.

Olivia dropped to her knees beside Boomer as he struggled to his feet.

"She doesn't know what she's talking about, does she, Boomer?" Olivia said, holding his lovable jowls in her hands. "I'm just fine with the way things are, aren't I?"

Boomer gave Olivia a slobbery lick at the corner of her mouth.

"Oh, for heaven's sake," she cried. "Even the dog knows."

Then she flopped back onto the pile of soft leaves and let out a hearty laugh.

TYLER PULLED UP in front of the clinic early enough to avoid the walking club and his uncle's arrival. His uncle's antics had once amused him, but for the last few weeks he'd felt like all joy had been sucked from the world. Since he'd poured out his feelings to Olivia, he hadn't seen or heard a peep from her.

Nearly a dozen times he'd picked up his cell phone to dial her. Almost twice as many times, he'd taken the long way home from work, deciding at the very last second not to pull onto the street that would lead him to Hattie's cottage in the woods. While grabbing lunch at The Bayshore Bar or picking up dog treats from The Lollipop or hiking the trail on Falcon's Peak, he couldn't stop looking for her, believing that at any moment he might turn the corner and find her.

However, every day that that didn't happen was another day he felt more disconnected from her. It was easy to assume that with time, he'd learn to move on. Perhaps she already had.

"Mornin', Doc!" a chipper voice called. Tyler spotted and waved to Samantha and Caroline, jogging partners who approached quickly from up the block.

Caroline's cousin, Faith, had married Samantha's brother, John, who everyone affectionately called "Tully." Though Tyler had never seen the women together before, he could only assume the family bond had helped them become friends.

The women slowed to a stop in front of Tyler. Samantha, who exuded flirtatious energy with nearly everyone and had been doing so since at least the fourth grade, flashed a wide, pearly smile. She wore a bright purple jogging suit, white Converse sneakers and big, bangle hoop earrings.

"Mornin', ladies," Tyler said, fiddling with his keys. He couldn't help but feel like their encounter was about to slip him into walking club sidewalk chatter.

"You're up early," Samantha said.

"So are you."

"Eh," she said, shimmying her shoulders with a giggle. "You never know what the day might bring."

Tyler wished he felt her same optimistic

spirit. He hated to admit that he was up early because he hadn't been able to sleep, tossing and turning when he wasn't dreaming about Olivia.

"Is Micah still grounded?" Caroline asked.

"No, he started back a couple of weeks ago." Tyler didn't want to admit that he hadn't heard from Olivia since before that. Hattie had dropped into the clinic a few times when she'd dropped Micah off for work. She'd been the one to explain that Micah had not been driving the car that had killed Jeb. Tyler felt deeply happy to learn that Micah and Olivia were on the right track and could better heal alongside each other, the way Olivia had always wanted. Still, a part of him wished he was included in their little family.

Caroline pressed her forehead to the front window.

"Did you leave the light on in there?"

"Gary must have forgotten to shut it off. He has a habit of doing that."

"He's a hoot," Samantha said. "We need to fix him up with someone."

Caroline elbowed her friend before picking up the pace again. "Focus your attention on yourself, Sam. No one needs your matchmaking ideas. Bye, Tyler!"

Tyler went inside as the women jogged off.

With the newspaper tucked under his arm, he moved to the kitchen and started the coffee maker before wandering to his back office. He'd no sooner entered the room and made his way to his desk when he sensed someone watching him.

"Hi," a voice whispered from behind him.

Tyler didn't need to look. He knew that voice. It was the sweetest voice in the world, and it belonged to the one woman who had the power to shatter him like icicles hitting pavement.

"I'm glad you left the light on," he said turning around.

"I didn't want you to think I was a thief."

Olivia was perched on the arm of his love seat, fidgeting with a stuffed koala bear a patient had given him for Christmas. Wasn't she a thief? Hadn't she stolen his heart when he'd spent his entire adult life convincing himself that he would be better off alone?

"This is cute," she continued, nuzzling the koala. "I never pegged you as the wild animal sort."

"I love all animals," he said. "In my experience, it's people who are dangerous."

"I know," Olivia said, placing the koala on the love seat and making her way to him. "I know you've been hurt before, and I never wanted to hurt you, Tyler. As much as I tried not to, I think I did."

Tyler shrugged as if he hadn't spent the last several weeks wandering through each day only half-alive.

He sat back on the edge of his desk as she came close enough to reach out and touch him. He wanted so desperately for her to, though he only wanted it if she meant it. He couldn't put his heart on the line again and tell her how much he missed her if she was going to tout her desire to be friends again.

"Hattie told me about you and Micah," he said. "The fact that he wasn't driving in the accident...and that he made the photo collage... heck, that he's starting school..."

"Yeah, I asked her to."

Tyler frowned. "Why wouldn't you stop by to tell me yourself? You could have at least called me or texted."

She lowered her eyes. "I didn't want something as important as Micah's accident to be sent in a text. I also had to figure things out for myself before I spoke to you again."

"But why? One of the things I loved about being with you was how we were able to talk, really talk."

"I know. I liked that closeness, too."

"Then, why?"

Olivia dabbed at tears in her eyes and sucked a breath. She looked like she was steeling herself to explain. "I had to make sure that what I felt for you was real."

"As opposed to what? Every minute of it felt real to me. It didn't for you?" He wanted her to tell him it was real for her, too, at least while it lasted.

"I loved Jeb so deeply in the beginning," she said. "For as much as he hurt me over the years, whether intentionally or unintentionally, I continued to love him. If he hadn't died in that accident, I think he and I would have worked things out. Maybe there was a chance, even if it was a small chance, that we could have been happy."

Tyler bristled, uncertain where her train of thought was going. She pressed on.

"For the past two years I've felt justified that I started the divorce paperwork when I did. I thought Jeb wasn't capable of change, but now I see that he might have been."

"You miss him? Is that what you're trying to work through?"

Olivia shook her head. "I've spent the last few weeks saying goodbye to him. I'll never fully be able to do that. He was my husband for many years, and I see him every time I look at Micah. He'll always be with me—

the good, the bad, the missed opportunity of what might have been. But I had to close out that season of my life with him as best as I could, because I want things with us—you and me—to start off on the right foot."

"You and me?" Tyler said. "How do you mean that exactly?" He couldn't let himself hope that she meant something more than friendship. If his heart leaped too early, it might hit the ground harder than it could handle.

Olivia closed the gap between them, this time cupping his face the way he had cupped hers before their first kiss.

"I need things between us to go slowly, and I need you to be conscious of the fact that dating me is a two-for-one deal."

Tyler couldn't stop himself from kissing the inside of her wrist. "I'm well aware."

"These past few weeks without you have been excruciating," she said, her eyes now flooding with tears. "Let's never do that again."

His chest expanded with hope at her confession. "I'm glad it wasn't just me," he said.

Olivia wrapped her arms around him, and he felt himself melt fully into her embrace.

"It wasn't just you," she whispered. "I love you, Tyler."

His heart expanded tenfold. It would take time and trust to completely tear down his fear of falling in love, but at her words, he could feel it crumbling away.

Before she could kiss him, he muttered the words he never thought he'd ever tell another soul again. They slipped easily off his lips just as his mouth found hers.

"I love you, too."

EPILOGUE

TYLER HELD a finger to his lips. Both Olivia and Ranger stopped short as he pointed to a large mound of dirt at the top of a steep slope. After dozens of hikes up the trail, he'd only ever spotted fox cubs in this spot once.

It felt fitting that today, of all days, he would finally spot some again, with Olivia by his side.

Delight lit up her face. She held up three fingers, denoting the three cubs in view. Two lay in a sunny patch of grass, while the third sniffed at something near their den entrance. Tyler imagined their mother sleeping in the den, most likely exhausted after a night out hunting for her cubs. Mothers were self-sacrificing like that. He squeezed Olivia's hand. It was something he admired so much about her, too.

"Sandy texted," Olivia said, glancing briefly at her phone. "She bought us those redbud tree saplings you were admiring. She'll be by later to help plant them."

His relationship with Sandy was still far from being healthy, but he appreciated the small strides she'd made, especially when it came to being a step-grandma to Micah.

Though the calendar said spring had begun two months earlier, the mountain had just started to catch up, sprouting buds and grass, and filling out the trees with leaves in every shade of green. Overhead a male house finch cried out, its distinctive tweet crying once, twice, thrice before sloping up on an optimistic high note. As they approached the ledge of Falcon's Peak, Tyler took the finch's song as a good sign.

"Look familiar?" he said, releasing Ranger to wander for a few minutes off leash.

"You mean the place we first met?" She smiled.

"This place has more important meaning than that."

She let her other hand drift over his arm affectionately. "It's also where you asked me to marry you."

Tyler loved to recall the day he'd proposed to Olivia in this very spot, as well as the day Micah had stood by his side as his best man. Between giving Tyler his blessing to marry Olivia, helping him pick out the ring and standing up with him during the ceremony, Micah had been not only the *best* best man Tyler could have ever wished for, but the best stepson, too. There had been challenges as the three of them figured out how their new family functioned, but they were working through things together. Tyler was determined to always work through things together.

"Getting warmer."

Olivia frowned. "Did you come here when you were deciding about whether or not to propose to me?"

"Sweetheart," Tyler said. "There wasn't any decision involved. I wanted to marry you the moment I saw you looking better in my Falcon High baseball hat than I did…"

Olivia burst out laughing. "Now, *that's* love," she said.

Her rich brown eyes shone, lashes fluttering wildly like butterfly wings. When they'd begun their hike, the sky had been overcast, but her laughter made everything around him brighten. It was as if the sun had been standing at attention just to breach the tree line at her call.

"I might have saved you on this peak," Tyler said. "But ever since that day, I feel like you and Micah were the ones who saved me."

"Did you bring me here to tell me that?"

"To ask you something, too."

She gave him an assessing gaze. "I'm listening."

"I love our family the way it is—you, Micah and me." Tyler pulled Olivia toward him. "But lately I can't stop thinking about expanding our family."

"Really?" Olivia said, eyes growing wide.

"Yeah. I know it's a lot for you, going back to the baby stage again. But I wouldn't mind having a little girl with your big brown eyes and a smile that could melt my heart in two seconds flat."

Tears flooded Olivia's eyes as Tyler continued, "Plus, don't you think Micah would make an incredible big brother? I know we should talk about it a little more and, of course, it's up to you—"

Olivia leaped into Tyler's arms and clung to him so hard he thought she might knock them both off the peak.

"I think she likes the idea," he called to Ranger with a laugh. He pulled away and caressed curly wisps off her face. She had a wellspring of joy that bubbled from within, and in that moment, as she beamed up at him, he tried to lock every detail of her face into his memory. The way her skin glowed with golden undertones as the sunlight found it.

The little mouth twist he had spent the past eighteen months trying to kiss off. "Is that a yes, then?"

"You made this way too easy on me," she whispered. "I've spent the past two days trying to think of how to tell you..."

"Were you going to suggest the same thing?" Tyler said, perking. "Do you want to start trying?"

"No," Olivia said with a smile. "I want to tell you that our baby is already on the way."

* * * * *

Visit
ReaderService.com
Today!

As a valued member of the Harlequin Reader Service, you'll find these benefits and more at ReaderService.com:

- Try 2 free books from any series
- Access risk-free special offers
- View your account history & manage payments
- Browse the latest Bonus Bucks catalog

Don't miss out!

If you want to stay up-to-date on the latest at the Harlequin Reader Service and enjoy more content, make sure you've signed up for our monthly News & Notes email newsletter. Sign up online at ReaderService.com or by calling Customer Service at 1-800-873-8635.

RS20

COMING NEXT MONTH FROM

⬥ HARLEQUIN
HEARTWARMING

#423 THE COWBOY SEAL'S CHALLENGE
Big Sky Navy Heroes • by Julianna Morris

Navy SEAL Jordan Maxwell returns to Montana ready to take over the family ranch. Proving himself to his grandfather is one thing—proving himself to single mom and ranch manager Paige Bannerman is another story.

#424 HEALING THE RANCHER
The Mountain Monroes • by Melinda Curtis

City girl Kendall Monroe needs to cowboy it up to win a much-needed work contract. Rancher and single dad Finn McAfee is willing to teach her lessons of the land. But will lessons of the heart prevail?

#425 A FAMILY FOR KEEPS
by Janice Sims

Sebastian Contreras and Marley Syminette were inseparable growing up in their small fishing town. The tides of friendship changed to love, but neither could admit their true feelings—until a surprising offer changes everything...

#426 HIS HOMETOWN REDEMPTION
by LeAnne Bristow

Caden Murphy can't start over without making amends for the biggest mistake of his life. But Stacy Tedford doesn't need an apology—she needs help at her family's cabin rentals! Can this temporary handyman find a permanent home?

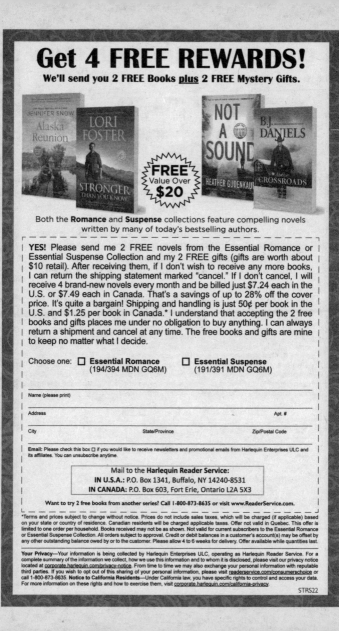

COUNTRY LEGACY COLLECTION

Get 4 FREE REWARDS!

We'll send you 2 FREE Books plus 2 FREE Mystery Gifts.

FREE
Value Over
$20

Both the **Love Inspired®** and **Love Inspired® Suspense** series feature compelling novels filled with inspirational romance, faith, forgiveness, and hope.